AF613650

Earle Ashley Walcott

Blindfolded

e-artnow 2020

Earle Ashley Walcott
Blindfolded

Murder Mystery Novel

e-artnow, 2020
Contact: info@e-artnow.org

ISBN 978-80-273-3942-6

Contents

CHAPTER I. A DANGEROUS ERRAND

A city of hills with a fringe of houses crowning the lower heights; half-mountains rising bare in the background and becoming real mountains as they stretched away in the distance to right and left; a confused mass of buildings coming to the water's edge on the flat; a forest of masts, ships swinging in the stream, and the streaked, yellow, gray-green water of the bay taking a cold light from the setting sun as it struggled through the wisps of fog that fluttered above the serrated sky-line of the city-these were my first impressions of San Francisco.

The wind blew fresh and chill from the west with the damp and salt of the Pacific heavy upon it, as I breasted it from the forward deck of the ferry steamer, *El Capitan*. As I drank in the air and was silent with admiration of the beautiful panorama that was spread before me, my companion touched me on the arm.

"Come into the cabin," he said. "You'll be one of those fellows who can't come to San Francisco without catching his death of cold, and then lays it on to the climate instead of his own lack of common sense. Come, I can't spare you, now I've got you here at last. I wouldn't lose you for a million dollars."

"I'll come for half the money," I returned, as he took me by the arm and led me into the close cabin.

My companion, I should explain, was Henry Wilton, the son of my father's cousin, who had the advantages of a few years of residence in California, and sported all the airs of a pioneer. We had been close friends through boyhood and youth, and it was on his offer of employment that I had come to the city by the Golden Gate.

"What a resemblance!" I heard a woman exclaim, as we entered the cabin. "They must be twins."

"There, Henry," I whispered, with a laugh; "you see we are discovered." Though our relationship was not close we had been cast in the mold of some common ancestor. We were so nearly alike in form and feature as to perplex all but our intimate acquaintances, and we had made the resemblance the occasion of many tricks in our boyhood days.

Henry had heard the exclamation as well as I. To my surprise, it appeared to bring him annoyance or apprehension rather than amusement.

"I had forgotten that it would make us conspicuous," he said, more to himself than to me, I thought; and he glanced through the cabin as though he looked for some peril.

"We were used to that long ago," I said, as we found a seat. "Is the business ready for me? You wrote that you thought it would be in hand by the time I got here."

"We can't talk about it here," he said in a low tone. "There is plenty of work to be done. It's not hard, but, as I wrote you, it needs a man of pluck and discretion. It's delicate business, you understand, and dangerous if you can't keep your head. But the danger won't be yours. I've got that end of it."

"Of course you're not trying to do anything against the law?" I said.

"Oh, it has nothing to do with the law," he replied with an odd smile. "In fact, it's a little matter in which we are-well, you might say-outside the law."

I gave a gasp at this disturbing suggestion, and Henry chuckled as he saw the consternation written on my face. Then he rose and said:

"Come, the boat is getting in."

"But I want to know—" I began.

"Oh, bother your 'want-to-knows.' It's not against the law-just outside it, you understand. I'll tell you more of it when we get to my room. Give me that valise. Come along now." And as the boat entered the slip we found ourselves at the front of the pressing crowd that is always surging in and out of San Francisco by the gateway of the Market-Street ferry.

As we pushed our way through the clamoring hack-drivers and hotel-runners who blocked the entrance to the city, I was roused by a sudden thrill of the instinct of danger that warns one when he meets the eye of a snake. It was gone in an instant, but I had time to trace effect to cause. The warning came this time from the eyes of a man, a lithe, keen-faced man who flashed a look of triumphant malice on us as he disappeared in the waiting-room of the ferry-shed. But the keen face, and the basilisk glance were burned into my mind in that moment as deeply as though I had known then what evil was behind them.

My companion swore softly to himself.

"What's the matter?" I asked.

"Don't look around," he said. "We are watched."

"The snake-eyed man?"

"Did you see him, too?" His manner was careless, but his tone was troubled. "I thought I had given him the slip," he continued. "Well, there's no help for it now."

"Are we to hunt for a hiding-place?" I asked doubtfully.

"Oh, no; not now. I was going to take you direct to my room. Now we are going to a hotel with all the publicity we can get. Here we are."

"Internaytional! Internaytional!" shouted a runner by our side. "Yes, sir; here you are, sir. Free 'bus, sir." And in another moment we were in the lumbering coach, and as soon as the last lingering passenger had come from the boat we were whirling over the rough pavement, through a confusing maze of streets, past long rows of dingy, ugly buildings, to the hotel.

Though the sun had but just set, the lights were glimmering in the windows along Kearny Street as we stepped from the 'bus, and the twilight was rapidly fading into darkness.

"A room for the night," ordered Henry, as we entered the hotel office and saluted the clerk.

"Your brother will sleep with you?" inquired the clerk.

"Yes."

"That's right-if you are sure you can tell which is which in the morning," said the clerk, with a smile at his poor joke.

Henry smiled in return, paid the bill, took the key, and we were shown to our room. After removing the travel-stains, I declared myself quite ready to dine.

"We won't need this again," said Henry, tossing the key on the bureau as we left. "Or no, on second thought," he continued, "it's just as well to leave the door locked. There might be some inquisitive callers." And we betook ourselves to a hasty meal that was not of a nature to raise my opinion of San Francisco.

"Are you through?" asked my companion, as I shook my head over a melancholy piece of pie, and laid down my fork. "Well, take your bag. This door-look pleasant and say nothing."

He led the way to the bar and then through a back room or two, until with a turn we were in a blind alley. With a few more steps we found ourselves in a back hall which led into another building. I became confused after a little, and lost all idea of the direction in which we were going. We mounted one flight of stairs, I remember, and after passing through two or three winding hallways and down another flight, came out on a side street.

After a pause to observe the street before we ventured forth, Henry said:

"I guess we're all right now. We must chance it, anyhow." So we dodged along in the shadow till we came to Montgomery Street, and after a brief walk, turned into a gloomy doorway and mounted a worn pair of stairs.

The house was three stories in height. It stood on the corner of an alley, and the lower floor was intended for a store or saloon; but a renting agent's sign and a collection of old show-bills ornamenting the dirty windows testified that it was vacant. The liquor business appeared to be overdone in that quarter, for across the alley, hardly twenty feet away, was a saloon; across Montgomery Street was another; and two more held out their friendly lights on the corner of the street above.

In the saloons the disreputability was cheerful, and cheerfully acknowledged with lights and noise, here of a broken piano, there of a wheezy accordion, and, beyond, of a half-drunken man singing or shouting a ribald song. Elsewhere it was sullen and dark,—the lights, where there were lights, glittering through chinks, or showing the outlines of drawn curtains.

"This isn't just the place I'd choose for entertaining friends," said Henry, with a visible relief from his uneasiness, as we climbed the worn and dirty stair.

"Oh, that's all right," I said, magnanimously accepting his apology.

"It doesn't have all the modern conveniences," admitted Henry as we stumbled up the second flight, "but it's suitable to the business we have in hand, and —"

"What's that?" I exclaimed, as a creaking, rasping sound came from the hall below.

We stopped and listened, peering into the obscurity beneath.

Nothing but silence. The house might have been a tomb for any sign of life that showed within it.

"It must have been outside," said Henry. "I thought for a moment perhaps —" Then he checked himself. "Well, you'll know later," he concluded, and opened the door of the last room on the right of the hall.

As we entered, he held the door ajar for a full minute, listening intently. The obscurity of the hall gave back nothing to eye or ear, and at last he closed the door softly and touched a match to the gas.

The room was at the rear corner of the building. There were two windows, one looking to the west, the other to the north and opening on the narrow alley.

"Not so bad after you get in," said Henry, half as an introduction, half as an apology.

"It's luxury after six days of railroading," I replied.

"Well, lie down there, and make the most of it, then," he said, "for there may be trouble ahead." And he listened again at the crack of the door.

"In Heaven's name, Henry, what's up?" I exclaimed with some temper. "You're as full of mysteries as a dime novel."

Henry smiled grimly.

"Maybe you don't recognize that this is serious business," he said.

"I don't understand it at all."

"Well, I'm not joking. There's mischief afoot, and I'm in danger."

"From whom? From what?"

"Never mind that now. It's another person's business-not mine, you understand-and I can't explain until I know whether you are to be one of us or not."

"That's what I came for, isn't it?"

"Hm! You don't seem to be overly pleased with the job."

"Which isn't surprising, when I haven't the first idea what it is, except that it seems likely to get me killed or in jail."

"Oh, if you're feeling that way about it, I know of another job that will suit you better in —"

"I'm not afraid," I broke in hotly. "But I want to see the noose before I put my head in it."

"Then I'm sure the assistant bookkeeper's place I have in mind will —"

"Confound your impudence!" I cried, laughing in spite of myself at the way he was playing on me. "Assistant bookkeeper be hanged! I'm with you from A to Z; but if you love me, don't keep me in the dark."

"I'll tell you all you need to know. Too much might be dangerous."

I was about to protest that I could not know too much, when Henry raised his hand with a warning to silence. I heard the sound of a cautious step outside. Then Henry sprang to the door, flung it open, and bolted down the passage. There was the gleam of a revolver in his hand. I hurried after him, but as I crossed the threshold he was coming softly back, with finger on lips.

"I must see to the guards again. I can have them together by midnight."

"Can I help?"

"No. Just wait here till I get back. Bolt the door, and let nobody in but me. It isn't likely that they will try to do anything before midnight. If they do-well, here's a revolver. Shoot through the door if anybody tries to break it down."

I stood in the door, revolver in hand, watched him down the hall, and listened to his footsteps as they descended the stairs and at last faded away into the murmur of life that came up from the open street.

CHAPTER II. A CRY FOR HELP

I hastily closed and locked the door. It shut out at least the eyes and ears that, to my excited imagination, lurked in the dark corners and half-hidden doorways of the dimly-lighted hall. And as I turned back to the room my heart was heavy with bitter regret that I had ever left my home.

This was not at all what I had looked for when I started for the Golden Gate at my friend's offer of a "good place and a chance to get rich."

Then I rallied my spirits with something of resolution, and shamed myself with the reproach that I should fear to share any danger that Henry was ready to face. Wearied as I was with travel, I was too much excited for sleep. Reading was equally impossible. I scarcely glanced at the shelf of books that hung on the wall, and turned to a study of my surroundings.

The room was on the corner, as I have said, and I threw up the sash of the west window and looked out over a tangle of old buildings, ramshackle sheds, and an alley that appeared to lead nowhere. A wooden shutter swung from the frame-post of the window, reaching nearly to a crazy wooden stair that led from the black depths below. There were lights here and there in the back rooms. Snatches of drunken song and rude jest came up from an unseen doggery, and vile odors came with them. Shadows seemed to move here and there among the dark places, but in the uncertain light I could not be sure whether they were men, or only boxes and barrels.

Some sound of a drunken quarrel drew my attention to the north window, and I looked out into the alley. The lights from Montgomery Street scarcely gave shape to the gloom below the window, but I could distinguish three or four men near the side entrance of a saloon. They appeared quiet enough. The quarrel, if any there was, must be inside the saloon. After an interval of comparative silence, the noise rose again. There were shouts and curses, sounds as of a chair broken and tables upset, and one protesting, struggling inebriate was hurled out from the front door and left, with threats and foul language, to collect himself from the pavement.

This edifying incident, which was explained to me solely by sound, had scarcely come to an end when a noise of creaking boards drew my eyes to the other window. The shutter suddenly flew around, and a human figure swung in at the open casing. Astonishment at this singular proceeding did not dull the instinct of self-defense. The survey of my surroundings and the incident of the bar-room row had in a measure prepared me for any desperate doings, and I had swung a chair ready to strike a blow before I had time to think.

"S-h-h!" came the warning whisper, and I recognized my supposed robber. It was Henry.

His clothes and hair were disordered, and his face and hands were grimy with dust.

"Don't speak out loud," he said in suppressed tones. "Wait till I fasten this shutter. The other one's gone, but nobody can get in from that side unless they can shin up thirty feet of brick wall."

"Shall I shut the window?" I asked, thoroughly impressed by his manner.

"No, you'll make too much noise," he said, stripping off his coat and vest. "Here, change clothes with me. Quick! It's a case of life and death. I must be out of here in two minutes. Do as I say, now. Don't ask questions. I'll tell you about it in a day or two. No, just the coat and vest. There-give me that collar and tie. Where's your hat?"

The changes were completed, or rather his were, and he stood looking as much like me as could be imagined.

"Don't stir from this room till I come back," he whispered. "You can dress in anything of mine you like. I'll be in before twelve, or send a messenger if I'm not coming. By-by."

He was gone before I could say a word, and only an occasional creaking board told me of his progress down the stairs. He had evidently had some practice in getting about quietly. I could only wonder, as I closed and locked the door, whether it was the police or a private enemy that he was trying to avoid.

I had small time to speculate on the possibilities, for outside the window I heard the single word, "Help!"

The cry was half-smothered, and followed by a gurgling sound and noise as of a scuffle in the alley.

I rushed to the window and looked out. A band of half a dozen men was struggling and pushing away from Montgomery Street into the darker end of the alley. They were nearly under the window.

"Give it to him," said a voice.

In an instant there came a scream, so freighted with agony that it burst the bonds of gripping fingers and smothering palms that tried to close it in, and rose for the fraction of a second on the foul air of the alley. Then a light showed and a tall, broad-shouldered figure leaped back.

"These aren't the papers," it hissed. "Curse on you, you've got the wrong man!"

There was a moment's confusion, and the light flashed on the man who had spoken and was gone. But that flash had shown me the face of a man I could never forget—a man whose destiny was bound up for a brief period with mine, and whose wicked plans have proved the master influence of my life. It was a strong, cruel, wolfish face-the face of a man near sixty, with a fierce yellow-gray mustache and imperial—a face broad at the temples and tapering down into a firm, unyielding jaw, and marked then with all the lines of rage, hatred, and chagrin at the failure of his plans.

It took not a second for me to see and hear and know all this, for the vision came and was gone in the dropping of an eyelid. And then there echoed through the alley loud cries of "Police! Murder! Help!" I was conscious that there was a man running through the hall and down the rickety stairs, making the building ring to the same cries. My own feelings were those of overmastering fear for my friend. He had gone on his mysterious, dangerous errand, and I felt that it was he who had been dragged into the alley, and stabbed, perhaps to death. Yet it seemed I could make no effort, nor rouse myself from the stupor of terror into which I was thrown by the scene I had witnessed.

It was thus with a feeling of surprise that I found myself in the street, and came to know that the cries for help had come from me, and that I was the man who had run through the hall and down the stairs shouting for the police.

Singularly enough there was no crowd to be seen, and no excitement anywhere. Some one was playing a wheezy melodeon in the saloon, and men were singing a drunken song. The alley was dark, and I could see no one in its depths. The house through which I had flown shouting was now silent, and if any one on the street had heard me he had hurried on and closed his ears, lest evil befall him. Fortunately the policeman on the beat was at hand, and I hailed him excitedly.

"Only rolling a drunk," he said lightly, as I told of what I had seen.

"No, it's worse than that," I insisted. "There was murder done, and I'm afraid it's my friend."

He listened more attentively as I told him how Henry had left the house just before the cry for help had risen.

The policeman took me by the shoulders, turned me to the gaslight, and looked in my face.

"Excuse me, sor," he said. "I see you're not one of that kind. Some of 'em learns it from the blitherin' Chaneymen."

I was mystified at the moment, but I found later that he suspected me of having had an opium dream. The house, I learned, was frequented by the "opium fiends," as they figure in police slang.

"It's a nasty place," he continued. "It's lucky I've got a light." He brought up a dark lantern from his overcoat pocket, and stood in the shelter of the building as he lighted it. "There's not many as carries 'em," he continued, "but they're mighty handy at times."

We made our way to the point beneath the window, where the men had stood.

There was nothing to be seen-no sign of struggle, no shred of torn clothing, no drop of blood. Body, traces and all had disappeared.

CHAPTER III. A QUESTION IN THE NIGHT

I was stricken dumb at this end to the investigation, and half doubted the evidence of my eyes.

"Well," said the policeman, with a sigh of relief, "there's nothing here."

I suspected that his doubts of my sanity were returning.

"Here is where it was done," I asserted stoutly, pointing to the spot where I had seen the struggling group from the window. "There were surely five or six men in it."

The policeman turned his lantern on the spot. The rough pavement had taken no mark of the scuffle.

"It's hard to make sure of things from above in this light," said the policeman, hinting once more his suspicion that I was confusing dreams with reality.

"There was no mistaking that job," I said. "See here, the alley leads farther back. Bring your light."

"Aisy, now," said the policeman. "I'll lead the way. Maybe you want one yourself, as your friend has set the fashion."

A few paces farther the alley turned at a right angle to the north, yawning dark behind the grim and threatening buildings, and filled with noisome odors. We looked narrowly for a body, and then for traces that might give hint of the passage of a party.

"Nothing here," said the policeman, as we came out on the other street. "Maybe they've carried him into one of these back-door dens, and maybe they whisked him into a hack here, and are a mile or two away by now."

"But we must follow them. He may be only wounded and can be rescued. And these men can be caught." I was almost hysterical in my eagerness.

"Aisy, aisy, now," said the policeman. "Go back to your room, now. That's the safest place for you, and you can't do nothin' at all out here. I'll report the case to the head office, an' we'll send out the alarm to the force. Now, here's your door. Just rest aisy, and they'll let you know if anything's found."

And he passed on, leaving me dazed with dread and despair in the entrance of the fateful house.

The sounds of drunken pleasure were lessening about me. The custom had fallen off in the saloon across the street to such extent that the proprietor was putting up the shutters. The saloon on the corner of the alley was still waiting for stray customers and I crossed over to it with the thought that the inmates might give me a possible clue. A man half-asleep leaned back in a chair by the stove with his chin on his breast. Two rough-looking men at a table who were talking in low tones pretended not to notice my entrance, but their furtive glances gave more eloquent evidence of their interest than the closest stare.

The barkeeper eyed me with apparent openness. I called for a glass of wine, partly as an excuse for my visit, and partly to revive my shaken spirits.

"Any trouble about here to-night?" I asked in my most affable tone.

The barkeeper looked at me with cold suspicion.

"No, sir," he said shortly. "This is the quietest neighborhood in town."

"I should think there would be a disturbance every time that liquor was sold," was my private comment, as I got the aftertaste of the dose. But I merely wished him good night as I paid for the drink, and sauntered out.

I promptly got into my doorway before any one could reach the street to see whither I went, and listened to a growling comment and a mirthless laugh that followed my departure. Hardly had I gained my concealment when the swinging doors of the saloon opened cautiously, and a face peered out into the semi-darkness. With a muttered curse it went back, and I heard the barkeeper's voice in some jest about a failure to be "quick enough to catch flies."

Once more in the room to wait till morning should give me a chance to work, I looked about the dingy place with a heart sunk to the lowest depths. I was alone in the face of this mystery. I had not one friend in the city to whom I could appeal for sympathy, advice or money. Yet

I should need all of these to follow this business to the end-to learn the fate of my cousin, to rescue him, if alive and to avenge him, if dead.

Then, in the hope that I might find something among Henry's effects to give me a clue to the men who had attacked him, I went carefully through his clothes and his papers. But I found that he did not leave memoranda of his business lying about. The only scrap that could have a possible bearing on it was a sheet of paper in the coat he had changed with me. It bore a rough map, showing a road branching thrice, with crosses marked here and there upon it. Underneath was written:

"Third road-cockeyed barn-iron cow."

Then followed some numerals mixed in a drunken dance with half the letters of the alphabet-the explanation of the map, I supposed, in cipher, and as it might prove the clue to this dreadful business, I folded the sheet carefully in an envelope and placed it in an inmost pocket.

The search having failed of definite results, I sat with chair tilted against the wall to consider the situation. Turn it as I would, I could make nothing good of it. There were desperate enterprises afoot of which I could see neither beginning nor end, purpose nor result. I repented of my consent to mix in these dangerous doings and resolved that when the morning came I would find other quarters, take up the search for Henry, and look for such work as might be found.

It was after midnight when I had come to this conclusion, and, barring doors and windows as well as I could, I flung myself on the bed to rest. I did not expect to sleep after the exciting events through which I had passed; yet after a bit the train of mental pictures drawn out by the surging memories of the night became confused and faded away, and I sank into an uneasy slumber.

When I awoke it was with a start and an oppressive sense that somebody else was in the room. The gas-light that I had left burning had been put out. Darkness was intense. The beating of my own heart was the only sound I could distinguish. I sat upright and felt for the matches that I had seen upon the stand.

In another instant I was flung back upon the bed. Wiry fingers gripped my throat, and a voice hissed in my ear:

"Where is he? Where is the boy? Give me your papers, or I'll wring the life out of you!"

I was strong and vigorous, and, though taken at a disadvantage, struggled desperately enough to break the grip on my throat and get a hold upon my assailant.

"Where is the boy?" gasped the voice once more; and then, as I made no reply, but twined my arms about him, my assailant saved all his breath for the struggle.

We rolled to the floor with a thud that shook the house, and in this change of base I had the luck to come out uppermost. Then my courage rose as I found that I could hold my man. I feared a knife, but if he had one he had not drawn it, and I was able to keep his hands too busy to allow him to get possession of it now. Finding that he was able to accomplish nothing, he gave a short cry and called:

"Conn!"

I heard a confusion of steps outside, and a sound as of a muffled oath. Then the door opened, there was a rush of feet behind me, and the flash of a bull's-eye lantern. I released my enemy, and sprang back to the corner where I could defend myself at some advantage. It was a poor chance for an unarmed man, but I found a chair and set my teeth to give an account of myself to the first who advanced, and reproached the lack of foresight that had allowed me to lay the revolver under the pillow instead of putting it in my pocket.

I could distinguish four dark figures of men; but, instead of rushing upon me as I stood on the defensive, they seized upon my assailant. I looked on panting, and hardly able to regain my breath. It was not half a minute before my enemy was securely bound and gagged and carried out. One of the men lingered.

"Don't take such risks," he said. "I wouldn't have your job, Mr. Wilton, for all the old man's money. If we hadn't happened up here, you'd have been done for this time."

"In God's name, man, what does all this mean?" I gasped.

The man looked at me in evident surprise.

"They've got a fresh start, I guess," he said. "You'd better get some of the men up here. Mr. Richmond sent us up to bring this letter."

He was gone silently, and I was left in the darkness. I struck a match, lighted the gas once more, and, securing the revolver, looked to the letter. The envelope bore no address. I tore it open. The lines were written in a woman's hand, and a faint but peculiar perfume rose from the paper, it bore but these words:

"Don't make the change until I see you. The money will be ready in the morning. Be at the bank at 10:30."

The note, puzzling as it was, was hardly an addition to my perplexities. It was evident that I had been plunged into the center of intrigue, plot and counterplot. I was supposed to have possession of somebody's boy. A powerful and active enemy threatened me with death. An equally active friend was working to preserve my safety. People of wealth were concerned. I had dimly seen a fragment of the struggling forces, and it was plain that only a very rich person could afford the luxury of hiring the bravos and guards who threatened and protected me.

How wide were the ramifications of the mystery? Whose was the boy, and what was wanted of him? Had he been stolen from home and parents? Or was he threatened with mortal danger and sent into hiding to keep him from death?

The fate of Henry showed the power of those who were pursuing me. Armed as he was with the knowledge of his danger, knowing, as I did not, what he had to guard and from what he had to guard it, he had yet fallen a victim.

I could not doubt that he was the man assaulted and stabbed in the alley below. But the fact that no trace of him or of a tragedy was to be found gave me hope that he was still alive. Yet, at best, he was wounded and in the hands of his enemies, a prisoner to the men who had sought his life. It must be, however, that he was not yet recognized. The transfer of the chase to me was proof that the scoundrels had been misled by the resemblance between us, and by the letters found in the coat. They were convinced that he was Giles Dudley, and that I was Henry Wilton. As long as there was hope that he was alive I would devote myself to searching for him and to helping him to recover his liberty.

As I was hoping, speculating, planning thus, I was startled to hear a step on the stair.

The sound was not one that need be thought out of place in such a house and neighborhood even though the hour was past four in the morning. But it struck a chill through me, and I listened with growing apprehension as it mounted step by step.

The dread silence of the house that had cast its shadow of fear upon me now seemed to become vocal with protest against this intrusion, and to send warning through the halls. At last the step halted before my door and a loud knock startled the echoes.

With a great bound my heart threw off its tremors, and I grasped the revolver firmly:

"Who's there?"

"Open the door, sor; I've news for ye."

"Who are you?"

"Come now, no nonsense; I'm an officer."

I unlocked the door and stepped to one side. My bump of caution had developed amazingly in the few hours I had spent in San Francisco, and, in spite of his assurance, I thought best to avoid any chance of a rush from my unknown friends, and to put myself in a good position to use my revolver if necessary.

The man stepped in and showed his star. He was the policeman I had met when I had run shouting into the street.

"I suspicion we've found your friend," he said gravely. "You're wanted at the morgue."

"Dead!" I gasped.

"Dead as Saint Patrick-rest his sowl!"

CHAPTER IV. A CHANGE OF NAME

"Here's your way, sor," said the policeman, turning into the old City Hall, as it was even then known, and leading me to one of the inner rooms of the labyrinth of offices.

The odors of the prison were heavy upon the building. The foul air from the foul court-rooms and offices still hung about the entrance, and the fog-laden breeze of the early morning hours was powerless to freshen it.

The policeman opened an office door, saluted, and motioned me to enter.

"Detective Coogan," he said, "here's your man."

Detective Coogan, from behind his desk, nodded with the careless dignity of official position.

"Glad to see you, Mr. Wilton," he said affably.

If I betrayed surprise at being called by Henry's name, Detective Coogan did not notice it. But I hastened to disclaim the dangerous distinction.

"I am not Wilton," I declared. "My name is Dudley-Giles Dudley."

At this announcement Detective Coogan turned to the policeman. "Just step into Morris' room, Corson, and tell him I'm going up to the morgue."

"Now," he continued, as the policeman closed the door behind him, "this won't do, Wilton. We've had to overlook a good deal, of course, but you needn't think you can play us for suckers all the time."

"But I tell you I'm not—" I began, when he interrupted me.

"You can't make that go here," he said contemptuously. "And I'll tell you what, Wilton, I shall have to take you into custody if you don't come down to straight business. We don't want to chip in on the old man's play, of course, especially as we don't know what his game is." Detective Coogan appeared to regret this admission that he was not omniscient, and went on hastily: "You know as well as we do that we don't want any fight with *him*. But I'll tell you right now that if you force a fight, we'll make it so warm for him that he'll have to throw *you* overboard to lighten ship."

Here was a fine prospect conveyed by Detective Coogan's picturesque confusion of metaphors. If I persisted in claiming my own name and person I was to be clapped into jail, and charged with Heaven-knows-what crimes. If I took my friend's name, I was to invite the career of adventure of which I had just had a taste. And while this was flashing through my mind, I wondered idly who the "old man" could be. The note I had received was certainly in a lady's hand. But if the lady was Henry's employer, it was evident that he had dealt with the police as the representative of a man of power.

My decision was of necessity promptly taken.

"Oh, well, if that's the way you look at it, Coogan," I said carelessly, "it's all right. I thought it was agreed that we weren't to know each other."

This was a chance shot, but it hit.

"Yes, yes," said the detective, "I remember. But, you see, this is serious business. Here's a murder on our hands, and from all I can learn it's on account of your confounded schemes. We've got to know where we stand, or there will be the Old Nick to pay. The papers will get hold of it, and then-well, you remember that shake-up we had three years ago."

"But you forget the 'old man,'" I returned. The name of that potent Unknown seemed to be my only weapon in the contest with Detective Coogan, and I thought this a time to try its force.

"Not much, I don't!" said Coogan, visibly disturbed. "But if it comes to a choice, we'll have to risk a battle with him."

"Well, maybe we're wasting time over a trifle," said I, voicing my hope. "Perhaps your dead man belongs somewhere else."

"Come along to the morgue, then," said he.

"Where was he found?" I asked as we walked out of the City Hall.

"He was picked up at about three o'clock in the back room of the Hurricane Deck-the water-front saloon, you know-near the foot of Folsom Street."

Detective Coogan asked a number of questions as we walked, and in a few minutes we came to the undertaker's shop that served as the city morgue. At the best of times it could not be a place of cheer. In the hour before daybreak, with the chill air of the morning almost suppressing the yellow gaslights, the errand on which I had come made it the abode of dread. Yet I hoped-hoped in such an agony of fear that I became half-insensible to my surroundings.

"Here it is," said Coogan, opening a door.

The low room was dark and chill and musty, but its details started forth from the obscurity as he turned up the lights.

Detective Coogan's words seemed to come from a great distance as he said: "Here, you see, he was stabbed. The knife went to the heart. Here he was hit with something heavy and blunt; but it had enough of an edge to cut the scalp and lay the cheek open. The skull is broken. See here —"

I summoned my resolution and looked.

Disfigured and ghastly as it was, I recognized it. It was the face of Henry Wilton.

The next I knew I was sitting on a bench, and the detective was holding a bottle to my lips.

"There, take another swallow," he said, not unkindly. "I didn't know you weren't used to it."

"Oh," I gasped, "I'm all right now." And I was able to look steadily at the gruesome surroundings and the dreadful burden on the slab.

"Is this the man?" asked the detective.

"Yes."

"His name?"

"Dudley-James Dudley." I was not quite willing to transfer the whole of my identity to the dead, and changed the Giles to James.

"Was he a relative?"

I shook my head, though I could not have said why I denied it. Then, in answer to the detective's question, I told the story of the scuffle in the alley, and of the events that followed.

"Did you see any of the men? To recognize them, I mean?"

I described the leader as well as I was able-the man with the face of the wolf that I had seen in the lantern-flash.

Detective Coogan lost his listless air, and looked at me in astonishment.

"I don't see your game, Wilton," he said.

"I'm giving you the straight facts," I said sullenly, a little disturbed by his manner and tone.

"Well, in that case, I'd expect you to keep the straight facts to yourself, my boy."

It was my turn to be astonished.

"Well, that's my lookout," I said with assumed carelessness.

"I don't see through you," said the detective with some irritation. "If you're playing with me to stop this inquiry by dragging in-well, we needn't use names-you'll find yourself in the hottest water you ever struck."

"You can do as you please," I said coolly.

The detective ripped out an oath.

"If I knew you were lying, Wilton, I'd clap you in jail this minute."

"Well, if you want to take the risks —" I said smiling.

He looked at me for a full minute.

"Candidly, I don't, and you know it," he said. "But this is a stunner on me. What's your game, anyhow?"

I wished I knew.

"So accomplished a detective should not be at a loss to answer so simple a question."

"Well, there's only one course open, as I see," he said with a groan. "We've got to have a story ready for the papers and the coroner's jury."

This was a new suggestion for me and I was alarmed.

"You can just forget your little tale about the row in the alley," he continued. "There's nothing to show that it had anything to do with this man here. Maybe it didn't happen. Anyhow, just think it was a dream. This was a water-front row-tough saloon-killed and robbed by parties unknown. Maybe we'll have you before the coroner for the identification, but maybe it's better not."

I nodded assent. My mind was too numbed to suggest another course.

The gray dawn was breaking through the chill fog, and people were stirring in the streets as Detective Coogan led the way out of the morgue. As we parted he gave me a curious look.

"I suppose you know your own business, Wilton," he said, "but I suspect you'd be a sight safer if I'd clap you in jail."

And with this consoling comment he was gone, and I was left in the dawn of my first morning in San Francisco, mind and body at the nadir of depression after the excitement and perils of the night.

CHAPTER V. DODDRIDGE KNAPP

It was past ten o'clock of the morning when the remembrance of the mysterious note I had received the preceding night came on me. I took the slip from my pocket, and read its contents once more:

"Don't make the change until I see you. The money will be ready in the morning. Be at the bank at 10:30."

This was perplexing enough, but it furnished me with an idea. Of course I could not take money intended for Henry Wilton. But here was the first chance to get at the heart of this dreadful business. The writer of the note, I must suppose, was the mysterious employer. If I could see her I could find the way of escape from the dangerous burden of Henry Wilton's personality and mission.

But which bank could be meant? The only names I knew were the Bank of California, whose failure in the previous year had sent echoes even into my New England home, and the Anglo-Californian Bank, on which I held a draft. The former struck me as the more likely place of appointment, and after some skilful navigating I found myself at the corner of California and Sansome Streets, before the building through which the wealth of an empire had flowed.

I watched closely the crowd that passed in and out of the treasure-house, and assumed what I hoped was an air of prosperous indifference to my surroundings.

No one appeared to notice me. There were eager men and cautious men, and men who looked secure and men who looked anxious, but neither man nor woman was looking for me.

Plainly I had made a bad guess. A hasty walk through several other banks that I could see in the neighborhood gave no better result, and I had to acknowledge that this chance of penetrating the mystery was gone. I speculated for the moment on what the effects might be. To neglect an order of this kind might result in the withdrawal of the protection that had saved my life, and in turning me over to the mercies of the banditti who thought I knew something of the whereabouts of a boy.

As I reflected thus, I came upon a crowd massed about the steps of a great granite building in Pine Street; a whirlpool of men, it seemed, with crosscurrents and eddies, and from the whole rose the murmur of excited voices.

It was the Stock Exchange, the gamblers' paradise, in which millions were staked, won and lost, and ruin and affluence walked side by side. As I watched the swaying, shouting mass with wonder and amusement, a thrill shot through me.

Upon the steps of the building, amid the crowd of brokers and speculators, I saw a tall, broad-shouldered man of fifty or fifty-five, his face keen, shrewd and hard, broad at the temples and tapering to a strong jaw, a yellow-gray mustache and imperial half-hiding and half-revealing the firm lines of the mouth, with the mark of the wolf strong upon the whole. It was a face never to be forgotten as long as I should hold memory at all. It was the face I had seen twelve hours before in the lantern flash in the dreadful alley, with the cry of murder ringing in my ears. Then it was lighted by the fierce fires of rage and hatred, and marked with the chagrin of baffled plans. Now it was cool, good-humored, alert for the battle of the Exchange that had already begun. But I knew it for the same, and was near crying aloud that here was a murderer.

I clutched my nearest neighbor by the arm, and demanded to know who it was.

"Doddridge Knapp," replied the man civilly. "He's running the Chollar deal now, and if I could only guess which side he's on, I'd make a fortune in the next few days. He's the King of Pine Street."

While I was looking at the King of the Street and listening to my neighbor's tales of his operations, Doddridge Knapp's eyes met mine. To my amazement there was a look of recognition in them. Yet he made no sign, and in a moment was gone. This, then, was the enemy I was to meet! This was the explanation of Detective Coogan's hint that I should be safer in jail than free on the streets to face this man's hatred or revenge.

I must have stood in a daze on the busy street, for I was roused by some one shaking my arm with vigor.

"Come! are you asleep?" said the man, speaking in my ear. "Can't you hear?"

"Yes, yes," said I, rousing my attention.

"The chief wants you." His voice was low, almost a whisper.

"The chief? Who? Where?" I asked. "At the City Hall?" I jumped to the conclusion that it was, of course, the chief of police, on the scent of the murder.

"No. Of course not. In the second office, you know."

This was scarcely enlightening. Doubtless, however, it was a summons from my unknown employer.

"I'll follow you," said I promptly.

"I don't think I'd better go," said the messenger dubiously. "He didn't say anything about it, and you know he's rather—"

"Well, I order it," I cut in decisively. "I may need you."

I certainly needed him at that moment if I was to find my way.

"Go ahead a few steps," I said.

My tone and manner impressed him, and he went without another word. I sauntered after him with as careless an air as I could assume. My heart was beating fast. I felt that I was close to the mystery and that the next half-hour would determine whether I was to take up Henry Wilton's work or to find my way in safety back to my own name and person.

My unconscious guide led the way along Montgomery Street into an office building, up a flight of stairs, and into a back hallway.

"Stay a moment," I said, as he had his hand on the door knob. "On second thoughts you can wait down stairs."

He turned back, and as his footsteps echoed down the stair I opened the door and entered the office.

As I crossed the threshold my heart gave a great bound, and I stopped short. Before me sat Doddridge Knapp, the King of the Street, the man for whom above all others in the world I felt loathing and fear.

Doddridge Knapp finished signing his name to a paper on his desk before he looked up.

"Come in and sit down," he said. The voice was alert and businesslike-the voice of a man accustomed to command. But I could find no trace of feeling in it, nothing that could tell me of the hatred or desperate purpose that should inspire such a tragedy as I had witnessed, or warn me of danger to come.

"Do you hear?" he said impatiently; "shut the door and sit down. Just spring that lock, will you? We might be interrupted."

I was not at all certain that I should not wish very earnestly that he might be interrupted in what Bret Harte would call the "subsequent proceedings." But I followed his directions.

Doddridge Knapp was not less impressive at close view than at long range. The strong face grew stronger when seen from the near distance.

"My dear Wilton," he said, "I've come to a place where I've got to trust somebody, so I've come back to you." The voice was oily and persuasive, but the keen gray eyes shot out a glance from under the bushing eyebrows that thrilled me as a warning.

"It's very kind of you," I said, swallowing my astonishment with an effort.

"Well," said Knapp, "the way you handled that Ophir matter was perfectly satisfactory; but I'll tell you that it's on Mrs. Knapp's say-so, as much as on your own doings, that I select you for this job."

"I'm much obliged to Mrs. Knapp," I said politely. I was in deep waters. It was plainly unsafe to do anything but drift.

"Oh, you can settle that with her at your next call," he said good humoredly.

The jaded nerves of surprise refused to respond further. If I had received a telegram informing me that the dispute over the presidency had been settled by shelving both Hayes and Tilden and giving the unanimous vote of the electors to me, I should have accepted it as a matter of course. I took my place unquestioningly as a valued acquaintance of Doddridge Knapp's and a particular friend of Mrs. Knapp's.

Yet it struck me as strange that the keen-eyed King of the Street had failed to discover that he was not talking to Henry Wilton, but to some one else who resembled him. There were enough differences in features and voice to distinguish us among intimate friends, though there were not enough to be seen by casual acquaintances. I had the key in the next sentence he spoke.

"I have decided that it is better this time to do our business face to face. I don't want to trust messengers on this affair, and even cipher notes are dangerous, —confoundedly dangerous."

Then we had not been close acquaintances.

"Oh, by the way, you have that other cipher yet, haven't you?" he asked.

"No, I burnt it," I said unblushingly.

"That's right," he said. "It was best not to take risks. Of course you understand that it won't do for us to be seen together."

"Certainly not," I assented.

"I have arranged for another office. Here's the address. Yours is Room 15. I have the key to 17, and 16 is vacant between with a 'To Let' sign on it. They open into each other. You understand?"

"Perfectly," I said.

"You will be there by nine o'clock for your orders. If you get none by twelve, there will be none for the day."

"If I can't be there, I'll let you know." I was off my guard for a moment, thinking of the possible demands of Henry's unknown employer.

"You will do nothing of the kind," said Doddridge Knapp shortly. His voice, so smooth and businesslike a moment before, changed suddenly to a growl. His heavy eyebrows came down, and from under them flashed a dangerous light. "You will be there when I tell you, young man, or you'll have to reckon with another sort of customer than the one you've been dealing with. This matter requires prompt and strict obedience to orders. One slip may ruin the whole plan."

"You can depend on me," I said with assumed confidence. "Am I to have any discretion?"

"None whatever."

I had thus far been able to get no hint of his purposes. If I had not known what I knew, I should have supposed that his mind was concentrated on the apparent object before him-to secure the zeal and fidelity of an employee in some important business operation.

"And what am I to do?" I asked.

"Be a capitalist," he said with an ironical smile. "Buy and sell what I tell you to buy and sell. Keep under cover, but not too much under cover. You can pick your own brokers. Better begin with Bockstein and Eppner, though. Your checks will be honored at the Nevada Bank. Oh, here's a cipher, in case I want to write you. I suppose you'll want some ready money."

Doddridge Knapp was certainly a liberal provider, for he shoved a handful of twenty-dollar gold pieces across the desk in a way that made my eyes open.

"By the way," he continued, "I don't think I have your signature, have I?"

"No, sir," I replied with prompt confidence.

"Well, just write it on this slip then. I'll turn it into the bank for your identification. You can take this check-book with you."

"Anything more?"

"That's all," he replied with a nod of dismissal. "Maybe it's to-morrow—maybe it's next month."

And I walked out into Montgomery Street, bewildered among the conflicting mysteries in which I had been entangled.

CHAPTER VI. A NIGHT AT BORTON'S

Room 15 was a plain, comfortable office in a plain, comfortable building on Clay Street, not far from the heart of the business district. It was on the second floor, and its one window opened to the rear, and faced a desolate assortment of back yards, rear walls, and rickety stairways. The floor had a worn carpet, and there was a desk, a few chairs and a shelf of law books. The place looked as though it had belonged to a lawyer in reduced circumstances, and I could but wonder how it had come into the possession of Doddridge Knapp, and what had become of its former occupant.

I tried to thrust aside a spirit of melancholy, and looked narrowly to the opportunities offered by the room for attack and defense. The walls were solidly built. The window-casement showed an unusual depth for a building of that height. The wall had been put in to withstand an earthquake shock. The door opening into the hall, the door into Room 16, and the window furnished the three avenues of possible attack or retreat. The window upon examination appeared impracticable. There was a sheer drop of twenty feet, without a projection of any kind below it. The ledge was hardly an inch wide. The iron shutters by which it might be closed did not swing within ten feet of any other window. The one chance of getting in by this line was to drop a rope ladder from the roof. The door opening into Room 16 was not heavy, and the lock was a cheap affair. A good kick would send the whole thing into splinters. As it swung into Number 16 and not into my room it could not be braced with a barricade. Plainly it was not a good place to spend the night should Doddridge Knapp care to engineer another case of mysterious disappearance.

The depression of spirits that progressed with my survey of the room deepened into gloom as I flung myself into the arm-chair before the desk, and tried to plan some way out of the tangle in which I was involved. How was I, single-handed, to contend against the power of the richest man in the city, and bring home to him the murder of Henry Wilton? I could look for no assistance from the police. The words of Detective Coogan were enough to show that only the most convincing proof of guilt, backed by fear of public sentiment, could bring the department to raise a finger against him. And how could I hope to rouse that public sentiment? What would my word count against that of the King of the Street?

Where was the motive for the crime? Until that was made clear I could not hope to piece together the scraps of evidence into a solid structure of proof. And what motive could there be that would reconcile the Doddridge Knapp who sought the life of Henry Wilton, with the Doddridge Knapp of this morning, who was ready to engage him in his confidential business? And had I the right to accept any part in his business? It had the flavor of treachery about it; yet it seemed the only possible chance to come upon the secret springs of his acts, to come in touch with the tools and accomplices in his crime. And the unknown mission, that had brought Henry to his death? How was I to play his part in that? And even if I could take his place, how was I to serve the mysterious employer and Doddridge Knapp at the same time, when Doddridge Knapp was ready to murder me to gain the Unknown's secret.

Fatigue and loss of sleep deepened the dejection of mind that oppressed me with these insistent questions, and as I vainly struggled against it, carried me at last into the oblivion of dreamless slumber.

The next I knew I was awaking to the sound of breaking glass. It was dark but for a feeble light that came from the window. Every bone in my body ached from the cramped position in which I had slept, and it seemed an age before I could rouse myself to act. It was, however, but a second before I was on my feet, revolver in hand, with the desk between me and a possible assailant.

Silence, threatening, oppressive, surrounded me as I stood listening, watching, for the next move. Then I heard a low chuckle, as of some one struggling to restrain his laughter; and so far from sympathizing with his mirth, I was tempted to try the effect of a shot as an assistance in suppressing it.

"I thought the transom was open," said a low voice, which still seemed to be struggling with suppressed laughter.

"I guess it woke him up," said another and harsher voice. "I heard a noise in there."

"You're certain he's there?" asked the first voice with another chuckle.

"Sure, Dicky. I saw him go in, and Porter and I have taken turns on watch ever since."

"Well, it's time he came out," said Dicky. "He can't be asleep after that racket. Say!" he called, "Harry! What's the matter with you? If you're dead let us know."

They appeared friendly, but I hesitated in framing an answer.

"We'll have to break down the door, I guess," said Dicky. "Something must have happened." And a resounding kick shook the panel.

"Hold on!" I cried. "What's wanted?"

"Oh," said Dicky sarcastically. "You've come to life again, have you."

"Well, I'm not dead yet."

"Then strike a light and let us in. And take a look at that reminder you'll find wrapped around the rock I heaved through the transom. I thought it was open." And Dicky went off into another series of chuckles in appreciation of his mistake.

"All right," I said. I was not entirely trustful, and after I had lighted the gas-jet I picked up the stone that lay among the fragments of glass, and unwrapped the paper. The sheet bore only the words:

"At Borton's, at midnight. Richmond."

This was the name of the agent of the Unknown, who had sent the other note. Dicky and his companion must then be protectors instead of enemies. I hastened to unlock the door, and in walked my two visitors.

The first was a young man, tall, well-made, with a shrewd, good-humored countenance, and a ready, confident air about him. I had no trouble in picking him out as the amused Dicky. The other was a black-bearded giant, who followed stolidly in the wake of the younger man.

"You've led me a pretty chase," said Dicky. "If it hadn't been for Pork Chops here, I shouldn't have found you till the cows come home."

"Well, what's up now?" I asked.

"Why, you ought to know," said Dicky with evident surprise. "But you'd better be hurrying down to Borton's. The gang must be there by now."

I could only wonder who Borton might be, and where his place was, and what connection he might have with the mystery, as Dicky took me by the arm and hurried me out into the darkness. The chill night air served to nerve instead of depress my spirits, as the garrulous Dicky unconsciously guided me to the meeting-place, joyously narrating some amusing adventure of the day, while the heavy retainer stalked in silence behind.

Down near the foot of Jackson Street, where the smell of bilge-water and the wash of the sewers grew stronger, and the masts of vessels could just be seen in the darkness outlined against the sky, Dicky suddenly stopped and drew me into a doorway. Our retainer disappeared at the same instant, and the street was apparently deserted. Then out of the night the shape of a man approached with silent steps.

"Five-sixteen," croaked Dicky.

The man gave a visible start.

"Sixteen-five," he croaked in return.

"Any signs?" whispered Dicky.

"Six men went up stairs across the street. Every one of them did the sailor-drunk act."

"Sure they weren't sailors?"

"Well, when six coves goes up the same stairs trying the same dodge, all inside of ten minutes, I has a right to my suspicions. And Darby Meeker ain't been to sea yet that I knows on."

"Darby Meeker!" exclaimed Dicky in a whisper. And he drew a whistle under his breath. "What do you think of that, Wilton? I had no idea he was back from that wild-goose chase you sent him on."

"It looks bad," I admitted cautiously. "I dare say he isn't in good temper."

"You'll have to settle with him for that piece of business," said Dicky with a chuckle.

I failed to see the amusing side of the prospect. I wished I knew what Mr. Meeker looked like.

The guard had melted away into the darkness without another word, and we hurried forward with due caution. Just past the next corner was a lighted room, and the sound of voices broke the quiet. A triangular glass lantern projected from above the door, and such of the paint as had not weathered away made the announcement:

{Illustration: BORTON'S Meals Liquors Lodgings}

We pushed open the door and walked in. The room was large and dingy, the ceiling low. Tables were scattered about the sanded floor. A bar took up the side of the room next the entrance, and a general air of disreputability filled the place. The only attempts at ornament, unless the arrangement of various-colored bottles behind the bar came under that head, were the circles and festoons of dirty cut paper hanging from the ceiling.

About the room, some at the tables, some at the bar, were numbers of stout, rough-looking men, with a few Greek fishermen and two or three sailors.

Behind the bar sat a woman whose appearance in that place almost startled me. She might have been nearing seventy, and a hard and evil life had left its marks on her bent frame and her gaunt face. Her leathery cheeks were lined deep, and a hawk-like nose emphasized the unpleasant suggestions conveyed by her face and figure. But the most remarkable feature about her was her eyes. There was no trace of age in them. Bright and keen as the eyes of a rat, they gave me an unpleasant thrill as I felt her gaze fixed upon me when I entered the door, arm in arm with Dicky. It was as though they had pierced me through, and had laid bare something I would have concealed. It was a relief to pass beyond her into a recessed part of the room where her gaze might waste itself on the back of my head.

"Mother Borton's up late to-night," said Dicky thoughtfully, as he ordered wine.

"You can't blame her for thinking that this crowd needs watching," I suggested with as much of airiness as I could throw into my manner.

Dicky shook his head for a second, and then resumed his light-hearted, bantering way. Yet I could see that he was perplexed and anxious about something that had come to his attention on our arrival.

"You'll not want to attend to business till all the boys are here?" asked Dicky.

"Not unless there's something to be done," I responded dryly.

Dicky gave me a quick glance.

"Of course," he said with a laugh that was not quite easy, "not unless there's something to be done. But I thought there was something."

"You've got a fine mind for thinking, Dicky," I replied. "You'd better cultivate it."

"Well, they say there's nothing like society for that sort of cultivation," said Dicky with another laugh. "They don't say what kind, but I've got a pretty good stock here to choose from." He was at his ease in banter again, but it struck unpleasantly on me that there was something behind.

"Oh, here's a queer friend," he said suddenly, looking to the door. "I'd better speak to him on the matter of countersigns."

"By all means," I said, turning in my chair to survey the new-comer.

I saw the face for an instant. The man wore a sou'wester, and he had drawn his thick, rough coat up as though he would hide his head under the collar. Cheek and chin I could see were covered by a thick blond beard. His movements were apparently clumsy, but his figure was lithe and sinuous. And his eyes! Once seen they never could be forgotten. At their glance, beard and sou'wester dropped away before my fancy, and I saw in my inner vision the man of the serpent glance who had chilled my spirit when I had first put foot in the city. It flashed on me in an instant that this was the same man disguised, who had ventured into the midst of his enemies to see what he might learn of their plans.

As I watched Dicky advance and greet the new-comer with apparent inquiry, a low harsh voice behind gave me a start of surprise.

"This is your wine, I think,"—and a lean, wrinkled arm passed over my shoulder, and a wrinkled face came near my own.

I turned quickly. It was Mother Borton, leering at me with no apparent interest but in her errand.

"What are you doing here?" asked the crone in a voice still lower. "You're not the one they take you to be, but you're none the less in danger. What are you doing with his looks, and in this place? Look out for that man you're with, and the other. Yes, sir," her voice rose. "A small bottle of the white; in a minute, sir."

I understood her as Dicky and the new-comer came to the table and took seats opposite. I commanded my face to give no sign of suspicion, but the warning put me on the alert. I had come on the supposition that I was to meet the band to which Henry Wilton belonged. Instead of being among friends, however, it seemed now that I was among enemies.

"It's all right," said Dicky carelessly. "He's been sent."

"That's lucky," said I with equal unconcern. "We may need an extra hand before morning."

The new-comer could not repress a triumphant flash in the serpent eyes.

"I'm the one for your job," he said hoarsely, his face as impassive as a stone wall.

"What do you know about the job?" I asked suspiciously.

"Only what I've been told," he answered.

"And that is—"

"That it's a job for silence, secrecy, and—"

"Spondulicks," said Dicky with a laugh, as the other hesitated for a word.

"Just so," said the man.

"And what else?" I continued, pressing him firmly.

"Well," he admitted hoarsely, "I learned as how there was to be a change of place to-night, and I might be needed."

I looked at him inquiringly. Perhaps I was on the threshold of knowledge of this cursed business from the mouth of the enemy.

"I heard as how the boy was to be put in a safer place," he said, wagging his head with affected gravity.

Some imp put it into my brain to try him with an unexpected bit of news.

"Oh," I said coolly, "that's all attended to. The change was made yesterday."

The effect of this announcement was extraordinary. The man started with an oath.

"The hell you say!" he exclaimed in a low, smooth voice, far different from the harsh tone he had used thus far. Then he leaped to his feet, with uncontrollable rage.

"Tricked-by God!" he shouted impulsively, and smote the table with his fist.

His outburst threw the room into confusion. Men sprang from their chairs. Glasses and bottles fell with clinking crash. Oaths and shouts arose from the crowd.

"Damn you, I'll have it out of you!" said the man with suppressed fury, his voice once again smooth and low. "Where is the boy?"

He smote the table again; and with that stroke the false beard fell from his chin and cheek, and exposed the malignant face, distorted with rage. A feeling of horrible repulsion came over me, and I should have struck at that serpent's head but for a startling occurrence. As he spoke, a wild scream rose upon the air, and as it echoed through the room the lights went out.

The scream was repeated, and after an instant's silence there rose a chorus of shouts and oaths, mingled with the crash of tables and the clink of breaking glass and crockery, as the men in the room fought their way to the door.

“Oh, my God, I’m cut!” came in a shriek out of the darkness and clamor; and there followed the flash of a pistol and a report that boomed like a cannon in that confined place.

My eyes had not been idle after the warning of Mother Borton, and in an instant I had decided what to do. I had figured out what I conceived to be the plan of the house, and thought I knew a way of escape. There were two doors at the rear of the room, and facing me. One led, as I knew, to the kitchen; the other opened, I reasoned, on a stair to the lodging-rooms above.

Before the scream that accompanied the extinction of the lights had died away, I had made a dive beneath the table, and, lifting with all my might, had sent it crashing over with my enemy under it. With one leap I cleared the remaining table that lay between me and the door. And with the clamor behind me, I turned the knob and bounded up the stairs, three steps at a time.

CHAPTER VII. MOTHER BORTON

The noise of the struggle below continued. Yells and curses rose from the maddened men. Three shots were fired in quick succession, and a cry of "Oh, my Lord!" penetrated through the closed door with the sound of one sorely hurt.

I lingered for a little, listening to the tumult. I was in a strange and dangerous position. Enemies were behind me. There were friends, too, but I knew no way to tell one from the other, and my ignorance had nearly brought me to my death. I hesitated to move, but I could not remain in the open hall; and as the sounds of disturbance from below subsided, I felt my way along the wall and moved cautiously forward.

I had progressed perhaps twenty steps when a door, against which my hand pressed, yielded at the touch and swung slowly open. I strove to stop it, for the first opening showed a dim light within. But the panel gave no hold for my fingers, and my efforts to close the door only swung it open the faster. I drew back a little into the shadow, for I hesitated to dash past the sight of any who might occupy the room.

"Come in!" called a harsh voice.

I hesitated. Behind, the road led to the eating-room with its known dangers. A dash along the hall for the front door meant the raising of an alarm, and probably a bullet as a discourager of burglary. Should I escape this, I could be certain of a warm reception from the enemies on watch outside. Prudence lay in facing the one rather than risking the many. I accepted the invitation and walked into the room.

"I was expecting you," said the harsh voice composedly. "Good evening."

"Good evening," I returned gravely, swallowing my amazement as best I could.

By the table before me sat Mother Borton, contemplating me as calmly as though this meeting were the most commonplace thing in the world. A candle furnished a dim, flickering light that gave to her hard wicked countenance a diabolic leer that struck a chill to my blood.

"Excuse me," I said, "I have lost my way, I fear."

"Not at all," said Mother Borton. "You are in the right place."

"I was afraid I had intruded," I said apologetically.

"I expected you," she repeated. "Shut the door."

I glanced about the room. There was no sign of another person to be seen, and no other door. I obeyed her.

"You might as well sit down," she said with some petulance. "There's nothing up here to hurt you." There was so much meaning in her tone of the things that would hurt me on the floor below that I hastened to show my confidence in her, and drew up a chair to the table.

"At your service," I said, leaning before her with as much an appearance of jaunty self-possession as I could muster.

"Who are you, and what are you doing here?" she asked grimly.

What should I answer? Could I tell her the truth? "Who are you?" she repeated impatiently, gazing on me. "You are not Wilton. Tell me. Who are you?"

The face, hard as it was, seamed with the record of a rough and evil life, as it appeared, had yet a kindly look as it was turned on me.

"My name is Dudley,—Giles Dudley."

"Where is Wilton?"

"Dead."

"Dead? Did you kill him?" The half-kindly look disappeared from her eyes, and the hard lines settled into an expression of malevolent repulsiveness.

"He was my best friend," I said sadly; and then I described the leading events of the tragedy I had witnessed.

The old woman listened closely, and with hardly the movement of a muscle, to the tale I told.

"And you think he left his job to you?" she said with a sneer.

"I have taken it up as well as I can. To be frank with you, Mrs. Borton, I know nothing about his job. I'm going along on blind chance, and trying to keep a whole skin."

The old woman looked at me in amazement.

"Poor boy!" she exclaimed half-pityingly, half-admiringly. "You put your hands to a job you know nothing about, when Henry Wilton couldn't carry it with all his wits about him."

"I didn't do it," said I sullenly. "It has done itself. Everybody insists that I'm Wilton. If I'm to have my throat slit for him I might as well try to do his work. I wish to Heaven I knew what it was, though."

Mother Borton leaned her head on her hand, and gazed on me thoughtfully for a full minute.

"Young man," said she impressively, "take my advice. There's a train for the East in the mornin'. Just git on board, and never you stop short of Chicago."

"I'm not running away," said I bitterly. "I've got a score to settle with the man who killed Henry Wilton. When that score is settled, I'll go to Chicago or anywhere else. Until that's done, I stay where I can settle it."

Mother Borton caught up the candle and moved it back and forth before my face. In her eyes there was a gleam of savage pleasure.

"By God, he's in earnest!" she said to herself, with a strange laugh. "Tell me again of the man you saw in the alley."

I described Doddridge Knapp.

"And you are going to get even with *him*?" she said with a chuckle that had no mirth in it.

"Yes," said I shortly.

"Why, if you should touch him the people of the city would tear you to pieces."

"I shall not touch him. I'm no assassin!" I exclaimed indignantly. "The law shall take him, and I'll see him hanged as high as Haman."

Mother Borton gave a low gurgling laugh.

"The law! oh, my liver, —the law! How young you are, my boy! Oh, ho, oh ho!" And again she absorbed her mirthless laugh, and gave me an evil grin. Then she became grave again, and laid a claw on my sleeve. "Take my advice now, and git on the train."

"Not I!" I returned stoutly.

"I'm doing it for your own good," she said, with as near an approach to a coaxing tone as she could command. It was long since she had used her voice for such a purpose and it grated. "For my sake I'd like to see you go on and wipe out the whole raft of 'em. But I know what'll happen to ye, honey. I've took a fancy to ye. I don't know why. But there's a look on your face that carries me back for forty years, and-don't try it, dearie."

There were actually tears in the creature's eyes, and her hard, wicked face softened, and became almost tender and womanly.

"I can't give up," I said. "The work is put on me. But can't you help me? I believe you want to. I trust you. Tell me what to do-where I stand. I'm all in the dark, but I must do my work." It was the best appeal I could have made.

"You're right," she said. "I'm an old fool, and you've got the real sand. You're the first one except Henry Wilton that's trusted me in forty years, and you won't be sorry for it, my boy. You owe me one, now. Where would you have been to-night if I hadn't had the light doused on ye?"

"Oh, that was your doing, was it? I thought my time had come."

"Oh, I was sure you'd know what to do. It was your best chance."

"Then will you help me, now?" The old crone considered, and her face grew sharp and cunning in its look.

"What can I do?"

"Tell me, in God's name, where I stand. What is this dreadful mystery? Who is this boy? Why is he hidden, and why do these people want to know where he is? Who is behind me, and who threatens me with death?"

I burst out with these questions passionately, almost frantically. This was the first time I had had chance to demand them of another human being.

Mother Borton gave me a leer.

"I wish I could tell you, my dear, but I don't know."

"You mean you dare not tell me," I said boldly. "You have done me a great service, but if I am to save myself from the dangers that surround me I must know more. Can't you see that?"

"Yes," she nodded. "You're in a hard row of stumps, young man."

"And you can help me."

"Well, I will," she said, suddenly softening again. "I took a shine to you when you came in, an' I says to myself, 'I'll save that young fellow,' an' I done it. And I'll do more. Mr. Wilton was a fine gentleman, an' I'd do something, if I could, to git even with those murderin' gutter-pickers that laid him out on a slab."

She hesitated, and looked around at the shadows thrown by the flickering candle.

"Well?" I said impatiently. "Who is the boy, and where is he?"

"Never you mind that, young fellow. Let me tell you what I know. Then maybe we'll have time to go into the things I don't know."

It was of no use to urge her. I bowed my assent to her terms.

"I'll name no names," she said. "My throat can be cut as quick as yours, and maybe a damned sight quicker."

Mother Borton had among her failings a weakness for profanity. I have omitted most of her references to sacred and other subjects of the kind in transcribing her remarks.

"The ones that has the boy means all right. They're rich. The ones as is looking for the boy is all wrong. They'll be rich if they gits him."

"How?"

"Why, I don't know," said Mother Borton. "I'm tellin' you what Henry Wilton told me."

This was maddening. I began to suspect that she knew nothing after all.

"Do you know where he is?" I asked, taking the questioning into my own hands.

"No,"—sullenly.

"Who is protecting him?"

"I don't know."

"Who is trying to get him?"

"It's that snake-eyed Tom Terrill that's leading the hunt, along with Darby Meeker; but they ain't doing it for themselves."

"Is Doddridge Knapp behind them?"

The old woman looked at me suddenly in wild-eyed alarm.

"S-s-h!" she whispered. "Don't name no names."

"But I saw—"

She put her hand over my mouth.

"He's in it somewhere, or the devil is, but I don't know where. He's an awful man. He's everywhere at once. He's—oh Lord! What was that?"

I had become infected with her nervousness, and at a cracking or creaking sound turned around with half an expectation of seeing Doddridge Knapp himself coming in the door.

There was no one there-nothing to be seen but the flickering shadows, and no sound broke the stillness as we listened.

"It's nothing," I said.

"I reckon I ain't got no call to be scared at any crackings in this old house," said Mother Borton with a nervous giggle. "I've hearn 'em long enough. But that man's name gives me the shivers."

"What did he ever do to you?" I asked with some curiosity.

"He never did nothing," she said, "but I hearn tell dreadful things that's gone on of nights,—how Doddridge Knapp or his ghost was seen killing a Chinaman over at North Beach, while Doddridge Knapp or his ghost,—whichever was the other one,—was speaking at a meeting, at the Pavilion. And I hearn of his drinkin' blood—"

"Nonsense!" said I; "where did you get such stories?"

"Well, they're told me for true, and by ones I believe," she said stoutly. "Oh, there's queer things goes on. Doddridge Knapp or the devil, it's all one. But it's ill saying things of them that can be in two places at once." And the old dame looked nervously about her. "They've hushed things up in the papers, and fixed the police, but people have tongues."

I wondered what mystification had given rise to these absurd reports, but there was nothing to be gained by pursuing them. The killing of the Chinaman might have been something to my hand, but if Doddridge Knapp had such a perfect alibi it was a waste of time to look into it.

"And is this all you know?" I asked in disappointment.

Mother Borton tried to remember some other point.

"I don't see how it's going to keep a knife from between my ribs," I complained.

"You keep out of the way of Tom Terrill and his hounds, and you'll be all right, I reckon."

"Am I supposed to be the head man in this business?"

"Yes."

"Who are my men?"

"There's Wilson and Fitzhugh and Porter and Brown," and she named ten or a dozen more.

"And what is Dicky?"

"It's a smart man as can put his finger on Dicky Nahl," said Mother Borton spitefully.

"Nahl is his name?"

"Yes. And I've seen him hobnob with Henry Wilton, and I've seen him thick as thieves with Tom Terrill, and which he's thickest with the devil himself couldn't tell. I call him Slippery Dicky."

"Why did he bring me here to-night?"

"I hearn there's orders come to change the place-the boy's place, you know. You was to tell 'em where the new one was to be, I reckon, but Tom Terrill spoiled things. He's lightning, is Tom Terrill. But I guess he got it all out of Dicky, though where Dicky got it the Lord only knows."

This was all that was to be had from Mother Borton. Either she knew no more, or she was sharp enough to hide a knowledge that might be dangerous, even fatal, to reveal. She was willing to serve me, and I was forced to let it pass that she knew no more.

"Well, I'd better be going then," said I at last. "It's nearly four o'clock, and everything seems to be quiet hereabouts. I'll find my way to my room."

"You'll do no such thing," said Mother Borton. "They've not given up the chase yet. Your men have gone home, I reckon, but I'll bet the saloon that you'd have a surprise before you got to the corner."

"Not a pleasant prospect," said I grimly.

"No. You must stay here. The room next to this one is just the thing for you. See?"

She drew me into the adjoining room, shading the candle as we passed through the hall that no gleam might fall where it would attract attention.

"You'll be safe here," she said. "Now do as I say. Go to sleep and git some rest. You ain't had much, I guess, since you got to San Francisco."

The room was cheerless, but in the circumstances the advice appeared good. I was probably safer here than in the street, and I needed the rest.

"Good night," said my strange protectress, "You needn't git up till you git ready. This is a beautiful room-beautiful. I call it our bridal chamber, though we don't get no brides down here. There won't be no sun to bother your eyes in the mornin', for that window don't open up outside. So there, can't nobody git in unless he comes from inside the house. There, git to bed. Look out you don't set fire to nothing. And put out the candle. Now good night, dearie."

Mother Borton closed the door behind her, and left me to the shadows.

Her departure did not leave me wholly at my ease. I had escaped from my foes, but I was no closer to being in touch with those who would be my friends; and before daylight I might be lying here with my throat slit. At the reflection I hastily bolted the door, and tried the fastenings of the window. All seemed secure, but the sound of a footstep in the passageway gave me a start for an instant.

"Only Mother Borton going down stairs," I thought, with a smile at my fears.

There was nothing to be gained by sitting up, and the candle was past its final inch. I felt that I could not sleep, but I would lie down on the bed and rest my tired limbs, that I might refresh myself for the demands of the day. I kicked off my boots, put my revolver under my hand, and lay down.

Heedless of Mother Borton's warning I left the candle to burn to the socket, and watched the flickering shadows chase each other over walls and ceiling. The shadows grew larger and blacker, and took fantastic shapes of men and beasts. And then with a confused impression of deadly fear and of an effort to escape from peril, a blacker shadow swallowed up all that had gone before, and carried me with it.

CHAPTER VIII. IN WHICH I MEET A FEW SURPRISES

I awoke with the sense of threatened danger strong in my mind. For a moment I was unable to recall where I was, or on what errand I had come. Then memory returned in a flood, and I sprang from the bed and peered about me.

A dim light struggled in from the darkened window, but no cause for apprehension could be seen. I was the only creature that breathed the air of that bleak and dingy room.

I drew aside the curtain, and threw up the window. It opened merely on a light-well, and the blank walls beyond gave back the cheery reflection of a patch of sunlight that fell at an angle from above.

The fresher air that crept in from the window cleared my mind, a dash of water refreshed my body, and I was ready once more to face whatever might befall.

I looked at my watch. It was eight o'clock, and I had slept four hours in this place. Truly I had been imprudent after my adventure below, but I had been right in trusting Mother Borton. Then I began to realize that I was outrageously hungry, and I remembered that I should be at the office by nine to receive the commands of Doddridge Knapp, should he choose to send them.

I threw back the bolt, but when I tried to swing the door open it resisted my efforts. The key had been missing when I closed it, but a sliding bolt had fastened it securely. Now I saw that the door was locked.

Here was a strange predicament. I had heard nothing of the noise of the key before I lost myself in slumber. Mother Borton must have turned it as an additional precaution as I slept. But how was I to get out? I hesitated to make a noise that could attract attention. It might bring some one less kindly disposed than my hostess of the night. But there was no other way. I was trapped, and must take the risk of summoning assistance.

I rapped on the panel and listened. No sound rewarded me. I rapped again more vigorously, but only silence followed. The house might have been the grave for all the signs of life it gave back.

There was something ominous about it. To be locked, thus, in a dark room of this house in which I had already been attacked, was enough to shake my spirit and resolution for the moment. What lay without the door, my apprehension asked me. Was it part of the plot to get the secret it was supposed I held? Had Mother Borton been murdered, and the house seized? Or had Mother Borton played me false, and was I now a prisoner to my own party for my enforced imposture, as one who knew too much to be left at large and too little to be of use? On a second and calmer thought it was evidently folly to bring my jailers about my ears, if jailers there were. I abandoned my half-formed plan of breaking down the door, and turned to the window and the light-well. Another window faced on the same space, not five feet away. If it were but opened I might swing myself over and through it; but it was closed, and a curtain hid the unknown possibilities and dangers of the interior. A dozen feet above was the roof, with no projection or foothold by which it might be reached. Below, the light-well ended in a tinned floor, about four feet from the window sill.

I swung myself down, and with two steps was trying the other window. It was unlocked. I raised the sash cautiously, but its creaking protest seemed to my excited ears to be loud enough to wake any but the dead. I stopped and listened after each squeak of the frame. There was no sign of movement.

Then I pushed aside the curtain cautiously, and looked within. The room appeared absolutely bare. Gaining confidence at the sight, I threw the curtain farther back, and with a bound climbed in, revolver in hand.

A scurrying sound startled me for an instant, and with a scramble I gained my feet, prepared to face whatever was before me. Then I saw the disappearing form of a great rat, and laughed at my fears.

The room was, as I had thought, bare and deserted. There was a musty smell about it, as though it had not been opened for a long time, and dust and desolation lay heavy upon it. A dark stain on the floor near the window suggested to my fancy the idea of blood. Had some wayfarer less fortunate than I been inveigled to his death in this evil place?

There was, however, nothing here to linger for, and I hastened to try the door. It was locked. I stooped to examine the fastening. It was of the cheapest kind, attached to door and casement by small screws. With a good wrench it gave way, and I found myself in a dark side-hall between two rooms. Three steps brought me to the main hall, and I recognized it for the same through which I had felt my way in the darkness of the night. It was not improved by the daylight, and a strange loneliness about it was an oppression to the spirits. There were six or eight rooms on the floor, and the doors glowered threateningly on me, as though they were conscious that I was an intruder in fear of his life.

The intense stillness within the house, instead of reassuring me, served as a threat. After my experience of the night, it spoke of treachery, not of peace.

I took my steps cautiously down the stairs, following the way that led to the side entrance. The saloon and restaurant room I was anxious to evade, for there would doubtless be a barkeeper and several loiterers about. It could not be avoided, however. As I neared the bottom of the stairs, I saw that a door led from the hallway to the saloon, and that it was open.

I moved slowly down, a step at a time, then from over-cautiousness tripped and came down the last three steps at once with the clatter of a four-horse team.

But nobody stirred. Then I glanced through the open door, and was stricken cold with astonishment. The room was empty!

The chairs and tables that a few hours ago I had seen scattered about were gone. There was no sign that the place had been occupied in months.

I stepped into the room that I had seen crowded with eager friends and enemies, eating, drinking, ready for desperate deeds. My step echoed strangely with the echo of an untenanted house. The bar and the shelves behind it were swept clear of the bottles and glasses that had filled them. Dust was thick over the floor and walls. The windows were stained and dirty, and a paper sign on each pane informed the passers-by that the house was "To Let."

Bewildered and apprehensive, I wondered whether, after all, the events of the night, the summons from Dicky Nahl, the walk in the darkness, the scene in the saloon, the encounter with the snake-eyed man, the riot, the rush up the dark stair, and the interview with the old crone, were not a fantastic vision from the land of dreams.

I looked cautiously through the other rooms on the first floor. They were as bare as the main room. The only room in the whole house that held a trace of furniture or occupancy must be the one from which I had escaped. It seemed that an elaborate trap had been set for my benefit with such precautions that I could not prove that it ever had been.

There was, however, no time to waste in prying into this mystery. By my watch it was close on nine o'clock, and Doddridge Knapp might even now be making his way to the office where he had stationed me.

The saloon's front doors were locked fast, but the side door that led from the stairway to the street was fastened only with a spring lock, and I swung it open and stepped to the sidewalk.

A load left my spirits as the door closed behind me. The fresh air of the morning was like wine after the close and musty atmosphere I had been breathing.

The street was but a prosaic place after the haunt of mystery I had just left. It was like stepping from the Dark Ages into the nineteenth century. Yet there was something puzzling about it. The street had no suggestion of the familiar, and it appeared somehow to have been turned end for end. I had lost my sense of direction. The hills were where the bay ought to be. I seemed to have changed sides of the street, and it took me a little time to readjust the points of the compass. I reasoned at last that Dicky Nahl had led me to the street below before turning to the place, and I had not noticed that we had doubled on our course.

I hurried along the streets with but a three-minute stop to swallow a cup of coffee and a roll, and once more mounted the stairs to the office and opened the door to Number 15.

The place was in disorder. The books that had been arranged on the desk and shelves were now scattered about in confusion, as though they had been hurriedly examined and thrown aside in a fruitless search. This was a disturbing incident, and I was surprised to discover that the door into the adjoining room was ajar. I pushed it wide open, and started back. Before me stood Doddridge Knapp, his face pale as the face of a corpse, and his eyes starting as though the dead had risen before him.

CHAPTER IX. A DAY IN THE MARKET

The King of the Street stood for a moment staring at me with that strange and fearsome gaze. What was there in that dynamic glance that struck a chill to my spirit as though the very fountain of life had been attacked? Was it the manifestation of the powerful will behind that mask? Or was it terror or anger that was to be read in the fiery eyes that gleamed from beneath those bushy brows, and in the play of the cruel mouth, which from under that yellow-gray mustache gave back the sign of the Wolf?

"Have you any orders, sir?" I asked in as calm a voice as I could command.

"Oh, it's you, is it?" said the Wolf slowly, covering his fangs.

It flashed on me that the attack in the Borton den was of his planning, that Terrill was his tool, and that he had supposed me dead. It was thus that I could account for his startled gaze and evident discomposure.

"Nine o'clock was the time, you said," I suggested deferentially. "I believe it's a minute or two past."

"Oh, yes," said Doddridge Knapp, pulling himself together. "Come in here."

He looked suspiciously at me as he took a seat at his desk, and motioned me to another.

"I had a little turn," he said, eying me nervously; "a vertigo, I believe the doctor called it. Just reach my overcoat pocket there, will you?—the left-hand side. Yes, bring me that flask."

He poured out a small glass of liquor, and the rich odor of brandy rose through the room. Then he took a vial from an inside pocket, counted a few drops into the glass, and drank it at a swallow.

I marveled at the actions of the man, and wondered if he was nerving himself to some deed that he lacked courage to perform.

When he had cleared his throat of the fiery liquor, the Wolf turned to me with a more composed and kindly expression.

"I never drink during business hours," he said with a trace of apology in his tone. "It's bad for business, and for the drink, too. But this is a little trouble I've had a touch of in the last two months. Just remember, young man, that I expect you to do your drinking after business is over-and not too much then. And now to business," said my employer with decision. "Take down these orders."

The King of the Street was himself once more, and I marveled again at the quickness and clearness of his directions. I was to buy one hundred shares of this stock, sell five hundred of that stock, buy one thousand of another in blocks of one hundred, and sell the same in a single block at the last session.

"And the last thing you do," he continued, "buy every share of Omega that is offered. There'll be a big block of it thrown on the market, and more in the afternoon. Buy it, whatever the price. There's likely to be a big slump. Don't bid for it-don't keep up the price, you understand-but get it."

"If somebody else is snapping it up, do I understand that I'm not to bid over them?"

"You're not to understand anything of the kind," he said, with a little disgust in his tone. "You're to get the stock. You've bought and sold enough to know how to do that. But don't start a boom for the price. Let her go down. Sabe?"

I felt that there was deep water ahead.

"Perfectly," I said. "I think I see the whole thing."

The King of the Street looked at me with a grim smile.

"Maybe you do, but all the same you'd better keep your money out of this little deal unless you can spare it as well as not. Well, get back to your room. You've got your check-book all right?"

Alone once more I was in despair of unraveling the tangle in which I was involved. I felt convinced that Doddridge Knapp was the mover in the plots that sought my life. He had, I felt sure, believed me dead, and was startled into fear at my unheralded appearance. Yet why should he trust me with his business? I could not doubt that the buying and selling he had given to my care were important. I knew nothing about the price of stocks but I was sure that the orders he had given me involved many thousands of dollars. Yet it might be-the thought struck home to me-that the credit had not been provided for me, and my checks on the Nevada Bank would serve only to land me in jail.

The disturbed condition of the books attracted my attention once more. The volumes were scattered over the desk and thrown about the room as though somebody had been seeking for a mislaid document. I looked curiously over them as I replaced them on the shelves. They were law-books, California Reports, and the ordinary text-books and form-books of the attorney. All bore on the fly-leaf the name of Horace H. Plymire, but no paper or other indication of ownership could I find.

I wondered idly who this Plymire might be, and pictured to myself some old attorney who had fallen into the hands of Doddridge Knapp, and had, through misfortune, been forced to sell everything for the mess of pottage to keep life in him. But there was small time for musing, and I went out to do Doddridge Knapp's bidding in the stock-gambling whirlpool of Pine Street.

There was already a confused murmur of voices about the rival exchanges that were the battlegrounds of millionaires. The "curbstone boards" were in session. The buyers who traded face to face, and the brokers who carried their offices under their hats, were noisily bargaining, raising as much clamor over buying and selling a few shares as the most important dealer in the big boards could raise over the transfer of as many thousands.

It was easy to find Bockstein and Eppner, and there could be no mistaking the prosperity of the firm. The indifference of the clerks to my presence, and the evident contempt with which an order for a hundred shares of something was being taken from an apologetic old gentleman were enough to assure me of that.

Bockstein and Eppner were together, evidently consulting over the business to be done. Bockstein was tall and gray-haired, with a stubby gray beard. Eppner was short and a little stooped, with a blue-black mustache, snapping blue-black eyes, and strong blue-black dots over his face where his beard struggled vainly against the devastating razor. Both were strongly marked with the shrewd, money-getting visage. I set forth my business.

"You wand to gif a larch order?" said Bockstein, looking over my memoranda. "Do you haf references?"

"Yes," echoed Eppner. "References are customary, you know." He spoke in a high-keyed voice that had irritating suggestions in it.

"Is there any reference better than cash?" I asked.

The partners looked at each other. "None," they replied.

"How much will secure you on the order?"

They named a heavy margin, and the sum total took my heart into my mouth. How large a balance I could draw against I had not the faintest idea. Possibly this was a trap to throw me into jail as a common swindler attempting to pass worthless checks. But there was no time to hesitate. I drew a check for the amount, signed Henry Wilton's name, and tossed it over to Bockstein.

"All ridt," said the senior partner. "Zhust talk it ofer vit Misder Eppner. He goes on der floor."

I knew well enough what was wanted. My financial standing was to be tested by the head of the firm, while the junior partner kept me amused.

Eppner was quick to take my ideas. A few words of explanation, and he understood perfectly what I wanted.

"You have not bought before?" It was an interrogation, not an assertion.

"Oh, yes," I said carelessly, "but not through you, I believe."

"No, no, I think not. I should have remembered you."

I thought this might be a favorable opportunity to glean a little information of what was going on in the market.

"Are there any good deals in prospect?" I ventured.

I could see in the blue-black depths of his eyes that an unfavorable opinion he had conceived of my judgment was deepened by this question. There was doubtless in it the flavor of the amateur.

"We never advise our customers," was the high-keyed reply.

"Certainly not," I replied. "I don't want advice-merely to know what is going on."

"Excuse me, but I never gossip. It is a rule I make."

"It might interfere with your opportunities to pick up a good bargain now and then," I suggested, as the blue-black man seemed at a loss for words.

"We never invest in stocks," was the curt reply.

"Excellent idea," said I, "for those who know too much or too little."

Eppner failed to smile, and could think of nothing to say. I was a little abashed, notwithstanding the tone of haughty indifference I took. I began to feel very young before this machine-like impersonation of the market.

Bockstein relieved the embarrassment of the situation by coming in out of breath, with a brave pretense of having been merely consulting a customer in the next room.

"You haf exblained to Misder Eppner?" he inquired. "Den all is done. Here is a card to der Board Room. If orders you haf to gif, Eppner vill dake dem on der floor. Zhust gif him der check for margin, and all is vell."

At the end of this harangue I found myself outside the office, with Bockstein's back waddling toward the private room where the partners were to have their last consultation before going to the Board.

My check had been honored, then, and Bockstein had assured himself of my solvency. In the rebound from anxiety, I swelled with the pride of a capitalist-on Doddridge Knapp's money.

In the Board Room of the big Exchange the uproar was something astonishing. The confusion outside had given me a suggestion that the business of buying and selling stocks was carried on in a somewhat less conventional manner than the trade in groceries. But it had not quite prepared me for the scene in the Exchange.

The floor was filled with a crowd of lunatics, howling, shaking fists, and pushing and scrambling from one place to another with the frenzy of a band of red men practising the scalp dance by the bright glow of the white man's fire-water. A confused roar rose from the mob, and whenever it showed signs of flagging a louder cry from some quarter would renew its strength, and a blast of shouts and screams, a rush of struggling men toward the one who had uttered the cry, and a waving of fists, arms, and hats, suggested visions of lynching and sudden death.

After a little I was able to discover a method in the outbreaks of apparent lunacy, and found that the shouts and yells and screams, the shaking of fists, and the waving of arms were merely a more or less energetic method of bidding for stocks; that the ringing of gongs and the bellow of the big man who smiled on the bear-garden from the high desk were merely the audible signs that another stock was being called; and that the brazen-voiced reading of a roll was merely the official announcement of the record of bargains and sales that had been going on before me.

It was my good fortune to make out so much before the purchase of the stocks on my order list was completed. The crisis was at hand in which I must have my wits about me, and be ready to act for myself. Eppner rushed up and reported the bargains made, handing me a slip with the figures he had paid for the stocks. He was no longer the impassive engine of business that he had appeared in the back room of his office. He was now the embodiment of the riot I had been observing. His blue-black hair was rumpled and on end. His blue-black eyes flashed with animation. The blue-black dots that showed where his beard would be if he had let it were almost overwhelmed by the glow that excitement threw into his sallow cheeks.

"Any more orders?" he gasped. He was trembling with excitement and suppressed eagerness for the fray.

"Yes," I shouted above the roar about me. "I want to buy Omega."

He gave a look that might have been a warning, if I could have read it; but it was gone with a shrug as though he would say, "Well, it's no business of mine."

"How much?" he asked. "Wait!"

He started away at a scream from the front, but returned in a moment. He had bought or sold something, but I had not the least idea what it was, or which he had done.

"It's coming!" he yelled in my ear.

The gong rang. There was a confused cry from the man at the big desk. And pandemonium let loose.

I had thought the riot that had gone before as near the climax of noise as it was possible to get. I was mistaken. The roar that followed the call was to the noise that had gone before as is the hurricane to the zephyr. There was a succession of yells, hoots, cries and bellows; men rushed wildly at each other, swung in a mad dance, jumped up and down; and the floor became a frantic sea of fists, arms, hats, heads, and all things movable.

"Omega opens at sixty-five," shouted Eppner.

"Bid sixty," I shouted in reply, "but get all you can, even if you have to pay sixty-five."

Eppner gave a bellow, and skated into a group of fat men, gesticulating violently. The roar increased, if such a thing were possible.

In a minute Eppner was back, perspiring, and I fancied a trifle worried.

"They're dropping it on me," he gasped in my ear. "Five hundred at sixty-two and one thousand at sixty. Small lots coming fast and big ones on the way."

"Good! Bid fifty-five, and then fifty, but get them."

With a roar he rushed into the midst of a whirling throng. I saw twenty brokers about him, shouting and threatening. One in his eagerness jumped upon the shoulders of a fat man in front of him, and shook a paper under his nose.

I could make out nothing of what was going on, except that the excitement was tremendous.

Twice Eppner reported to me. The stock was being hammered down stroke by stroke. There was a rush to sell. Fifty-five —fifty-three —fifty, came the price-then by leaps to forty-five and forty. It was a panic. At last the gong sounded, and the scene was over. Men staggered from the Exchange, white as death, some cursing, some angry and red, some despairing, some elate. I could see that ten had lost for one who had gained.

Eppner reported at the end of the call. He had bought for me twelve thousand five hundred shares, over ten thousand of them below fifty. The total was frightful. There was half a million dollars to pay when the time for settlement came. It was folly to suppose that my credit at the Nevada was of this size. But I put a bold face on it, gave a check for the figure that Eppner named, and rose.

"Any more orders?" he asked.

"Not till afternoon."

As I passed into the street I was astonished at the swift transformation that had come over it. The block about the Exchange was crowded with a tossing throng, hundreds upon hundreds pushing toward its fateful doors. But where cheerfulness and hope had ruled, fear and gloom now vibrated in electric waves before me. The faces turned to the pitiless, polished granite front of the great gambling-hall were white and drawn, and on them sat Ruin and Despair. The men were for the most part silent, with here and there one cursing; the women, who were there by scores, wept and mourned; and from the multitudes rose that peculiar whisper of crowds that tells of apprehension of things worse to come. And this, I must believe, was the work of Doddridge Knapp.

CHAPTER X. A TANGLE OF SCHEMES

Doddridge Knapp was seated calmly in my office when I opened the door. There was a grim smile about the firm jaws, and a satisfied glitter in the keen eyes. The Wolf had found his prey, and the dismay of the sheep at the sight of his fangs gave him satisfaction instead of distress.

The King of the Street honored me with a royal nod.

"There seems to have been a little surprise for somebody on the Board this morning," he suggested.

"I heard something about it on the street," I admitted.

"It was a good plan and worked well. Let me see your memoranda of purchases."

I gave him my slips.

He looked over them with growing perplexity in his face.

"Here's twelve thousand five hundred shares of Omega."

"Yes."

"You paid too much for that first lot." He was still poring over the list.

"It's easier to see that now than then," I suggested dryly.

"Humph! yes. But there's something wrong here." He was comparing my list with another in his hand.

"There!" I thought; "my confounded ignorance has made a mess of it." But I spoke with all the confidence I could assume: "What's the matter, now?"

"Eleven thousand and twelve thousand five hundred make twenty three thousand five hundred; and here are sales of Omega this morning of thirty-three thousand eight hundred and thirty." He seemed to be talking more to himself than to me, and to be far from pleased.

"How's that? I don't understand." I was all in the dark over his musings.

"I picked up eleven thousand shares in the other Boards this morning, and twelve thousand five hundred through you, but somebody has taken in the other ten thousand." The King of the Street seemed puzzled and, I thought, a little worried.

"Well, you got over twenty-three thousand shares," I suggested consolingly. "That's a pretty good morning's work."

The King of the Street gave me a contemptuous glance.

"Don't be a fool, Wilton. I sold ten thousand of those shares to myself."

A new light broke upon me. I was getting lessons of one of the many ways in which the market was manipulated.

"Then you think that somebody else —"

The King of the Street broke in with a grim smile.

"Never mind what I think. I've got the contract for doing the thinking for this job, and I reckon I can 'tend to it."

The great speculator was silent for a few moments.

"I might as well be frank with you," he said at last. "You'll have to know something, to work intelligently. I must get control of the Omega Company, and to do it I've got to have more stock. I've been afraid of a combination against me, and I guess I've struck it. I can't be sure yet, but when those ten thousand shares were gobbled up on a panicky market, I'll bet there's something up."

"Who is in it?" I asked politely.

"They've kept themselves covered," said the King of the Street, "but I'll have them out in the open before the end. And then, my boy, you'll see the fur fly."

As these words were uttered I could see the yellow-gray goatee rise like bristles, and the fangs of the Wolf shine white under the yellow-gray mustache.

"I've got a few men staked out," he continued slowly, "and I reckon I'll know something about it by this time to-morrow." There was the growl of the Wolf in his voice.

"Now for this afternoon," he continued. "There's got to be some sharp work done. I reckon the falling movement is over. We've got to pay for what we get from now on. I've got a man looking after the between-Board trading. With the scare that's on in the chipper crowd out there, I look to pick up a thousand shares or so at about forty."

"Well, what's the program?" I asked cheerfully.

"Buy," he said briefly. "Take everything that's offered this side of seventy-five."

"Um-there's a half-million wanted already to settle for what I bought this morning."

The bushy brows drew down, but the King of the Street answered lightly:

"Your check is good for a million, my boy, as long as it goes to settle for what you're ordered to buy." Then he added grimly: "I don't think you'd find it worth much for anything else."

There was a knock at the door beyond, and he hastily rose.

"Be here after the two-thirty session," he said. And the Wolf, huge and masterful, disappeared with a stealthy tread, and the door closed softly behind him.

A million dollars! My check honored for unlimited amounts! Doddridge Knapp trusting me with a great fortune! I was overwhelmed, intoxicated, with the consciousness of power.

Yet this was the man who had brought death to Henry Wilton, and had twice sought my life in the effort to wrest from me a packet of information I did not have. This was the man whose face had gleamed fierce and hateful in the lantern's flash in the alley. This was the man I had sworn to bring to the gallows for a brutal crime. And now I was his trusted agent, with control, however limited, of millions.

It was a puzzle too deep for me. I was near coming to Mother Borton's view that there was something uncanny about Doddridge Knapp. Did two spirits animate that body? What was the thread that should join all parts of the mystery into one harmonious whole?

I wondered idly who Doddridge Knapp's visitor might be, but as I could see no way of finding out, and felt no special concern over his identity or purposes, I rose and left the office. As I stepped into the hall I discovered that somebody had a deeper curiosity than I. A man was stooping to the keyhole of Doddridge Knapp's room in the endeavor to see or hear. As he heard the sound of my opening door he started up, and with a bound, was around the turn of the hall and pattering down the stairs.

In another bound I was after him. I had seen his form for but a second, and his face not at all. But in that second I knew him for Tim Terrill of the snake-eyes and the murderous purpose.

When I reached the head of the stairs he was nowhere to be seen, but I heard the patter of his feet below and plunged down three steps at a time and into Clay street, nearly upsetting a stout gentleman in my haste. The street was busy with people, but no sign of the snake-eyed man greeted me.

Much disturbed in mind at this apparition of my enemy, I sought in vain for some explanation of his presence. Was he spying on Doddridge Knapp? Did he not stand on a better footing with his employer than this? He was, I must suppose, trusted with the most secret and evil purposes of that strange man, and should be able to speak with him on even terms. Yet here he was, doing the work of the merest spy. What wickedness was he planning? What treachery was he shaping in his designs on the man whose bread he was eating and whose plans of crime he was the chief agent to assist or execute?

I must have stood gaping in the street like a countryman at a fair as I revolved these questions in my mind without getting an answer to them, for I was roused by a man bumping into me roughly.

I suspected that he had done it on purpose, but I begged his pardon and felt for my watch. I could find none of my personal property missing, but I noticed the fellow reeling back toward me, and doubled my fist with something of an intention to commit a breach of the peace if he repeated his trick. I thought better of it, and started by him briskly, when he spoke in a low tone:

"You'd better go to your room, Mr. Wilton." He said something more that I did not catch, and, reeling on, disappeared in the crowd before I could turn to mark or question him.

I thought at first that he meant the room I had just left. Then it occurred to me that it was the room Henry had occupied-the room in which I had spent my first dreadful night in San Francisco, and had not revisited in the thirty hours since I had left it.

The advice suited my inclination, and in a few minutes I was entering the dingy building and climbing the worn and creaking stairs. The place lost its air of mystery in the broad sunshine and penetrating daylight, and though its interior was as gloomy as ever, it lacked the haunting suggestions it had borrowed from darkness and the night.

Slipped under the door I found two notes. One was from Detective Coogan, and read:

"Inquest this afternoon. Don't want you. Have another story. Do you want the body?"

The other was in a woman's hand, and the faint perfume of the first note I had received rose from the sheet. It read:

"I do not understand your silence. The money is ready. What is the matter?"

The officer's note was easy enough to answer. I found paper, and, assuring Detective Coogan of my gratitude at escaping the inquest, I asked him to turn the body over to the undertaker to be buried at my order.

The other note was more perplexing. I could make nothing of it. It was evidently from my unknown employer, and her anxiety was plain to see. But I was no nearer to finding her than before, and if I knew how to reach her I knew not what to say. As I was contemplating this state of affairs with some dejection, and sealing my melancholy note to Detective Coogan, there was a quick step in the hall and a rap at the panel. It was a single person, so I had no hesitation in opening the door, but it gave me a passing satisfaction to have my hand on the revolver in my pocket as I turned the knob.

It was a boy, who thrust a letter into my hand.

"Yer name Wilton?" he inquired, still holding on to the envelope.

"Yes."

"That's yourn, then." And he was prepared to make a bolt.

"Hold on," I said. "Maybe there's an answer."

"No, there ain't. The bloke as gave it to me said there weren't."

"Well, here's something I want you to deliver," said I, taking up my note to Detective Coogan. "Do you know where the City Hall is?"

"Does I know-what are yer givin' us?" said the boy with infinite scorn in his voice.

"A quarter," I returned with a laugh, tossing him the coin. "Wait a minute."

"Yer ain't bad stuff," said the boy with a grin. I tore open the envelope and read on the sheet that came from it:

"Sell everything you bought-never mind the price. Other orders off. D. K."

I gasped with amazement. Had Doddridge Knapp gone mad? To sell twelve thousand five hundred shares of Omega was sure to smash the market, and the half-million dollars that had been put into them would probably shrink by two hundred thousand or more if the order was carried out.

I read the note again.

Then a suspicion large enough to overshadow the universe grew up in my brain. I recalled that Doddridge Knapp had given me a cipher with which he would communicate with me, and I believed, moreover, that he had no idea where I might be at the present moment.

"It's all right, sonny," I said. "Trot along."

"Where's yer letter?" asked the boy, loyally anxious to earn his quarter.

"It won't have to go now," I said coolly. I believed that the boy meant no harm to me, but I was not taking any risks.

The boy sauntered down the hall, singing *My Name Is Hildebrandt Montrose*, and I was left gazing at the letter with a melancholy smile.

"Well, I must look like a sucker if they think I can be taken in by a trick like that," was my mental comment. I charged the scheme up to my snake-eyed friend and had a poorer opinion of his intelligence than I had hitherto entertained. Yet I was astonished that he should, even with the most hearty wish to bring about my downfall, contrive a plan that would inflict a heavy loss on his employer and possibly ruin him altogether. There was more beneath than I could fathom. My brain refused to work in the maze of contradictions and mysteries, plots and counterplots, in which I was involved.

I took my way at last toward the market, and, hailing a boy to whom I intrusted my letter to Detective Coogan, walked briskly to Pine Street.

CHAPTER XI. THE DEN OF THE WOLF

The street had changed its appearance in the two or three hours since I had made my way from the Exchange through the pallid, panic-stricken mob. There were still thousands of people between the corner of Montgomery Street and Leidesdorff, and the little alley itself was packed full of shouting, struggling traders. The thousands were broken into hundreds of groups, and men were noisily buying and selling, or discussing the chances of the market when the "big Board" should open once more. But there was an air of confidence, almost of buoyancy, in place of the gloom and terror that had lowered over the street at noon. Plainly the panic was over, and men were inspirited by a belief that "stocks were going up."

I made a few dispositions accordingly. Taking Doddridge Knapp's hint, I engaged another broker as a relief to Eppner, a short fat man, with the baldest head I ever saw, a black beard and a hook-nose, whose remarkable activity and scattering charges had attracted my attention in the morning session.

Wallbridge was his name, I found, and he proved to be as intelligent as I could wish—a merry little man, with a joke for all things, and a flow of words that was almost overwhelming.

"Omega? Yes," chuckled the stout little broker, after he had assured himself of my financial standing. "But you ought to have bought this morning, if that's what you want. It was hell popping and the roof giving 'way all at once." The little man had an abundant stock of profanity which he used unconsciously and with such original variations that one almost forgot the blasphemy of it while listening to him. "You ought to have been there," he continued, "and watched the boys shell 'em out!"

"Yes, I heard you had lively times."

"Boiling," he said, with coruscating additions in the way of speech and gesture. "If it hadn't been for Decker and some fellow we haven't had a chance to make out yet the bottom of the market would have been resting on the roof of the lower regions." The little man's remark was slightly more direct and forcible, but this will do for a revised version.

"Decker!" I exclaimed, pricking up my ears. "I thought he had quit the market."

As I had never heard of Mr. Decker before that moment this was not exactly the truth, but I thought it would serve me better.

"Decker out of it!" gasped Wallbridge, his bald head positively glistening at the absurdity of the idea. "He'll be out of it when he's carried out."

"I meant out of Omega. Is he getting up a deal?"

The little broker looked vexed, as though it crossed his mind that he had said too much.

"Oh, no. Guess not. Don't think he is," he said rapidly. "Just wanted to save the market, I guess. If Omega had gone five points lower, there would have been the sickest times in the Street that we've seen since the Bank of California closed and the shop across the way,"—pointing his thumb at the Exchange,—"had to be shut up. But maybe it wasn't Decker, you know. That's just what was rumored on the Street, you know."

I suspected that my little broker knew more than he was willing to tell, but I forbore to press him further; and giving him the order to buy all the Omega stock he could pick up under fifty, I made my way to Eppner.

The blue-black eyes of that impassive agent snapped with a glow of interest when I gave him my order to sell the other purchases of the morning and buy Omega, but faded into a dull stare when I lingered for conversation.

I was not to be abashed.

"I wonder who was picking up Omega this morning?" I said.

"Oh, some of the shorts getting ready to fill contracts," he replied in his dry, uninterested tones.

"I heard that Decker was in the market for the stock," I said.

The blue-black eyes gave a flash of genuine surprise.

"Decker!" he exclaimed. Then his eyes fell, and he paused a moment before replying in his high inflexible voice. "He might be."

"Is he after Omega, or is he just bracing up the market?"

"Excuse me," said Eppner with the cold reflection of an apologetic tone, "but we never advise customers. Are you walking over to the Exchange?"

In the Exchange all was excitement, and the first call brought a roar of struggling brokers. I could make nothing of the clamor, but my nearest neighbor shouted in my ear:

"A strong market!"

"It looks that way," I shouted back. It certainly was strong in noise.

I made out at last that prices were being held to the figures of the morning's session, and in some cases were forced above them.

The excitement grew as the call approached Omega. There was an electric tension in the air that told of the anxious hopes and fears that centered in the coming struggle. The stock was called at last, and I looked for a roar that would shake the building and a scene of riot on the floor that would surpass anything I had witnessed yet.

It failed to come. There was almost a pause in the proceedings.

I caught a glimpse of Doddridge Knapp across the room, looking on with a grim smile on the wolf jaws and an apparently impassive interest in the scene. I marveled at his coolness when his fortune, perhaps, turned on the events of the next five minutes. He gave no sign, nor once looked in my direction.

The clamor on the floor began and swelled in volume, and a breath of visible relief passed over the anxious assembly.

Wallbridge and Eppner made a dive at once for a yelling broker, and a cold chill ran down my back. I saw then that I had set my brokers bidding against each other for the same stock.

"Great Mammon!" I thought. "If Doddridge Knapp ever finds it out, what a circus there will be!"

"She's going up!" said my neighbor with a shout of joy. He owned none of the stock, but like the rest of the populace he was a bull on principle.

I nodded with a dubious attempt to imitate his signs of satisfaction.

Forty-five —forty-seven —fifty-five —it was going up by leaps. I blessed the forethought that had suggested to me to put a limit on Wallbridge and stop the competition between my agents at fifty. The contest grew warmer. I could follow with difficulty the course of the proceedings, but I knew that Omega was bounding upward.

The call closed amid animation; but the excitement was nothing compared to the scene that had followed the fall in the morning. Omega stood at eighty asked, and seventy-eight bid, and the ship of the stock gamblers was again sailing on an even keel. Some hundreds had been washed overboard, but there were thousands left, and nobody foresaw the day when the market would take the fashion of a storm-swept hulk, with only a chance survivor clinging here and there to the wreckage and exchanging tales of the magnificence that once existed.

The session was over at last, and Wallbridge and Eppner handed me their memoranda of purchases.

"You couldn't pick Omega off the bushes this afternoon, Mr. Wilton," said Wallbridge, wiping his bald head vigorously. "There's fools at all times, and some of 'em were here and ready to drop what they had; but not many. I gathered in six hundred for you, but I had to fight for it."

I thanked the merry broker, and gave him a check for his balance.

Eppner had done some better with a wider margin, but all told I had added but three thousand one hundred shares to my list. I wondered how much of this had been sold to me by my employer. Plainly, if Doddridge Knapp was needing Omega stock he would have to pay for it.

There was no one to be seen as I reached Room 15. The connecting door was closed and locked, and no sound came from behind it. I turned to arrange the books, to keep from a bad habit of thinking over the inexplicable. But there was nothing exciting enough, in the statutes or reports of court decisions or text-books, to cover up the questions against which I had been beating in vain ever since I had entered this accursed city.

An hour passed, and no Doddridge Knapp. It was long past office hours. The sun had disappeared in the bank of fog that was rolling up from the ocean and coming in wisps and streamers over the hills, and the light was fast failing.

Just as I was considering whether my duty to my employer constrained me to wait longer, I caught sight of an envelope that had been slipped under the door. I wondered, as I hastily opened it and brought its inclosure to the failing light, how it could have got there. It was in cipher, but it yielded to the key with which Doddridge Knapp had provided me. I made it out to be this:

"Come to my house to-night.
Bring your contracts with you.
Knapp."

I was thrown into some perplexity by this order. For a little I suspected a trap, but on second thought this seemed unlikely. The office furnished as convenient a place for homicidal diversions as he could wish, if these were in his intention, and possibly a visit to Doddridge Knapp in his own house would give me a better clue to his habits and purposes, and a better chance of bringing home to him his awful crime, than a month together on the Street.

The clocks were pointing past eight when I mounted the steps that led to Doddridge Knapp's door. Doddridge Knapp's house fronted upper Pine Street much as Doddridge Knapp himself fronted lower Pine Street. There was a calmly aggressive look about it that was typical of the owner. It defied the elements with easy strength, as Doddridge Knapp defied the storms of the market. I had the fancy that even if the directory had not given me its position I might have picked it out from its neighbors by its individuality, its impression of reserve force.

I had something of trepidation, after all, as I rang the bell, for I was far from being sure that Doddridge Knapp was above carrying out his desperate purposes in his own house, and I wondered whether I should ever come out again, once I was behind those massive doors. I had taken the precaution to find a smaller revolver, "suitable for an evening call," as I assured myself, but it did not look to be much of a protection in case the house held a dozen ruffians of the Terrill brand. However, I must risk it. I gave my name to the servant who opened the door.

"This way," he said quietly.

I had hardly time as I passed to note the large hall, the handsome staircase, and the wide parlors that hung rich with drapery, but in darkness. I was led beyond and behind them, and in a moment was ushered into a small, plainly-furnished room; and at a desk covered with papers sat Doddridge Knapp, the picture of the Wolf in his den.

"Sit down, Wilton," said he with grim affability, giving his hand. "You won't mind if an old man doesn't get up."

I made some conventional reply.

"Sorry to disappoint you this afternoon, and take up your evening," he said; "but I found some business that needed more immediate attention. There was a little matter that had to be looked after in person." And the Wolf's fangs showed in a cruel smile, which assured me that the "little matter" had terminated unhappily for the other man.

I airily professed myself happy to be at his service at any time.

"Yes, yes," he said; "but let's see your memoranda. Did you do well this afternoon?"

"No-o," I returned apologetically. "Not so well as I wished."

He took the papers and looked over them carefully.

"Thirty-one hundred," he said reflectively. "Those sales were all right. Well, I was afraid you couldn't get above three thousand. I didn't get more than two thousand in the other Boards and on the Street."

"That was the best I could do," I said modestly. "They average at sixty-five. Omega got away from us this afternoon like a runaway horse."

"Yes, yes," said the King of the Street, studying his papers with drawn brows. "That's all right. I'll have to wait a bit before going further." I bowed as became one who had no idea of the plans ahead.

"And now," said Doddridge Knapp, turning on me a keen and lowering gaze, "I'd like to know what call you have to be spying on me?"

I opened my eyes wide in wonder.

"Spying? I don't understand."

"No?" said he, with something between a growl and a snarl. "Well, maybe you don't understand that, either!" And he tossed me a bit of paper.

I felt sure that I did not. My ignorance grew into amazement as I read. The slip bore the words:

> "I have bought Crown Diamond. What's the limit?
> Wilton."

"I certainly don't understand," I said. "What does it mean?"

"The man who wrote it ought to know," growled Doddridge Knapp, with his eyes flashing and the yellow-gray mustache standing out like bristles. The fangs of the Wolf were in sight.

"Well, you'll have to look somewhere else for him," I said firmly. "I never saw the note, and never bought a share of Crown Diamond."

Doddridge Knapp bent forward, and looked for an instant as though he would leap upon me. His eye was the eye of a wild beast in anger. If I had written that note I should have gone through the window without stopping for explanations. As I had not written it I sat there coolly and looked him in the face with an easy conscience.

"Well, well," he said at last, relaxing his gaze, "I almost believe you."

"There's no use going any further, Mr. Knapp, unless you believe me altogether."

"I see you understand what I was going to say," he said quietly. "But if you didn't send that, who did?"

"Well, if I were to make a guess, I should say it was the man who wrote this."

I tossed him in turn the note I had received in the afternoon, bidding me sell everything.

The King of the Street looked at it carefully, and his brows drew lower and lower as its import dawned on him. The look of angry perplexity deepened on his face.

"Where did you get this?"

I detailed the circumstances.

The anger that flashed in his eyes was more eloquent than the outbreak of curses I expected to hear.

"Um!" he said at last with a grim smile. "It's lucky, after all, that you had something besides cotton in that skull of yours, Wilton."

"A fool might have been caught by it," I said modestly.

"There looks to be trouble ahead," he said, "There's a rascally gang in the market these days." And the King of the Street sighed over the dishonesty that had corrupted the stock gamblers' trade. I smiled inwardly, but signified my agreement with my employer.

"Well, who wrote them?" he asked almost fiercely. "They seem to come from the same hand."

"Maybe you'd better ask that fellow who had his eye at your keyhole when I left the office this noon."

"Who was that?" The Wolf gave a startled look. "Why didn't you tell me?"

"He was a well-made, quick, lithe fellow, with an eye that reminded me of a snake. I gave chase to him, but couldn't overhaul him. He squirmed away in the crowd, I guess."

The last part of my tale was unheard. At the description of the snake-eyed man, Doddridge Knapp sank back in his chair, the flash of anger died out of his eyes, and his mind was far away.

Was it terror, or anxiety, or wonder, that swept in shadow across his face? The mask that never gave up a thought or purpose before the changing fortunes of the market was not likely to fail its owner here. I could make nothing out of the page before me, except that the vision of Terrill had startled him.

"Why didn't you tell me?" he said at last, in a steady voice.

"I didn't suppose it was worth coming back for, after I got into the street. And, besides, you were busy."

"Yes, yes, you were right: you are not to come-of course, of course."

The King of the Street looked at me curiously, and then said smoothly:

"But this isn't business." And he plunged into the papers once more. "There were over nine thousand shares sold this afternoon, and I got only five thousand of them."

"I suppose Decker picked the others up," I said.

The King of the Street did me the honor to look at me in amazement.

"Decker!" he roared. "How did you —" Then he paused and his voice dropped to its ordinary tone. "I reckon you're right. What gave you the idea?"

I frankly detailed my conversation with Wallbridge. As I went on, I fancied that the bushy brows drew down and a little anxiety showed beneath them.

I had hardly finished my account when there was a knock at the door, and the servant appeared.

"Mrs. Knapp's compliments, and she would like to see Mr. Wilton when you are done," he said.

I could with difficulty repress an exclamation, and my heart climbed into my throat. I was ready to face the Wolf in his den, but here was a different matter. I recalled that Mrs. Knapp was a more intimate acquaintance of Henry Wilton's than Doddridge Knapp had been, and I saw Niagara ahead of my skiff.

"Yes, yes; quite likely," said my employer, referring to my story of Wallbridge. "I heard something of the kind from my men. I'll know to-morrow for certain, I expect. I forgot to tell you that the ladies would want to see you. They have missed you lately." And the Wolf motioned me to the door where the servant waited.

Here was a predicament. I was missed and wanted-and by the ladies. My heart dropped back from my throat, and I felt it throbbing in the lowest recesses of my boot-heels as I rose and followed my guide.

CHAPTER XII. LUELLA KNAPP

As the door swung open, my heart almost failed me. If there had been a chance of escape I should have made the bolt, then and there.

I had not counted on an interview with the women of Doddridge Knapp's family. I had, to be sure, vaguely foreseen the danger to come from meeting them, but I had been confident that it would be easy to avoid them. And now, in the face of the emergency, my resources had failed me, and I was walking into Mrs. Knapp's reception-room without the glimmer of an idea of how I should find my way out.

Two women rose to greet me as I entered the room.

"Good evening," said the elder woman, holding out her hand. "You have neglected us for a long time." There was something of reproach as well as civility in the voice.

Mrs. Doddridge Knapp, for I had no doubt it was she who greeted me, was large of frame but well-proportioned, and stood erect, vigorous, with an air of active strength rare in one of her years. Her age was, I supposed, near forty-five. Her face was strong and resolute, yet it was with the strength and resolution of a woman, not of a man. Altogether she looked a fit mate for Doddridge Knapp.

"Yes," I replied, adjusting my manner nicely to hers, "I have been very busy."

As she felt the touch of my hand and heard the sound of my voice, I thought I saw a look of surprise, apprehension and hesitation in her eyes. If it was there it was gone in an instant, and she replied gaily:

"Busy? How provoking of you to say so! You should never be too busy to take the commands of the ladies."

"That is why I am here," I interrupted with my best bow. But she continued without noting it:

"Luella wagered with me that you would make that excuse. I expected something more original."

"I am very sorry," I said, with a reflection of the bantering air she had assumed.

"Oh, indeed!" exclaimed the younger woman, to whom my eyes had turned as Mrs. Knapp spoke her name. "How very unkind of you to say so, when I have just won a pair of gloves by it. Good evening to you!" And she held out her hand.

It was with a strong effort that I kept my self-possession, as for the first time I clasped the hand of Luella Knapp.

Was it the thrill of her touch, the glance of her eye, or the magnetism of her presence, that set my pulses beating to a new measure, and gave my spirit a breath from a new world? Whatever the cause, as I looked into the clear-cut face and the frank gray eyes of the woman before me, I was swept by a flood of emotion that was near overpowering my self-control.

Nor was it altogether the emotion of pleasure that was roused within me. As I looked into her eyes, I had the pain of seeing myself in a light that had not as yet come to me. I saw myself not the friend of Henry Wilton, on the high mission of bringing to justice the man who had foully sent him to death. In that flash I saw Giles Dudley hiding under a false name, entering this house to seek for another link in the chain that would drag this girl's father to the gallows and turn her life to bitterness and misery. And in the reflection from the clear depths of the face before me, I saw Imposter and Spy written large on my forehead.

I mastered the emotion in a moment and took the seat to which she had waved me.

I was puzzled a little at the tone in which she addressed me. There was a suggestion of resentment in her manner that grew on me as we talked.

Can I describe her? Of what use to try? She was not beautiful, and "pretty" was too petty a word to apply to Luella Knapp. "Fine looking," if said with the proper emphasis, might give some idea of her appearance, for she was tall in figure, with features that were impressive in their attractiveness. Yet her main charm was in the light that her spirit and intelligence threw on her face; and this no one can describe.

The brightness of her speech did not disappoint the expectation I had thus formed of her. It was a finely-cultivated mind that was revealed to me, and it held a wit rare to woman. I followed her lead in the conversational channel, giving but a guiding oar when it turned toward acquaintances she held in common with Henry Wilton, or events that had interested them together.

Through it all the idea that Miss Knapp was regarding me with a hidden disapproval was growing on me. I decided that Henry had made some uncommon blunder on his last visit and that I was suffering the penalty for it. The admiration I felt for the young woman deepened with every sentence she spoke, and I was ready to do anything to restore the good opinion that Henry might have endangered, and in lieu of apology exerted myself to the utmost to be agreeable.

I was unconscious of the flight of time until Mrs. Knapp turned from some other guests and walked toward us.

"Come, Henry," she said pointedly, "Luella is not to monopolize you all the time. Besides, there's Mr. Inman dying to speak to her."

I promptly hated Mr. Inman with all my heart and felt not the slightest objection to his demise; but at her gesture of command I rose and accompanied Mrs. Knapp, as a young man with eye-glasses and a smirk came to take my place. I left Luella Knapp, congratulating myself over my cleverness in escaping the pitfalls that lined my way.

"Now I've a chance to speak to you at last," said Mrs. Knapp.

"At your service," I bowed. "I owe you something."

"Indeed?" Mrs. Knapp raised her eyebrows in surprise.

"For your kind recommendation to Mr. Knapp."

"My recommendation? You have a little the advantage of me."

I was stricken with painful doubts, and the cold sweat started upon me. Perhaps this was not Mrs. Knapp after all.

"Oh, perhaps you didn't mean it," I said.

"Indeed I did, if it was a recommendation. I'm afraid it was unconscious, though. Mr. Knapp does not consult me about his business."

I was in doubt no longer. It was the injured pride of the wife that spoke in the tone.

"I'm none the less obliged," I said carelessly. "He assured me that he acted on your words."

"What on earth are you doing for Mr. Knapp?" she asked earnestly, dropping her half-bantering tone. There was a trace of apprehension in her eyes.

"I'm afraid Mr. Knapp wouldn't think your recommendations were quite justified if I should tell you. Just get him in a corner and ask him."

"I suppose it is that dreadful stock market."

"Oh, madam, let me say the chicken market. There is a wonderful opportunity just now for a corner in fowls."

"There are a good many to be plucked in the market that Mr. Knapp will look after," she said with a smile. But there was something of a worried look behind it. "Oh, you know, Henry, that I can't bear the market. I have seen too much of the misery that has come from it. It can eat up a fortune in an hour. A dear friend saw her home, the house over her head, all she possessed, go in a breath on a turn of the cards in that dreadful place. And her husband left her to face it with two little children. The coward escaped it with a bullet through his head, after he had brought ruin on his home and family."

She shuddered as she looked about her, as though in fancy she saw herself turned from the palace into the street.

"Mr. Knapp is not a man to lose," I said.

"Mr. Knapp is a strong man," she said with a proud straightening of her figure. "But the whirlpool can suck down the strongest swimmer."

"But I suspect Mr. Knapp makes whirlpools instead of swimming into them," I said meaningly.

"Ah, Henry," she said sadly, "how often have I told you that the best plan may come to ruin in the market? It may not take much to start a boulder rolling down the mountain-side, but who is to tell it to stop when once it is set going?"

"I think," said I, smiling, "that Mr. Knapp would ride the boulder and find himself in a gold mine at the end of the journey."

"Perhaps. But you're not telling me what Mr. Knapp is doing."

"He can tell you much better than I."

"No doubt," she said with a trace of sarcasm in her voice.

"And here he comes to do it, I expect," I said, as the tall figure of the King of the Street appeared in the doorway opposite.

"I'm afraid I shall have to depend on the newspapers," she said. "Mr. Knapp is as much afraid of a woman's tongue as you are. Oh," she continued after a moment's pause, "I was going to make you give an account of yourself; but since you will tell nothing I must introduce you to my cousin, Mrs. Bowser." And she led me, unresisting, to a short, sharp-featured woman of sixty or thereabouts, who rustled her silks, and in a high, thin voice professed herself charmed to see me.

She might have claimed and held the record as the champion of the conversational ring. I had never met her equal before, nor have I met one to surpass her since.

Had I been long in the city? She had been here only a week. Came from down Maine way. This was a dear, dreadful city with such nice people and such dreadful winds, wasn't it? And then she gave me a catalogue of the places she had visited, and the attractions of San Francisco, with a wealth of detail and a poverty of interest that was little less than marvelous.

Fortunately she required nothing but an occasional murmur of assent in the way of answer from me.

I looked across the room to the corner where Luella was entertaining the insignificant Inman. How vivacious and intelligent she appeared! Her face and figure grew on me in attractiveness, and I felt that I was being very badly used. As I came to this point I was roused by the sound of two low voices that just behind me were plainly audible under the shrill treble of Mrs. Bowser. They were women with their heads close in gossip.

"Shocking, isn't it?" said one.

"Dreadful!" said the other. "It gives me the creeps to think of it."

"Why don't they lock him up? Such a creature shouldn't be allowed to go at large."

"Oh, you see, maybe they can't be sure about it. But I've heard it's a case of family pride."

I was recalled from this dialogue by Mrs. Bowser's fan on my arm, and her shrill voice in my ear with, "What is your idea about it, Mr. Wilton?"

"I think you are perfectly right," I said heartily, as she paused for an answer.

"Then I'll arrange it with the others at once," she said.

This was a bucket of ice-water on me. I had not the first idea to what I had committed myself.

"No, don't," I said. "Wait till we have time to discuss it again."

"Oh, we can decide on the time whenever you like. Will some night week after next suit you?"

I had to throw myself on the mercy of the enemy.

"I'm afraid I'm getting rather absent-minded," I said humbly. "I was looking at Miss Knapp and lost the thread of the discourse for a minute."

"That's what I was talking about," she said sharply,—"about taking her and the rest of us through Chinatown."

"Yes, yes. I remember," I said unblushingly. "If I can get away from business, I'm at your service at any time."

Then Mrs. Bowser wandered on with the arrangements she would find necessary to make, and I heard one of the low voices behind me:

"Now this is a profound secret, you know. I wouldn't have them know for the world that any one suspects. I just heard it this week, myself."

"Oh, I wouldn't dare breathe it to a soul," said the other. "But I'm sure I shan't sleep a wink tonight." And they moved away.

I interrupted Mrs. Bowser to explain that I must speak to Mrs. Knapp, and made my escape as some one stopped to pass a word with her.

"Oh, must you go, Henry?" said Mrs. Knapp. "Well, you must come again soon. We miss you when you stay away. Don't let Mr. Knapp keep you too closely."

I professed myself happy to come whenever I could find the time, and looked about for Luella. She was nowhere to be seen. I left the room a little disappointed, but with a swelling of pride that I had passed the dreaded ordeal and had been accepted as Henry Wilton in the house in which I had most feared to meet disaster. My opinion of my own cleverness had risen, in the language of the market, "above par."

As I passed down the hall, a tall willowy figure stepped from the shadow of the stair. My heart gave a bound of delight. It was Luella Knapp. I should have the pleasure of a leave-taking in private.

"Oh, Miss Knapp!" I said. "I had despaired of having the chance to bid you good night." And I held out my hand.

She ignored the hand. I could see from her heaving bosom and shortened breath that she was laboring under great agitation. Yet her face gave no evidence of the effort that it cost her to control herself.

"I was waiting for you," she said in a low voice.

I started to express my gratification when she interrupted me.

"Who are you?" broke from her lips almost fiercely.

I was completely taken aback, and stared at her in amazement with no word at command.

"You are not Henry Wilton," she said rapidly. "You have come here with his name and his clothes, and made up to look like him, and you try to use his voice and take his place. Who are you?"

There was a depth of scorn and anger and apprehension in that low voice of hers that struck me dumb.

"Can you not answer?" she demanded, catching her breath with excitement. "You are not Henry Wilton."

"Well?" I said half-inquiringly. It was not safe to advance or retreat.

"Well—! well—!" She repeated my answer, with indignation and disdain deepening in her voice. "Is that all you have to say for yourself?"

"What should I say?" I replied quietly. "You make an assertion. Is there anything more to be said?"

"Oh, you may laugh at me if you please, because you can hoodwink the others."

I protested that laughter was the last thing I was thinking of at the moment.

Then she burst out impetuously:

"Oh, if I were only a man! No; if I were a man I should be hoodwinked like the rest. But you can not deceive me. Who are you? What are you here for? What are you trying to do?"

She was blazing with wrath. Her tone had raised hardly an interval of the scale, but every word that came in that smooth, low voice was heavy with contempt and anger. It was the true daughter of the Wolf who stood before me.

"I am afraid, Miss Knapp, you are not well tonight," I said soothingly.

"What have you done with Henry Wilton?" she asked fiercely. "Don't try to speak with his voice. Drop your disguise. You are no actor. You are no more like him than—"

The simile failed her in her wrath.

"Satyr to Hyperion," I quoted bitterly. "Make it strong, please."

I had thought myself in a tight place in the row at Borton's, but it was nothing to this encounter.

"Oh, where is he? What has happened?" she cried.

"Nothing has happened," I said calmly, determining at last to brazen it out. I could not tell her the truth. "My name is Henry Wilton."

She looked at me in anger a moment, and then a shadow of dread and despair settled over her face.

I was tempted beyond measure to throw myself on her mercy and tell all. The subtle sympathy that she inspired was softening my resolution. Yet, as I looked into her eyes, her face hardened, and her wrath blazed forth once more.

"Go!" she said. "I hope I may never see you again!" And she turned and ran swiftly up the stair. I thought I heard a sob, but whether of anger or sorrow I knew not.

And I went out into the night with a heavier load of depression than I had borne since I entered the city.

CHAPTER XIII. A DAY OF GRACE

The wind blew strong and moist and salt from the western ocean as I walked down the steps into the semi-darkness of Pine Street. But it was powerless to cool the hot blood that surged into my cheeks in the tumult of emotion that followed my dismissal by Luella Knapp. I was furious at the poor figure I had cut in her sight, at the insults I had been forced to bear without reply, and at the hopelessness of setting myself right. Yet, more than all was I sick at heart at the dreadful task before me. My spirit was bleeding from every stab that this girl had dealt me; yet I had to confess that her outburst of rage had challenged my admiration even more than her brightness in the hour that had gone before. How could I go through with my work? How could I bear to overwhelm her with the sorrow and disgrace that must crush on her if I proved to the world the awful facts that were burned on my brain?

Resolve, shame, despair, fought with each other in the tumult in my mind as I passed between the bronze lions and took my way down the street. I was called out of my distractions with a sudden start as though a bucket of cold water had been thrown over me. I had proceeded not twenty feet when I saw two dark forms across the street. They had, it struck me, been waiting for my appearance, for one ran to join the other and both hastened toward the corner as though to be ready to meet me.

I could not retreat to the house of the Wolf that loomed forbiddingly behind me. There was nothing to do but to go forward and trust to my good fortune, and I shifted my revolver to the side-pocket of my overcoat as I stepped briskly to the corner. Then I stopped under the lamp post to reconnoiter.

The two men who had roused my apprehensions did not offer to cross the street, but slackened their pace and strolled slowly along on the other side. I noted that it seemed a long way between street-lamps thereabouts. I could see none between the one under which I was standing and the brow of the hill below. Then it occurred to me that this circumstance might not be due to the caprice of the street department of the city government, but to the thoughtfulness of the gentlemen who were paying such close attention to my affairs. I decided that there were better ways to get down town than were offered by Pine Street.

To the south the cross-street stretched to Market with an unbroken array of lights, and as my unwary watchers had disappeared in the darkness, I hastened down the incline with so little regard for dignity that I found myself running for a Sutter Street car-and caught it, too. As I swung on to the platform I looked back; but I saw no sign of skulking figures before the car swept past the corner and blotted the street from sight.

The incident gave me a distaste for the idea of going back to Henry Wilton's room at this time of the night. So as Montgomery Street was reached I stepped into the Lick House, where I felt reasonably sure that I might get at least one night's sleep, free from the haunting fear of the assassin.

But, once more safe, the charms of Luella Knapp again claimed the major part of my thoughts, and when I went to sleep it was with her scornful words ringing in my ears. I awoke in the darkness-perhaps it was in but a few minutes-with the confused dream that Luella Knapp was seized in the grasp of the snake-eyed Terrill, and I was struggling to come to her assistance and seize him by his hateful throat. But, becoming calm from this exciting vision, I slept soundly until the morning sun peeped into the room with the cheerful announcement that a new day was born.

In the fresh morning air and the bright morning light, I felt that I might have been unduly suspicious and had fled from harmless citizens; and I was ashamed that I had lacked courage to return to Henry's room as I made my way thither for a change of clothes. I thought better of my decision, however, as I stepped within the gloomy walls of the house of mystery, and my footfalls echoed through the chilling silence of the halls. And I lost all regret over my night's lack of courage when I reached my door. It was swung an inch ajar, and as I approached I thought I saw it move.

"I'm certain I locked it," was my inward comment.

I stopped short and hunted my revolver from my overcoat pocket. I was nervous for a moment, and angry at the inattention that might have cost me my life.

"Who's there?" I demanded.

No reply.

I gave a knock on the door at long reach.

There was no sound and I gave it a push that sent it open while I prudently kept behind the fortification of the casing. As no developments followed this move, I peeped through the door in cautious investigation. The room was quite empty, and I walked in.

The sight that met my eyes was astonishing. Clothes, books, papers, were scattered over the floor and bed and chairs. The carpet had been partly ripped up, the mattress torn apart, the closet cleared out, and every corner of the room had been ransacked.

It was clear to my eye that this was no ordinary case of robbery. The search, it was evident, was not for money and jewelry alone, and bulkier property had been despised. The men who had torn the place to pieces must, I surmised, have been after papers of some kind.

I came at once to the conclusion that I had been favored by a visit from my friends, the enemy. As they had failed to find me in, they had looked for some written memoranda of the object of their search.

I knew well that they had found nothing among the clothing or papers that Henry had left behind. I had searched through these myself, and the sole document that could bear on the mystery was at that moment fast in my inside pocket. I was inclined to scout the idea that Henry Wilton had hidden anything under the carpet, or in the mattress, or in any secret place. The threads of the mystery were carried in his head, and the correspondence, if there had been any, was destroyed.

As I was engaged in putting the room to rights, the door swung back, and I jumped to my feet to face a man who stood on the threshold.

"Hello!" he cried. "House-cleaning again?"

It was Dicky Nahl, and he paused with a smile on his face.

"Ah, Dicky!" I said with an effort to keep out of my face and voice the suspicions I had gained from the incidents of the visit to the Borton place. "Entirely unpremeditated, I assure you."

"Well, you're making a thorough job of it," he said with a laugh.

"Fact is," said I ruefully, "I've been entertaining angels-of the black kind-unawares. I was from home last night, and I find that somebody has made himself free with my property while I was away."

"Whew!" whistled Dicky. "Guess they were after you."

I gave Dicky a sidelong glance in a vain effort to catch more of his meaning than was conveyed by his words.

"Shouldn't be surprised," I replied dryly, picking up an armful of books. "I'd expect them to be looking for me in the book-shelf, or inside the mattress-cover, or under the carpet."

Dicky laughed joyously.

"Well, they did rather turn things upside down," he chuckled. "Did they get anything?" And he fell to helping me zealously.

"Not that I can find out," I replied. "Nothing of value, anyhow."

"Not any papers, or anything of that sort?" asked Dicky anxiously.

"Dicky, my boy," said I; "there are two kinds of fools. The other is the man who writes his business on a sheet of paper and forgets to burn it."

Dicky grinned merrily.

"Gad, you're getting a turn for epigram! You'll be writing for the *Argonaut*, first we know."

"Well, you'll allow me a shade of common sense, won't you?"

"I don't know," said Dicky, considering the proposition doubtfully. "It might have been awkward if you had left anything lying about. But if you had real good sense you'd have had the guards here. What are you paying them for, anyhow?"

I saw difficulties in the way of explaining to Dicky why I had not ordered the guards on duty.

"Oh, by the way," said Dicky suddenly, before a suitable reply had come to me; "how about the scads-spondulicks-you know? Yesterday was pay-day, but you didn't show up."

I don't know whether my jaw dropped or not. My spirits certainly did.

"By Jove, Dicky!" I exclaimed, catching my breath. "It slipped my mind, clean. I haven't got at our-ahem-banker, either."

I saw now what that mysterious money was for-or a part of it, at all events. What I did not see was how I was to get it, and how to pay it to my men.

"That's rough," said Dicky sympathetically. "I'm dead broke."

It would appear then that Dicky looked to me for pay, whether or not he felt bound to me in service.

"There's one thing I'd like explained before a settlement," said I grimly, as I straightened out the carpet; "and that is the little performance for my benefit the other night."

Dicky cocked his head on one side, and gave me an uneasy glance.

"Explanation?" he said in affected surprise.

"Yes," said I sternly. "It looked like a plant. I was within one of getting a knife in me."

"What became of you?" inquired Dicky. "We looked around for you for an hour, and were afraid you had been carried off."

"That's all right, Dicky," I said. "I know how I got out. What I want to know is how I got in-taken in."

"I don't know," said Dicky anxiously. "I was regularly fooled, myself. I thought they were fishermen, all right enough, and I never thought that Terrill had the nerve to come in there. I was fooled by his disguise, and he gave the word, and I thought sure that Richmond had sent him." Dicky had dropped all banter, and was speaking with the tone of sincerity.

"Well, it's all right now, but I don't want any more slips of that sort. Who was hurt?"

"Trent got a bad cut in the side. One of the Terrill gang was shot. I heard it was only through the arm or leg, I forget which."

I was consumed with the desire to ask what had become of Borton's, but I suspected that I was supposed to know, and prudently kept the question to myself.

"Well, come along," said I. "The room will do well enough now. Oh, here's a ten, and I'll let you know as soon as I get the rest. Where can I find you?"

"At the old place," said Dicky; "three twenty-six."

"Clay?" I asked in desperation. Dicky gave me a wondering look as though he suspected my mind was going.

"No-Geary. What's the matter with you?"

"Oh, to be sure. Geary Street, of course. Well, let me know if anything turns up. Keep a close watch on things."

Dicky looked at me in some apparent perplexity as I walked up the stair to my Clay Street office, but gave only some laughing answer as he turned back.

But I was in far from a laughing humor myself. The problem of paying the men raised fresh prospects of trouble, and I reflected grimly that if the money was not found I might be in more danger from my unpaid mercenaries than from the enemy.

Ten o'clock passed, and eleven, with no sign from Doddridge Knapp, and I wondered if the news I had carried him of the activities of Terrill and of Decker had disarranged his plans.

I tried the door into Room 16. It was locked, and no sound came to my ears from behind it.

"I should really like to know," I thought to myself, "whether Mr. Doddridge Knapp has left any papers in his desk that might bear on the Wilton mystery."

I tried my keys, but none of them fitted the lock. I gave up the attempt-indeed, my mind shrank from the idea of going through my employer's papers-but the desire of getting a key that would open the door was planted in my brain.

Twelve o'clock came. No Doddridge Knapp had appeared, and I sauntered down to the Exchange to pick up any items of news. It behooved me to be looking out for Doddridge Knapp's movements. If he had got another agent to carry out his schemes, I should have to prepare my lines for attack from another direction.

Wallbridge was just coming rapidly out of the Exchange.

"No," said the little man, mopping the perspiration from his shining head, "quiet as lambs to-day. Their own mothers wouldn't have known the Board from a Sunday-school."

I inquired about Omega.

"Flat as a pancake," said the little man. "Nothing doing."

"What! Is it down?" I exclaimed with some astonishment.

"Lord bless you, no!" said Wallbridge, surprised in his turn. "Strong and steady at eighty, but we didn't sell a hundred shares to-day. Well, I'm in a rush. Good-by, if you don't want to buy or sell." And he hurried off without waiting for a reply.

So I was now assured that Doddridge Knapp had not displaced me in the Omega deal. It was a recess to prepare another surprise for the Street, and I had time to attend to a neglected duty.

The undertaker's shop that held the morgue looked hardly less gloomy in the afternoon sun than in the light of breaking day in which I had left it when I parted from Detective Coogan. The office was decorated mournfully to accord with the grief of friends who ordered the coffins, or the feelings of the surviving relatives on settling the bills.

"I am Henry Wilton," I explained to the man in charge. "There was a body left here by Detective Coogan to my order, I believe."

"Oh, yes," he said: "What do you want done with it?"

I explained that I wished to arrange to have it deposited in a vault for a time, as I might carry it East.

"That's easy done," he said; and he explained the details. "Would you like to see the body?" he concluded. "We embalmed it on the strength of Coogan's order."

I shrank from another look at the battered form. The awfulness of the tragedy came upon me with hardly less force than in the moment when I had first faced the mangled and bleeding body on the slab in the dead-room. Again I saw the scene in the alley; again his last cry for help rang in my ears; again I retraced the dreadful experiences of the night, and stood in the dim horror of the morgue with the questioning voice of the detective echoing beside me; and again did that wolf-face rise out of the lantern-flash over the body of the man whose death it had caused.

The undertaker was talking, but I knew not what he said. I was shaking with the horror and grief of the situation, and in that moment I renewed my vow to have blood for blood and life for life, if law and justice were to be had.

"We'll take it out any time," said the undertaker, with a decorous reflection of my grief upon his face. "Would you like to accompany the remains?"

I decided that I would.

"Well, there's nothing doing now. We can start as soon as we have sealed the casket."

"As soon as you can. There's nothing to wait for."

The ride to the cemetery took me through a part of San Francisco that I had not yet seen. Flying battalions of fog advanced swiftly upon us as we faced the West, and the day grew pale and ghostlike. The gray masses were pouring fast over the hills toward which we struggled, and the ranks thickened as we drew near the burial-place.

I paid little attention to the streets through which we passed. My mind was on the friend whose name I had taken, whose work I was to do. I was back with him in our boyhood days, and lived again for the fleeting minutes the life we had lived in common; and the resolve grew stronger on me that his fate should be avenged.

And yet a face came between me and the dead—a proud face, with varying moods reflected upon it, now gay, now scornful, now lighted with intelligence and mirth, now blazing with anger. But it was powerless to shake my resolve. Not even Luella Knapp should stand between me and vengeance.

"There's the place," said the undertaker, pointing to the vault. "I'll have it opened directly."

The scene was in accord with my feelings. The gray day gave a somber air to the trees and flowers that grew about. The white tombstones and occasional monuments to be seen were sad reminders of mortality.

Below me stretched the city, half-concealed by the magic drapery of the fog that streamed through it, turning it from a place of wood and stone into a fantastic illusion, heavy with gloom and sorrow.

It was soon over. The body of Henry Wilton was committed to the vault with the single mourner looking on, and we drove rapidly back in the failing light.

I had given my address at the undertaker's shop, and the hack stopped in front of my house of mystery before I knew where we were. Darkness had come upon the place, and the street-lamps were alight and the gas was blazing in the store-windows along the thoroughfares. As I stepped out of the carriage and gazed about me, I recognized the gloomy doorway and its neighborhood that had greeted me on my first night in San Francisco.

As I was paying the fare, a stout figure stepped up to me.

"Ah, Mr. Wilton, it's you again."

I turned in surprise. It was the policeman I had met on my first night in San Francisco.

"Oh, Corson, how are you?" I said heartily, recognizing him at last. I felt a sense of relief in the sight of him. The place was not one to quiet my nerves after the errand from which I had just come.

"All's well, sor, but I've a bit of paper for ye." And after some hunting he brought it forth. "I was asked to hand this to ye."

I took it in wonder. Was there something more from Detective Coogan? I tore open the envelope and read on its inclosure:

> "Kum tonite to the house. Shure if youre life is wurth savein.
> "Muther Borton."

CHAPTER XIV. MOTHER BORTON'S ADVICE

I studied the note carefully, and then turned to Policeman Corson.

"When did she give you this-and where?"

"A lady?" said Corson with a grin. "Ah, Mr. Wilton, it's too sly she is to give it to me. 'Twas a boy askin' for ye. 'Do you know him?' says he. 'I do that,' says I. 'Where is he?' says he. 'I don't know,' says I. 'Has 'e a room?' says he. 'He has,' says I. 'Where is it?' says he. 'What's that to you?' says I—"

"Yes, yes," I interrupted. "But where did he get the note?"

"I was just tellin' ye, sor," said the policeman amiably. "He shoves the note at me ag'in, an' says he, 'It's important,' says he. 'Go up there,' says I. 'Last room, top floor, right-hand side.' Before I comes to the corner up here, he's after me ag'in. 'He's gone,' says he. 'Like enough,' says I. 'When'll he be back?' says he. 'When the cows come home, sonny,' says I. 'Then there'll be the divil to pay,' says he. I pricks up my ears at this. 'Why?' says I. 'Oh, he'll be killed,' says he, 'and I'll git the derndest lickin',' says he. 'What's up?' says I, makin' a grab for him. But he ducks an' blubbers. 'Gimme that letter,' says I, 'and you just kite back to the folks that sent you, and tell them what's the matter. I'll give your note to your man if he comes while I'm on the beat,' says I. I knows too much to try to git anything more out of him. I says to meself that Mr. Wilton ain't in the safest place in the world, and this kid's folks maybe means him well, and might know some other place to look for him. The kid jaws a bit, an' then does as I tells him, an' cuts away. That's half an hour ago, an' here you are, an' here's your letter."

I hesitated for a little before saying anything. It was with quick suspicion that I wondered why Mother Borton had secured again that gloomy and deserted house for the interview she was planning. That mystery of the night, with its memories of the fight in the bar-room, the escape up the stair, the fearsome moments I had spent locked in the vacant place, came on me with nerve-shaking force. It was more likely to be a trap than a meeting meant for my advantage. There was, indeed, no assurance that the note was written by Mother Borton herself. It might well be the product of the gentlemen who had been lending such variety to an otherwise uninteresting existence.

All these considerations flashed through my mind in the seconds of hesitation that passed before my reply to Policeman Corson's account.

"That was very kind of you. You didn't know what was in the letter then?"

"No, sor," replied Corson with a touch of wounded pride. "It's not me as would open another man's letter, unless in the way of me duty."

"Do you know Mother Borton?" I continued.

"Know her? know her?" returned Corson in a tone scornful of doubt on such a point. "Do I know the slickest crook in San Francisco? Ah, it's many a story I could tell you, Mr. Wilton, of the way that ould she-divil has slipped through our fingers when we thought our hands were on her throat. And it's many of her brood we have put safe in San Quentin."

"Yes, I suppose so," said I dryly. "But the woman has done me a service-saved my life, I may say-and I'm willing to forget the bad in her."

"That's not for me to say, sor; but there's quare things happens, no doubt."

"This note," I continued, "is written over her name. I don't know whether it came from her, or not; but if she sent it I must see her. It may be a case of life or death for me."

"An' if it didn't come from her?" asked the policeman shrewdly.

"Then," said I grimly, "it's likely to be a case of death if I venture alone."

"I'll tell you what, Mr. Wilton," said Corson after a pause. "If you'll wait a bit, I'll go with you-that is, if there isn't somebody else you'd like better to have by your side to-night. You don't look to have any of your friends about."

"Just the thing," I said heartily. "There's no one I'd rather have. We'll go down as soon as we can get a bite to eat."

"I'll have to wait a bit, sor, till my relief comes. He'll be along soon. As for getting a bite, you can't do better than wait till you get to Mother Borton's. It's a rough place, but it's got a name for good cooking."

I was bewildered.

"I guess there's not much to be got in the way of eating in the house. There was nothing left in it yesterday morning but the rats." I spoke with considerable emphasis.

"That's square, now," he said, looking to see if there was a jest behind the words. "But 'twas all there when McPherson and I put a club to a drunk as was raising the Ould Nick in the place and smashing the bottles, not six hours ago. When we took him away in the ixpriss wagon the ould woman was rowling out those long black curses in a way that would warm the heart of the foul fiend himself."

There was some fresh mystery about this. I held my tongue with the reflection that I had better let it straighten itself out than risk a stumble by asking about things I ought to know.

Corson's relief soon appeared. "It's a nasty night," he said, buttoning up his overcoat closely, as Corson gave him a brief report of the situation on the beat.

"It's good for them as likes it dark," said Corson.

"It's just such a night as we had when Donaldson was murdered. Do you mind it?"

"Do I mind it? Am I likely to forgit it? Well, a pleasant time to you, me boy. Come along, sor. We'd better be moving. You won't mind stepping up to the hall with me, will ye, while I report?"

"Certainly not," I said with a shiver, half at the grim suggestion of murder and half at the chill of the fog and the cutting wind that blew the cold vapor through to the skin.

"You've no overcoat," said Corson. "We'll stop and get one. I'll have mine from the station."

The silence of the house of mystery was no less threatening now than on the night when Henry Wilton was walking through the halls on the way to his death. But the stout-hearted policeman by my side gave me confidence, and no sign showed the presence of an enemy as I secured Henry's heavy overcoat and the large revolver he had given me, and we took our way down the stairs.

A short visit to the grimy, foul-smelling basement of the City Hall, where a few policemen looked at me wonderingly, a brisk walk with the cutting wind at our backs and the fog currents hurrying and whirling in eddies toward the bay, and I felt rather than saw that we were in the neighborhood of the scene of my adventures of a night that had come so near costing me my life. I could not be certain of my bearings, but I trusted to the unconscious guidance of Corson, with a confused idea that we were bearing away from the place. Then with relief combined with bewilderment, I saw the lantern sign give forth its promise of the varied entertainment that could be had at Borton's.

"Here we are," said Corson.

We pushed open the door and entered. The place had the same appearance as the one to which I had been taken by Dicky Nahl.

"A fine night, Mother Borton," said Corson cheerily, as he was the first to enter, and then added under his breath, "—for the divil's business."

Mother Borton stared at him with a black look and muttered a curse.

"Good evening," I hastened to say. "I took the liberty to bring a friend; he doesn't come as an officer to-night."

The effect on the hag's features was marvelous. The black scowl lightened, the tight-drawn lips relaxed, and there was a sign of pleasure in the bright eyes that had flashed hatred at the policeman.

"Ah, it's you, is it?" she said sharply, but with a tone of kindness in her greeting. "I didn't see ye. Now sit down and find a table, and I'll be with ye after a bit."

"We want a dinner, and a good one. I'm half-starved."

"Are ye, honey?" said the woman with delight.

"Then it's the best dinner in town ye shall have. Here, Jim! Put these gentlemen over there at the corner table."

And if the cooking was not what we could have had at the Maison Dorée and the service was a little off color, neither of us was disposed to be critical.

"It's not the aristocracy of stoile ye get here," said Corson, lighting his pipe after the coffee, "but it's prime eating."

I nodded in lazy contentment, and then started up in remembrance of the occasion of our being in this place as the shadow of Mother Borton fell across the table. Her keen eyes fixed on me and her sharp beak nodding toward me gave her the uncanny aspect of a bird of prey, and I felt a sinking of courage as I met her glance.

"If you will go upstairs," she said sourly. "You know the way. I guess your friend can spare you."

"Is there anything that can't be told before him?" I asked.

The features of the old woman hardened.

"You'll be safer in my care than in his," she said, with warning in her tone.

"Yes, yes, I know I am safe here, but how is it with my friend if I leave him here? We came together and we'll go together."

The crone nodded with a laugh that ended in a snarl.

"If the gang knew he was here there would be more fun than you saw the other night."

"Don't worry about me, Mr. Wilton," said Corson with a grin. "I've stood her crowd off before, and I can do it again if the need comes. But I'd rather smoke a poipe in peace."

"You can smoke in peace, but it's not yourself you can thank for it," said Mother Borton sharply. "There'll be no trouble here to-night. Come along." And the old woman started for the door.

"Are you sure you're all right?" asked Corson in a low voice. "There's men gone up those stairs that came down with a sheet over them."

"It's all right-that is, unless there's any danger to you in leaving you here."

"No. Go ahead. I'll wait for ye. I'd as lief sit here as anywheres."

I hastened after Mother Borton, who was glowering at me from the doorway, and followed her footsteps in silence to the floor above. There was a dim light and a foul smell in the upper hall, both of which came from a lamp that burned with a low flame on a bracket by the forward stair. There were perhaps a dozen doors to be seen, all closed, but all giving the discomforting suggestion that they had eyes to mark my coming.

Mother Borton walked the passage cautiously and in silence, and I followed her example until she pushed open a door and was swallowed up in the blackness. Then I paused on the threshold while she lighted a candle; and as I entered, she swiftly closed and locked the door behind me.

"Sit down," she said in a harsh voice, motioning me to a chair by the stand that held the candle. Then this strange creature seated herself in front of me, and looked steadily and sternly in my face for a full minute. The gaze of the piercing, deep-sunken eyes of the old hag, the evil lines that marked the lean, sharp features, gaining a still more sinister meaning from the wavering, flickering light thrown upon her face by the candle, gave me a feeling of anything but ease in my position.

"What have you done that I should help you?" she broke forth in a harsh voice, her eyes still fixed on my face.

"I really couldn't say," I replied politely. "You have done me one or two services already. That's the best reason I know why you should do me another."

The hard lines on the face before me relaxed at the sound of my voice, and the old woman nodded approvingly.

"Ay, reason enough, I guess. Them as wants better can find it themselves. But why did you sneak out of the house the other night like a cop in plain clothes? Didn't I go bail you were safe? Do you want any better word than mine?" she had begun almost softly, but the voice grew higher and harsher as she went on.

"Why," I said, bewildered again, "the house sneaked away from me-or, at least you left me alone in it."

"How was that?" she asked grimly. And I described graphically my experience in the deserted building.

As I proceeded with my tale an amused look replaced the harsh lines of suspicion on Mother Borton's face.

"Oh, my lud!" she cried with a chuckle. "Oh, my lud! how very green you are, my boy. Oh ho! oh ho!" And then she laughed an inward, self-consuming laugh that called up anything but the feeling of sympathetic mirth.

"I'm glad it amuses you," I said with injured dignity.

"Oh, my liver! Don't you see it yet? Don't you see that you climbed into the next house back, and went through on to the other street?" And she relapsed into her state of silent merriment.

I felt foolish enough as the truth flashed over me. I had lost my sense of direction in the strange house, and had been deceived by the resemblance of the ground plan of the two buildings.

"But what about the plot?" I asked. "I got your note. It's very interesting. What about it?"

"What plot?"

"Why, I don't know. The one you wrote me about."

Mother Borton bent forward and searched my face with her keen glance.

"Oh," she said at last, "the one I wrote you about. I'd forgotten it."

This was disheartening. How could I depend on one whose memory was thus capricious?

"Yes," said I gloomily; "I supposed you might know something about it."

"Show me the note," she said sharply.

I fumbled through my pockets until I found it. Mother Borton clutched it, held it up to the candle, and studied it for two or three minutes.

"Where did you get it?"

I described the circumstances in which it had come into my possession, and repeated the essentials of Corson's story. Mother Borton's sharp, evil face was impassive during my recital. When it was done she muttered:

"Gimme a fool for luck." Then she appeared to consider for a minute or more.

"Well?" said I inquiringly.

"Well, honey, you're having a run of the cards," she said at last. "Between having the message trusted to a fool boy, and having a cop for your friend, an' maybe gitting this note before you're expected to, you're setting here genteel-like having agreeable conversation along with me, instead of being in company you mightn't like so well-or maybe floating out toward Fort Point."

"So you didn't write it?" I said coolly. "I had an idea of the kind. That's why my friend Corson is smoking his pipe down stairs."

Mother Borton gave me a pleased look and nodded. I hoped I had made her regret the cruel insinuation in her application of the proverb to me as the favorite of fortune.

"I see," I said. "I was to be waylaid on the road here and killed."

"Carried off, more likely. I don't say as it wouldn't end in killin' ye. But, you see, you'd be of mighty small use in tellin' tales if you was dead; but you might be got to talk if they had ye in a quiet place."

"Good reasoning. But Henry Wilton was killed."

"Yes," admitted Mother Borton; "they thought he carried papers, and maybe they ain't got over the idea yit. It's jest as well you're here instid of having a little passear with Tom Terrill and Darby Meeker and their pals."

"Well," said I, as cheerfully as I could under the depressing circumstances, "if they want to kill me, I don't see how I can keep them from getting a chance sooner or later."

Mother Borton looked anxious at this, and shook her head.

"You must call on your men," she said decidedly. "You must have guards."

"By the way," I said, "that reminds me. The men haven't been paid, and they're looking to me for money."

"Who's looking to you for money?"

"Dicky Nahl-and the others, I suppose."

"Dicky Nahl?"

"Why, yes. He asked me for it."

"And you gave it to him?" she asked sharply.

"No-o —that is, I gave him ten dollars, and told him he'd have to wait for the rest. I haven't got the money from the one that's doing the hiring yet, so I couldn't pay him."

Mother Borton gave an evil grin, and absorbed another inward laugh.

"I reckon the money'll come all right," said Mother Borton, recovering from her mirth. "There's one more anxious than you to have 'em paid, and if you ain't found out you'll have it right away. Now for guards, take Trent-no, he's hurt. Take Brown and Porter and Barkhouse and Fitzhugh. They're wide-awake, and don't talk much. Take 'em two and two, and never go without 'em, night or day. You stop here to-night, and I'll git 'em for you to-morrow."

I declined the proffered hospitality with thanks, and as a compromise agreed to call for my bodyguard in the early morning. Rejoining Corson, I explained Mother Borton's theory of the plot that had brought me thither.

"She's like to be right," said the policeman. "She knows the gang. Now, if you'll take my advice, you'll let the rats have your room for this night, and come along up to some foine hotel."

The advice appeared good, and fifteen minutes later Corson was drinking my health at the Lick House bar, and calling on the powers of light and darkness to watch over my safety as I slept.

Whether due to his prayers or not, my sleep was undisturbed, even by dreams of Doddridge Knapp and his charming but scornful daughter; and with the full tide of life and business flowing through the streets in the morning hours I found myself once more in Mother Borton's dingy eating-room, ordering a breakfast.

Mother Borton ignored my entrance, and, perched on a high stool behind the bar and cash-drawer, reminded me of the vulture guarding its prey. But at last she fluttered over to my table and took a seat opposite.

"Your men are here," she said shortly. And then, as I expressed my thanks, she warmed up and gave me a description by which I should know each and led me to the room where, as she said, they were "corralled."

"By the way," I said, halting outside the door, "they'll want some money, I suppose. Do you know how much?"

"They're paid," she said, and pushed open the door before I could express surprise or ask further questions. I surmised that she had paid them herself to save me from annoyance or possible danger, and my gratitude to this strange creature rose still higher.

The four men within the room saluted me gravely and with Mother Borton's directions in mind I had no hesitation in calling each by his name. I was pleased to see that they were robust, vigorous fellows, and soon made my dispositions. Brown and Barkhouse were to attend me during daylight, and Fitzhugh and Porter were to guard together at night. And, so much settled, I hastened to the office.

No sign of Doddridge Knapp disturbed the morning, and at the noon hour I returned to the room in the house of mystery that was still my only fixed abode.

All was apparently as I had left it, except that a letter lay on the table.

"I must get a new lock," was my comment, as I broke the seal. "This place is getting too public when every messenger has a key." I was certain that I had locked the door when Corson and I had come out on the evening before.

The letter was from my unknown employer, and read:

"Richmond has paid the men. Be ready for a move at any moment. Leave your address if you sleep elsewhere."

And now came three or four days of rest and quiet after the merry life I had been leading since my arrival in San Francisco.

No word did I get from Doddridge Knapp. I kept close watch of the stock market, and gossiped with speculators and brokers, for I wished to know at once if he had employed another agent. My work would lie in another direction if such should prove to be the case. But there was no movement in Omega, and I could hear no hint of another deal that might show a trace of his dexterous hand. "Quiet trading," was the report from all quarters.

"Fact is," said Wallbridge on the fourth day, trying to look doleful, "I haven't made enough this week to pay for the gas-and I don't burn any."

In the interval I improved my time by getting better acquainted with the city. Emboldened by my body-guard, I slept for two nights in Henry's room, and with one to watch outside the door, one lying on a mattress just inside, and a new lock and bolt, I was free from disturbance.

Just as I had formed a wild idea of looking up Doddridge Knapp in his home, I came to the office in the morning to find the door into Room 16 wide open and the farther door ajar.

"Come in, Wilton," said the voice of the King of the Street; and I entered his room to find him busied over his papers, as though nothing had occurred since I had last met him.

"The market has had something of a vacation." I ventured, as he failed to speak.

"I have been out of town," he said shortly. "What have you done?"

"Nothing."

He gave a grunt of assent.

"You didn't expect me to be buying up the market, did you?" The yellow-gray mustache went up, and the wolf-fangs gleamed from beneath.

"I reckon it wouldn't have been a very profitable speculation," he replied.

Then he leaned back in his chair and looked meditatively at the wall.

"It was for one fellow, though," he continued, mellowing as he mused in his recollections. "It was at the time of the Honest Injun deal—I guess you don't remember that. It must have been ten years ago. Well, I had a fellow named-why, what was his name?—oh, Riggs, or Rix, I forget which,—and he was handling about a hundred thousand dollars for me. We had Honest Injun run up from one dollar till it was over twenty dollars a share. I had to go up to Nevada City, and left ten thousand shares with him with orders to sell at twenty-five."

"Yes," I said, as the King of the Street paused and seemed inclined to drop the story. "At twenty-five."

"Well," he continued at this encouragement, "when I came back, Honest Injun was down to ten cents, or somewhere around there, which was just about as I expected. Riggs comes up to me as proud as a spotted pup, and tells me that he'd sold at thirty dollars, and cleared fifty thousand more than I'd expected."

"A pretty good deal," I suggested.

"It happened that way, but it wouldn't happen so once in ten years. The stock had gone up to thirty-one or thirty-two before it broke, and he had sold just in time."

"Did he get a reward?" I asked, as my employer appeared to wait for an observation from me.

"He did," said the Wolf with a growl. "I discharged him on the spot. And hanged if I didn't tell him that the fifty thousand was his-and let him have it, too. Oh, he was playing in great luck! That combination wouldn't come twice in a thousand years. The next man who tried it went to jail," he added with a snap of the jaws.

"Quite correct," I said. "Orders must be obeyed."

"Just remember that," he said significantly. "Have you heard anything more of Decker?"

"I've heard enough to satisfy me that he's the man who got the Omega stock."

"What other deal is he in?" asked the King of the Street.

"I don't know."

The King of the Street smiled indulgently.

"Well, you've got something to learn yet. I'll give you till next week to find the answer to that question."

I was convinced from his air that he had information on both these points himself, and was merely trying my knowledge.

"I'll not be back before next Wednesday," he concluded.

"Going away again?" I asked in surprise.

"I'm off to Virginia City," he replied after considering for a little. "I'm not sure about Omega, after all-and there's another one I want to look into. You needn't mention my going. When I come back we'll have a campaign that will raise the roof of every Board in town. No orders till then unless I telegraph you. That's all."

The King of the Street seemed straightforward enough in his statement of plans, and it did not occur to me to distrust him while I was in his presence. Yet, once more in my office, with the locked door between, I began to doubt, and tried to find some hidden meaning in each word and look. What plan was he revolving in that fertile brain? I could not guess. The mystery of the great speculator was beyond my power to fathom. And we worked, each in ignorance of the other's purposes, and went the appointed road.

CHAPTER XV. I AM IN THE TOILS

"Welcome once more, Mr. Wilton," said Mrs. Doddridge Knapp, holding out her hand. "Were you going to neglect us again?"

"Not at all, madam," said I with unblushing mendacity. "I am always at your command."

Mrs. Knapp bowed with regal condescension, and replied with such intimations of good will that I was glad I had come. I had vowed I would never set foot again in the place. The hot blood of shame had burned my cheeks whenever I recalled my dismissal from the lips of the daughter of the house. But I had received a letter from Mrs. Bowser, setting forth that I was wanted at the house of Doddridge Knapp, and her prolixity was such that I was unable to determine whether she, or Mrs. Knapp, or Luella, wished to see me. But as all three appeared to be concerned in it I pocketed pride and resentment, and made my bow with some nervous quavers at the Pine Street palace.

As I was speaking I cast my eyes furtively about the room. Mrs. Knapp interpreted my glance.

"She will be in presently." There was to my ear a trace of mocking laughter in her voice as she spoke, but her face betokened only a courteous interest.

"Thanks —I hope so," I said in a little confusion. I wished I knew whether she meant Luella or Mrs. Bowser.

"You got the note?" she asked.

"It was a great pleasure."

"Mrs. Bowser wished so much to see you again. She has been singing your praises-you were such an agreeable young man."

I cursed Mrs. Bowser in my heart.

"I am most flattered," I said politely.

There was a mischievous sparkle in Mrs. Knapp's eye, but her face was serenely gracious.

"I believe there was some arrangement between you about a trip to see the sights of Chinatown. Mrs. Bowser was quite worried for fear you had forgotten it, so I gave her your address and told her to write you a note."

I had not been conscious of expecting anything from my visit, but at this bit of information I found that I had been building air-castles which had been invisible till they came tumbling about my ears. I could not look for Miss Knapp's company on such an expedition.

"Oh," said I, with an attempt to conceal my disappointment, "the matter had slipped my mind. I shall be most happy to attend Mrs. Bowser, or to see that she has a proper escort."

We had been walking about the room during this conversation, and at this point had come to an alcove where Mrs. Knapp motioned me to a seat.

"I may not get a chance to talk with you alone again this evening," she continued, dropping her half-bantering tone, "and you come so little now. What are you doing?"

"Keeping out of mischief."

"Yes, but how?" she persisted. "You used to tell me everything. Now you tell me nothing."

"Mr. Knapp's work—" I began.

"Oh, of course I don't expect you to tell me about that. I know Mr. Knapp, and you're as close-mouthed as he, even when he's away."

"I should tell you anything of my own, but, of course, another's —"

"I understand." Mrs. Knapp, sitting with hands clasped in her lap, gave me a quick look. "But there was something else. You were telling me about your adventures, you remember. You told me two or three weeks ago about the way you tricked Darby Meeker and sent him to Sierra City." And she smiled at the recollection of Darby Meeker's discomfiture.

"Oh, yes," I said, with a laugh that sounded distressingly hollow to my ears. "That was a capital joke on Meeker."

Here was a fine pack of predicaments loosed on my trail. It was with an effort that I kept my countenance, and the cold sweat started on my forehead. How much had Henry told of his business? Had he touched on it lightly, humorously, or had he given a full account of his adventures to the wife of the man with whose secrets he was concerned, and whose evil plans had brought him to his death? The questions flashed through my mind in the instant that followed Mrs. Knapp's speech.

"How did it turn out?" asked Mrs. Knapp with lively interest. "Did he get back?"

I decided promptly on a judicious amount of the truth.

"Yes, he got back, boiling with wrath, and loaded to the guards with threats-that is, I heard so from my men. I didn't see him myself, or you might have found the rest of it in the newspaper."

"What did he do? Tell me about it." Mrs. Knapp gave every evidence of absorbed interest.

"Well, he laid a trap for me at Borton's, put Terrill in as advance guard, and raised blue murder about the place." And then I went on to give a carefully amended account of my first night's row at Borton's, and with an occasional question, Mrs. Knapp had soon extorted from me a fairly full account of my doings.

"It is dreadful for you to expose yourself to such dangers."

I was privately of her opinion.

"Oh, that's nothing," said I airily. "A man may be killed any day by a brick falling from a building, or by slipping on an orange peel on the crossing."

"But it is dreadful to court death so. Yet," she mused, "if I were a man I could envy you your work. There is romance and life in it, as well as danger. You are doing in the nineteenth century and in the midst of civilization what your forefathers may have done in the days of chivalry."

"It is a fine life," I said dryly. "But it has its drawbacks."

"But while you live no one can harm the child," she said. There was inquiry in her tone, I thought.

I suppressed a start of surprise. I had avoided mention of the boy. Henry had trusted Mrs. Knapp further than I had dreamed.

"He shall never be given up by me," I replied with conviction.

"That is spoken like a true, brave man," said Mrs. Knapp with an admiring look.

"Thank you," I said modestly.

"Another life than yours depends on your skill and courage. That must give you strength," she said softly.

"It does indeed," I replied. I was thinking of Doddridge Knapp's life.

"But here come Luella and Mrs. Bowser," said Mrs. Knapp. "I see I shall lose your company."

My heart gave a great bound, and I turned to see the queenly grace of Luella Knapp as she entered the room in the train of Mrs. Bowser.

Vows of justice and vengeance, visions of danger and death, faded away as I looked once more on the mobile, expressive face of the girl who had claimed so great a share of my waking thoughts and filled my dreams from the first moment her spirit had flashed on mine. I rose and my eyes followed her eagerly as I stood by the curtain of the alcove, oblivious of all else in the room.

Was it fancy, or had she grown paler and thinner since I had last seen her? Surely those dark hollows under her eyes that told of worry and lost sleep were not there when her brightness had chained my admiration. I could guess that she was grieving for Henry, and a jealous pang shot through my heart. She gave no glance in my direction as she walked into the room and looked about her. I dreaded her eye as I hungered for a look.

"Luella!" called Mrs. Knapp. I fancied she gave a low, musical laugh as she spoke, yet a glance showed me that her face was calm and serious. "Luella, here is some one you will like to see."

Luella Knapp turned and advanced. What was the look that lighted up her face and sparkled from her eyes? Before I could analyze the magnetic thrill that came from it, it was gone. A flush passed over her face and died away as she came.

"You honor our poor house once more?" she said, dropping a mock courtesy. "I thought you had deserted us."

I was surprised at this line of attack, and for a moment my little army of ideas was thrown into confusion. I felt, rather than heard, the undertone that carried the real meaning of her words.

"Not I," said I stoutly, recovering myself, and holding out my hand. I saw there was a little play to be carried on for the benefit of Mrs. Knapp. For some reason she had not confided in her mother. "Not I. I am always your very humble knight."

I saw that Mrs. Knapp was looking at us curiously, and pressed my advantage. Luella took my hand unwillingly. I was ready to dare a good deal for the clasp of her fingers, but I scarcely felt the thrill of their touch before she had snatched them away.

"There's nothing but pretty speeches to be had from you-and quotations at that," she said. There was malice under the seeming innocence of a pretended pout.

"There's nothing that could be so becoming in the circumstances."

"Except common sense," frowned Luella.

"The most uncommon of qualities, my dear," laughed Mrs. Knapp. "Sit down, children. I must see to Mr. Carter, who is lost by the portière and will never be discovered unless I rescue him."

"Take him to dear Aunt Julia," said Luella as her mother left us.

"Dear Aunt Julia," I inferred, was Mrs. Bowser.

I was certain that Mr. Carter would not find the demands of conversation too much for him if he was blest with the company of that charming dame.

Luella took a seat, and I followed her example. Then, with chin in hand and elbow on the arm of her chair, the young woman looked at me calmly and thoughtfully.

I grew a little uncomfortable as my self-possession melted away before this steady gaze. I had no observations to make, being uncertain about the weather, so I had the prudence to keep silent.

"Well," said Luella at last, in a cutting voice, "why don't you talk?"

"It's your lead," said I gloomily. "You took the last trick."

At this reference to our meeting, Luella looked surprised. Then she gave a little rippling laugh.

"Really," she said, "I believe I shall begin to like you, yet."

"That's very kind of you; but turn about is fair play."

"You mustn't do that," said she severely, "or I shan't."

"I meant it," said I defiantly.

"Then you ought to know better than to say it," she retorted.

"I'm in need of lessons, I fear."

"How delightful of you to confess it! Then shall I tell you what to do?"

This was very charming. I hastened to say:

"Do, by all means."

The young woman sank back in her chair, clasped her hands in her lap as her mother had done, and glanced hastily about. Then in a low voice she said:

"Be yourself."

It was an electric shock she gave me, not more by the words than by the tone.

I struggled for a moment before I regained my mental balance.

"Don't you think we could get on safer ground?" I suggested.

"No," said Luella. "There isn't any safe ground for us otherwise."

The sudden heart-sickness at the reminder of my mission with which these words overwhelmed me, tied my tongue and mastered my spirits. It was this girl's father that I was pursuing. It was to bring him to the halter that I must keep up my masquerade. It was to bring her to sorrow and disgrace that I was bound by the dead hand of my murdered friend. Oh, why was this burden laid upon me? Why was I to be torn on the rack between inclination and duty?

Luella watched my face narrowly through the conflict in my mind, and I felt as though her spirit struggled with mine to win me to the course of open, honest dealing. But it was impossible. She must be the last of all to know.

Her eyes sank as though she knew which had won the victory, and a proud, scornful look took the place of the grave good humor that had been there a moment before. Then, on a sudden, she began to speak of the theaters, rides, drives and what-not of the pleasures of the day. To an observer it would have seemed that we were deep in friendly discourse; but I, who felt her tone and manner, knew that she was miles away from me and talking but for the appearance of courtesy. Suddenly she stopped with a weary look.

"There's Aunt Julia waiting for you," she said with a gleam of malicious pleasure. "Come along. I deliver you over a prisoner of war."

"Wait a minute," I pleaded.

"No," she said, imperiously motioning me. "Come along." And with a sigh I was given, a helpless, but silently protesting, captive, to the mercies of Mrs. Bowser.

That eloquent lady received me with a flutter of feathers, if I may borrow the expression, to indicate her pleasure.

"Oh, Mr. Wilton, you'll pardon my boldness, I'm sure," she said with an amiable flirt of the head, as I seated myself beside her and watched Luella melt away into the next room; "but I was afraid you had forgotten all about us poor women, and it's a dreadful thing to be in this great house when there isn't a man about, though of course there are the servants, but you can't count them as men, besides some of them being Chinamen. And we —I —that is, I really did want to see you, and we ought to have so much to talk over, for I've heard that your mother's first cousin was a Bowser, and I do so want to see that dear, delightful Chinatown that I've heard so much about, though they do say it's horrid and dirty, but you'll let us see that for ourselves, won't you, and did you ever go through Chinatown, Mr. Wilton?"

Mrs. Bowser pulled up her verbal coach-and-six so suddenly that I felt as though she must have been pitched off the box.

"Oh," said I carelessly, "I've seen the place often enough."

"How nice!" Then suddenly looking grave, Mrs. Bowser spoke from behind her fan. "But I hope, Mr. Wilton, there's nothing there that a lady shouldn't see."

I hastened to assure her that it was possible to avoid everything that would bring a blush to the cheek of a matron of her years.

Mrs. Bowser at this rattled on without coming to any point, and, after waiting to learn when she expected to claim my services, and seeing no prospect of getting such information without a direct question, I allowed my eyes and attention to wander about the room, feeding the flow of speech, when it was checked, with a word or two of reply. I could see nothing of Luella, and Mrs. Knapp appeared to be too much taken up with other guests to notice me. I was listening to the flow of Mrs. Bowser's high-pitched voice without getting any idea from it, when my wandering attention was suddenly recalled by the words, "Mr. Knapp."

"What was that?" I asked in some confusion. "I didn't catch your meaning."

"I was saying I thought it strange Mr. Knapp wouldn't go with us, and he got awfully cross when I pressed him, and said-oh, Mr. Wilton, he said such a dreadful word-that he'd be everlastingly somethinged if he would ever go into such a lot of dens of-oh, I can't repeat his dreadful language-but wasn't it strange, Mr. Wilton?"

"Very," I said diplomatically; "but it isn't worth while to wait for him, then."

"Oh, laws, no! —he'll be home to-morrow, but he won't go."

"Home to-morrow!" I exclaimed. "I thought he wasn't to come till Wednesday."

Mrs. Bowser looked a little uncomfortable.

"I guess he's old enough to come and go when he likes," she said. But her flow of words seemed to desert her.

"Very true," I admitted. "I wonder what's bringing him back in such a hurry."

Mrs. Bowser's beady eyes turned on me in doubt, and for a moment she was dumb. Then she followed this miracle by another, and spoke in a low tone of voice.

"It's not for me to say anything against a man in his own house, but I don't like to talk of Doddridge Knapp."

"What's the matter?" I asked. "A little rough in his speech? Oh, Mrs. Bowser, you should make allowances for a man who has had to fight his way in the roughest business life in the world, and not expect too much of his polish."

"Oh, laws, he's polite enough," whispered Mrs. Bowser. "It ain't that-oh, I don't see how she ever married him."

I followed the glance that Mrs. Bowser gave on interrupting herself with this declaration, and saw Mrs. Knapp approaching us.

"Oh," she exclaimed cheerily, "is it all settled? Have you made all the arrangements, Cousin Julia?"

"Well, I declare! I'd forgotten all about telling him," cried Mrs. Bowser in her shrillest tone. "I'd just taken it for a fact that he'd know when to come."

"That's a little too much to expect, I'm afraid," said Mrs. Knapp, smiling gaily at Mrs. Bowser's management. "I see that I shall have to arrange this thing myself. Will Monday night suit you, Henry?"

"As well as another," said I politely, concealing my feelings as a victim of feminine diplomacy.

"You have told him who are going, haven't you?" said Mrs. Knapp to Mrs. Bowser.

"Laws, no! I never thought but what he knew."

"Oh!" exclaimed Mrs. Knapp. "What a gift as a mind-reader Mr. Wilton ought to have! Well, I suppose I'd better not trust to that, Henry. There's to be Mrs. Bowser, of course, and Mr. and Mrs. Carter, and Mr. Horton, and-oh, yes-Luella."

My heart gave a jump, and the trip to Chinatown suddenly became an object of interest.

"I, mama?" said an inquiring voice, and Luella herself stood by her mother.

"Yes," said Mrs. Knapp. "It's the Chinatown expedition for Monday night."

Luella looked annoyed, and tapped her foot to the floor impatiently.

"With Mr. Wilton," there was the slightest emphasis on the words, "to accompany the party, I shouldn't think it would be necessary for me to go."

"It is either you or I," said Mrs. Knapp.

"You will be needed to protect Mr. Horton," said I sarcastically.

"Oh, what a task!" she said gaily. "I shall be ready." And she turned away before I could put in another word, and I walked down the room with Mrs. Knapp.

"And so Mr. Knapp is coming home to-morrow?" I said.

Mrs. Knapp gave me a quick look.

"Yes," she said. There was something in her tone that set me to thinking that there was more than I knew behind Mr. Knapp's sudden return.

"I hope he is not ill," I said politely.

Mrs. Knapp appeared to be considering some point deeply, and did not answer for a little. Then she shook her head as though the idea was not to her liking.

"I think you will find him all right when you see him. But here-you must meet Mr. and Mrs. Carter. They are just from the East, and very charming people, and as you are to do them the honors on Monday evening, you should know them."

Mr. and Mrs. Carter had pleasant faces and few ideas, and as the conversational fire soon burned low I sought Mrs. Knapp and took my leave. Luella was nowhere to be seen.

"You must be sure that you are well-guarded," said Mrs. Knapp. "It quite gives me the terrors to think of those murderous fellows. And since you told me of that last plot to call you down to Borton's, I have a presentiment that some special danger is ahead of you. Be cautious as well as brave."

She had followed me into the hall, and spoke her warning freely. There was a sadness in her eyes that seemed as though she would dissuade me from my task.

I thanked her as she pressed my hand, and, with no Luella awaiting me by the stair, I took my way down the stone steps, between the bronze lions, and joined Porter and Barkhouse on the sidewalk.

CHAPTER XVI. AN ECHO OF WARNING

"All quiet?" I asked of my guards, as we took our way down the street.

"All quiet," said Porter.

"You'd better tell him," said Barkhouse.

"Oh, yes," said Porter, as if in sudden recollection. "Dicky Nahl was along here, and he said Terrill and Meeker and the other gang was holding a powwow at Borton's, and we'd best look out for surprises."

"Was that all?"

"Well, he said he guessed there was a new deal on hand, and they was a-buzzin' like a nest of hornets. It was hornets, wasn't it, Bob?"

"Hornets was what he said," repeated Barkhouse stolidly.

"Where's Dicky now?" I asked.

"I ain't good at guessing," said Porter, "and Bob's nothing at all at it."

"Well," said I, "we had better go down to Borton's and look into this matter."

There was silence for a time. My guards walked beside me without speaking, but I felt the protest in their manner. At last Barkhouse said respectfully:

"There's no use to do that, sir. You'd better send some one that ain't so likely to be nabbed, or that won't matter much if he is. We'd be in a pretty fix if you was to be took."

"Here comes Dicky, now," said Porter, as a dark figure came swinging lightly along.

"Hullo!" cried Dicky, halting and shading his eyes from the gaslight. "I was just going up to look for you again."

"What's up, Dicky?"

"I guess it's the devil," said Dicky, so gravely that I broke into a laugh.

"He's right at home if he's come to this town," I said.

"I'm glad you find it so funny," said Dicky in an injured tone. "You was scared enough last time."

I had put my foot in it, sure enough. I might have guessed that the devil was not his Satanic Majesty but some evil-minded person in the flesh whom I had to fear.

"Can it be Doddridge Knapp?" flashed across my mind but I dismissed the suspicion as without foundation. I spoke aloud:

"Well, I've kept out of his claws this far, and it's no use to worry. What's he trying to do now?"

"That's what I've been trying to find out all the evening. They're noisy enough, but they're too thick to let one get near where there's anything going on-that is, if he has a fancy for keeping a whole skin."

"Suppose we go down there now," I suggested. "We might find out something."

Dicky stopped short.

"Cæsar's ghost!" he gasped; "what next? Wouldn't you like to touch off a few powder-kegs for amusement? Won't you fire a pistol into your mouth to show how easy you can stop the bullet?"

"Why, you have been down there and are all right," I argued.

"Well, there's nothing much to happen to me, but where would you be if they got hold of you? You're getting off your *cabesa*, old fellow," said Dicky anxiously.

"If I could see Mother Borton I could fix it," I said confidently.

"What! That she-devil?" cried Dicky. "She'd give you up to have your throat cut in a minute if she could get a four-bit piece for your carcass. I guess she could get more than that on you, too."

Mother Borton's warnings against Dicky Nahl returned to me with force at this expression of esteem from the young man, and I was filled with doubts.

"I came up to tell you to look out for yourself," continued Dicky. "I'm afraid they mean mischief, and here you come with a wild scheme for getting into the thick of it."

"Well, I'll think better of it," I said. "But see if you can find out what is going on. Come up and let me know if you get an inkling of their plans."

"All right," said Dicky. "But just sleep on a hair-trigger to-night."

"Good night," I said, as I turned toward my room, and Dicky, with an answering word, took his way toward the Borton place.

I had grown used to the silent terrors of my house. The weird fancies that clung around the gloomy halls and dark doorways still whispered their threatening tales of danger and death. The air was still peopled with the ghosts of forgotten crimes, and the tragedy of the alley that had changed my life was heavy on the place. But habit, and the confidence that had come to me with the presence of my guards, had made it a tolerable spot in which to live. But as we stumbled up the stairway the apprehensions of Dicky Nahl came strong upon me, and I looked ahead to the murky halls, and glanced at every doorway, as though I expected an ambush. Porter and Barkhouse marched stolidly along, showing little disposition to talk.

"What's that?" I exclaimed, stopping to listen.

"What was it?" asked Barkhouse, as we stopped on the upper landing and gazed into the obscurity.

"I thought I heard a noise," said I. "Who's there?"

"It was a rat," said Porter. "I've heard 'em out here of nights."

"Well, just light that other gas-jet," I said. "It will help to make things pleasant in case of accidents."

The doors came out of the darkness as the second jet blazed up, but nothing else was to be seen.

Suddenly there was a scramble, and something sprang up before my door. Porter and I raised the revolvers that were ready in our hands, but Barkhouse sprang past us, and in an instant had closed with the figure and held it in his arms.

There was a volley of curses, oaths mingled with sounds that reminded me of nothing so much as a spitting cat, and a familiar voice screamed in almost inarticulate rage:

"Let me go, damn ye, or I'll knife ye!"

"Good heavens!" I cried. "Let her go, Barkhouse. It's Mother Borton."

Mother Borton freed herself with a vicious shake, and called down the wrath of Heaven and hell on the stalwart guard.

"You're the black-hearted spawn of the sewer rats, to take a respectable woman like a bag of meal," cried Mother Borton indignantly, with a fresh string of oaths. "It's fire and brimstone you'll be tasting yet, and you'd 'a' been there before now, you miserable gutter-picker, if it wasn't for me. And this is the thanks I git from ye!"

"I'll apologize for his display of gallantry," said I banteringly. "I've always told him that he was too fond of the ladies."

I was mistaken in judging that this tone would be the most effective to restore her to good humor. Mother Borton turned on me furiously.

"Oh, it's you that would set him on a poor woman as comes to do you a service. I was as wide-awake as any of ye. I never closed my eyes a wink, and you has to come a-sneakin' up and settin' your dogs on me." Mother Borton again drew on an apparently inexhaustible vocabulary of oaths. "Oh, you're as bad as him," she shouted, "and I reckon you'd be worse if you knowed how." And she spat out more curses, and shook her fist in impotent but verbose rage.

"Come in," I said, unlocking the door and lighting up my room. "You can be as angry as you like in here, and it won't hurt anything."

Mother Borton stormed a bit, and then sullenly walked in and took a chair. Silence fell on her as she crossed the threshold, but she glowered on us with fierce eyes.

"It's quite an agreeable surprise to see you," I ventured as cheerfully as I could, as she made no move to speak. My followers looked awkward and uncomfortable.

At the sound of my voice, Mother Borton's bent brows relaxed a little.

"If you'd send these fellows out, I reckon we could talk a bit better," she said sourly.

"Certainly. Just wait in the hall, boys; and close the door."

Porter and Barkhouse ambled out, and Mother Borton gave her chair a hitch that brought us face to face.

"You ain't so bad off here," she said, looking around critically. "Can any one git in them winders?"

I explained that the west window might be entered from the rear stairway by the aid of the heavy shutter, if it were swung back and the window were open. I added that we kept it closed and secured.

"And you say there's a thirty-foot drop from this winder?" she inquired, pointing to the north.

I described the outlook on the alley.

She nodded as if satisfied.

"I reckon you don't think I come on a visit of perliteness?" she said sharply, after a brief silence.

I murmured something about being glad to entertain her at any time.

"Nonsense!" she sniffed. "I'm a vile old woman that the likes of you would never put eyes on twice if it wasn't for your business-none knows it better than me. I don't know why I should put myself out to help ye." Her tone had a touch of pathos under its hardness.

"I know why," I said, a little touched. "It's because you like me."

She turned a softened eye on me.

"You're right," she said almost tenderly, with a flash of womanly feeling on her seamed and evil face. "I've took a fancy to ye and no mistake, and I'd risk something to help ye."

"I knew you would," I said heartily.

"And that's what I come to do," she said, with a sparkle of pleasure in her eye. "I've come to warn ye."

"New dangers?" I inquired cheerfully. My prudence suggested that I had better omit any mention of the warning from Dicky Nahl.

"The same ones," said Mother Borton shortly, "only more of 'em."

Then she eyed me grimly, crouching in her chair with the appearance of an evil bird of prey, and seemed to wait for me to speak.

"What is the latest plot?" I asked gravely, as I fancied that my light manner grated on my strange guest.

"I don't know," she said slowly.

"But you know something," I argued.

"Maybe you know what I know better than I knows it myself," growled Mother Borton with a significant glance.

I resigned myself to await her humor.

"Not at all," said I carelessly. "I only know that you've come to tell me something, and that you'll tell it in your own good time."

"It's fine to see that you've learned not to drive a woman," she returned with grim irony. "It's something to know at your age."

I smiled sympathetically upon her, and she continued:

"I might as well tell ye the whole of it, though I reckon my throat's jist as like to be slit over it as not."

"I'll never breathe a word of it," I replied fervently.

"I'd trust ye," she said. "Well, there was a gang across the street to-night —across from my place, I mean-and that sneaking Tom Terrill and Darby Meeker, and I reckon all the rest of 'em, was there. And they was runnin' back and forth to my place, and a-drinkin' a good deal, and the more they drinks the louder they talks. And I hears Darby Meeker say to one feller, 'We'll git him, sure!' and I listens with all my ears, though pretendin' to see nothin'. 'We'll fix it this time,' he said; 'the Old Un's got his thinkin' cap on.' And I takes in every word, and by one thing and another I picks up that there's new schemes afoot to trap ye. They was a-sayin' as it might be an idee to take ye as you come out of Knapp's to-night."

"How did they know I was at Knapp's?" I asked, somewhat surprised, though I had little reason to be when I remembered the number of spies who might have watched me.

"Why, Dicky Nahl told 'em," said Mother Borton. "He was with the gang, and sings it out as pretty as you please."

This gave me something new to think about, but I said nothing.

"Well," she continued, "they says at last that won't do, fer it'll git 'em into trouble, and I reckon they're argyfying over their schemes yit. But one thing I finds out."

Mother Borton stopped and looked at me anxiously.

"Well," I said impatiently, "what was it?"

"They're a-sayin' as how, if you're killed, the one as you knows on'll have to git some one else to look after the boy, and mebbe he won't be so smart about foolin' them."

"That's an excellent idea," said I. "If they only knew that I was the other fellow they could see at once what a bright scheme they had hit upon."

"Maybe they ain't a-goin' to do it," said Mother Borton. "There's a heap o' things said over the liquor that don't git no further, but you'll be a fool if you don't look out. Now, do as I tell you. You just keep more men around you. Keep eyes in the back of your head, and if you see there's a-goin' to be trouble, jest you shoot first and ax questions about it afterward. They talked of getting you down on the water-front or up in Chinatown with some bogus message and said how easy it would be to dispose of you without leaving clues behind 'em. Now, don't you sleep here without three or four men on guard, and don't you stir round nights with less than four. Send Porter out to git two more men, and tell him to look sharp and see if the coast's clear outside. I reckon I'll slide out if no one's lookin'."

"I've got some men on the next floor," I said. "I thought it would be just as well to have a few around in case of emergencies. I'll have two of them out, and send Porter to reconnoiter."

"Who told you to git your men together?"

"A little idea of my own."

"You've got some sense, after all."

The reinforcements were soon ready to take orders, and Porter returned to bring word that no suspicious person was in sight in the street.

"I reckon I'd best go, then," said Mother Borton. "I don't want no knife in me jest yit, but if there's no one to see me I'm all right."

I pressed Mother Borton to take two of my men as escort, but she sturdily refused.

"They'd know something was up if I was to go around that way, and I'd be a bloody ghost as soon as they could ketch me alone," she said. "Well, good night-or is it mornin'? And do take keer of yourself, dearie." And, so saying, Mother Borton muffled herself up till it was hard to tell whether she was man or woman, and trudged away.

Whatever designs were brewing in the night-meeting of the conspirators, they did not appear to concern my immediate peace of body. The two following days were spent in quiet, and, in spite of warnings, I began to believe that no new plan of action had been determined on.

"Don't you feel too sure of yourself," said Dicky Nahl, to whom I confided this view of the situation. "You won't feel so funny about it if you get prodded in the ribs with a bowie some dark night, or find your head wrapped up in a blanket when you think you're just taking a 'passy-ar' in Washington Square in the evening."

Dicky looked very much in earnest, and his bright and airy manner was gone for the moment.

"You seem to get along well enough with them," I suggested tartly, remembering Mother Borton's stories with some suspicion.

"Of course," said Dicky. "Why shouldn't I? They're all right if you don't rub the fur the wrong way. But I haven't got state secrets in my pockets, so they know it's no use to pick 'em."

I was not at all sure of Dicky's fidelity, in spite of his seeming earnestness, but I forbore to mention my doubts, and left the garrulous young man to go his way while I turned to the office that had been furnished by Doddridge Knapp. I hardly expected to meet the King of the Street.

He had, I supposed, returned to the city, but he had set Wednesday as the day for resuming operations in the market, and I did not think that he would be found here on Monday.

The room was cold and cheerless, and the dingy books in law-calf appeared to gaze at me in mute protest as I looked about me.

The doors that separated me from Doddridge Knapp's room were shut and locked. What was behind them? I wondered. Was there anything in Doddridge Knapp's room that bore on the mystery of the hidden boy, or would give the clue to the murder of Henry Wilton? As I gazed on the panels the questions became more and more insistent. Was it not my duty to find the answer? The task brought my mind to revolt. Yet the thought grew on me that it was necessary to my task. If vengeance was to be mine; if Doddridge Knapp was to pay the penalty of the gallows for the death of Henry Wilton, it must be by the evidence that I should wrest from him and his tools. I must not stop at rummaging papers, nor at listening at keyholes. I had just this morning secured the key that would fit the first door. I had taken the impression of the lock and had it made without definite purpose, but now I was ready to act.

With a sinking heart but a clear head I put the key cautiously to the lock and gently turned it. The key fitted perfectly, and the bolt flew back as it made the circle. I opened the door into the middle room. The second door, as I expected, was closed. Would the same key fit the second lock, or must I wait to have another made? I advanced to the second door and was about to try the key when a sound from behind it turned my blood to water.

Beyond that door, from the room I had supposed to be empty, I heard a groan.

I stood as if petrified, and, in the broad daylight that streamed in at the window, with the noise and rush of Clay Street ringing in my ears, I felt my hair rise as though I had come on a ghost. I listened a minute or more, but heard nothing.

"Nonsense!" I thought to myself; "it was a trick of the imagination."

I raised my hand once more to the lock, when the sound broke again, louder, unmistakable. It was the voice of one in distress of body or mind.

What was it? Could it be some prisoner of Doddridge Knapp's, brought hither by the desperate band that owned him as employer? Was it a man whom I might succor? Or was it Doddridge Knapp himself, overwhelmed by recollection and remorse, doing penance in solitude for the villainy he had done and dared not confess? I listened with all my ears. Then there came through the door the low, stern tones of a man's voice speaking earnestly, pleadingly, threateningly, but in a suppressed monotone.

Then the groan broke forth again, and it was followed by sobs and choked sounds, as of one who protested, yet, strangely, the voice was the same. There was one man, not two. It was self-accusation, self-excuse, and the sobs seemed to come in answer to self-reproaches.

Then there was sound as of a man praying, and the prayer was broken by sobs; and again I thought there were two men. And then there was noise of a man moving about, and a long smothered groan, as of one in agony of spirit. Fearful that the door might be flung open in my face, I tiptoed back to my room, and silently turned the key, as thoroughly mystified as ever I had been in the strange events that had crowded my life since I had entered the city.

CHAPTER XVII. IN A FOREIGN LAND

I stood long by my own door, irresolute, listening, hoping, fearing, my brain throbbing with the effort to seize some clue to the maze of mysteries in which I was entangled. Was the clue behind those locked doors? Did the man whose groans and prayers had startled me hold the heart of the mystery?

The groans and prayers, if they continued, could be heard no longer through the double doors, and I seated myself by the desk and took account of the events that had brought me to my present position. Where did I stand? What had I accomplished? What had I learned? How was I to reach the end for which I struggled and bring to justice the slayer of my murdered friend? As I passed in review the occurrences that had crowded the few weeks since my arrival, I was compelled to confess that I knew little more of the mysteries that surrounded me than on the night I arrived. I knew that I was tossed between two opposing forces. I knew that a mysterious boy was supposed to be under my protection, and that to gain and keep possession of him my life was sought and defended. I knew that Doddridge Knapp had caused the murder of Henry Wilton, and yet for some unfathomable reason gave me his confidence and employment under the belief that I was Henry Wilton. But I had been able to get no hint of who the boy might be, or where he was concealed, or who was the hidden woman who employed me to protect him, or why he was sought by Doddridge Knapp. Mother Borton's vague hints seemed little better than guess-work. If she knew the name of the boy and the identity of the woman, she had some good reason for concealing them. It flashed over my mind that Mother Borton might herself be the mysterious employer. I had never yet seen a line of her handwriting, and the notes might have come from her. It was she who first had told me that my men were already paid, and a few hours later I had found the note from my employer assuring me that the demands were fully settled. Could it be that she was the woman with whom Doddridge Knapp was battling with a desperate purpose that did not stop at murder? The idea was gone as soon as it came. It was preposterous to suppose that these two could feel so overwhelming an interest in the same child.

How long I sat by the desk waiting, thinking, planning, I know not. One scheme of action after another I had considered and rejected, when a sound broke on my listening ears. I started up in feverish anxiety. It was from the room beyond, and I stole toward the door to learn what it might mean.

Again it came, but, strain as I might, I could not determine its cause. What could be going on in the locked office? If two men were there was it a personal encounter? If one man, was he doing violence upon himself? Was the heart of the mystery to be found behind those doors if I had the courage to throw them open? Burning with impatience, I thrust aside the fears of the evil that might follow hasty action. I had drawn the key and raised it once more to the slot, when I heard a step in the middle room. I had but time to retreat to my desk when a key was fitted in the lock, the door was flung open, and Doddridge Knapp stepped calmly into the room.

"Ah, Wilton," said the King of the Street affably. "I was wondering if I should find you here."

There was no trace of surprise or agitation in the face before me. If this was the man whose prayers and groans and sobs had come to me through the locked door, if he had wrestled with his conscience or even had been the accusing conscience of another, his face was a mask that showed no trace of the agony of thoughts that might contort the spirit beneath it.

"I was attending to a little work of my own," I answered, after greeting. If I felt much like a disconcerted pickpocket I was careful to conceal the circumstance, and spoke with easy indifference. "You have come back before I expected you," I continued carelessly.

"Yes," said the King of the Street with equal carelessness. "Some family affairs called me home sooner than I had thought to come."

I had an inward start. Mrs. Knapp's troubled look, Mrs. Bowser's confusion, and the few words that had passed, returned to me. What was the connection between them?

"Mrs. Knapp is not ill, I trust?" I ventured.

"Oh, no."

"Nor Miss Knapp?"

"Oh, all are well at the house, but sometimes you know women-folks get nervous."

Was it possible that Mrs. Knapp had sent for her husband? What other meaning could I put on these words? But before I could pursue my investigations further along this line, the wolf came to the surface, and he waved the subject aside with a growl.

"But this is nothing to you. What you want to know is that I won't need you before Wednesday, if then."

"Does the campaign reopen?" I asked.

"If you don't mind, Wilton," said the Wolf with another growl, "I'll keep my plans till I'm ready to use them."

"Certainly," I retorted. "But maybe you would feel a little interest to know that Rosenheim and Bashford have gathered in about a thousand shares of Omega in the last four or five days."

Doddridge Knapp gave me a keen glance.

"There were no sales of above a hundred shares," he said.

"No-most of them ran from ten to fifty shares."

"Well," he continued, looking fixedly at me, "you know something about Rosenheim?"

"If it won't interfere with your plans," I suggested apologetically.

The Wolf drew back his lips over his fangs, and then turned the snarl into a smile. "Go on," he said, waving amends for the snub he had administered.

"Well, I don't know much about Rosenheim, but I caught him talking with Decker."

"Were the stocks transferred to Decker?"

"No; they stand to Rosenheim, trustee."

"Well, Wilton, they've stolen a march on us, but I reckon we'll give 'em a surprise before they're quite awake."

"And," I continued coolly, "Decker's working up a deal in Crown Diamond and toying a little with Confidence-you gave me a week to find out, you may remember."

"Very good, Wilton," said the King of the Street with grudging approval. "We'll sell old Decker quite a piece of Crown Diamond before he gets through. And now is there anything more in your pack?"

"It's empty," I confessed. "Well, you may go then."

I was puzzled to know why Doddridge Knapp should wish to get me out of the office. Was there some secret locked in his room that he feared I might surprise if I stayed? I looked at him sharply, but there was nothing to be read on that impassive face.

Doddridge Knapp followed me to the door, and stood on the threshold as I walked down the hall. There was no chance for spying or listening at keyholes, if I were so inclined, and it was not until I had reached the bottom stair that I thought I heard the sound of a closing door behind me.

As I stood at the entrance, almost oblivious of the throng that was hurrying up and down Clay Street, Porter joined me.

"Did you see him?" he asked.

"Him? Who?"

"Why, Tom Terrill sneaked down those stairs a little bit ago, and I thought you might have found him up there."

Could it be possible that this man had been with Doddridge Knapp, and that it was his voice I had heard? This in turn seemed improbable, hardly possible.

"There he is now," whispered Porter.

I turned my eyes in the direction he indicated, and a shock ran through me; for my eye had met the eye of a serpent. Yes, there again was the cruel, keen face, and the glittering, repulsive eye, filled with malice and hatred, that I had beheld with loathing and dread whenever it had come in my path. With an evil glance Terrill turned and made off in the crowd.

"Follow that man, Wainwright," said I to the second guard, who was close at hand. "Watch him to-night and report to me to-morrow."

I wondered what could be the meaning of Terrill's visit to the building. Was it to see Doddridge Knapp and get his orders? Or was it to follow up some new plan to wrest from me the secret I was supposed to hold? But there was no answer to these questions, and I turned toward my room to prepare for the excursion that had been set for the evening.

It was with hope and fear that I took my way to the Pine Street palace. It was my fear that was realized. Mrs. Bowser fell to my lot-indeed, I may say that I was surrounded by her in force, and surrendered unconditionally-while Luella joined Mr. Carter, and Mrs. Carter with Mr. Horton followed.

Corson was waiting for us at the old City Hall. I had arranged with the policeman that he should act as our guide, and had given him Porter and Barkhouse as assistants in case any should be needed.

"A fine night for it, sor," said Corson in greeting. "There's a little celebration goin' on among the haythens to-night, so you'll see 'em at their best."

"Oh, how sweet!" gushed Mrs. Bowser. "Is it that dear China New Year that I've heard tell on, and do they take you in to dinner at every place you call, and do they really eat rats? Ugh, the horrid things!" And Mrs. Bowser pulled up short in mid career.

"No, ma'am," said Corson, "leastways it ain't Chaney New Year for a couple of months yet. As for eatin' rats, there's many a thing gets eaten up in the dens that would be better by bein' turned into a rat."

Looking across the dark shrubbery of Portsmouth Square and up Washington Street, the eye could catch a line of gay-colored lanterns, swaying in the light wind, and casting a mellow glow on buildings and walks.

"Oh, isn't it sweet! So charming!" cried Mrs. Bowser, as we came into full view of the scene and crossed the invisible line that carries one from modern San Francisco into the ancient oriental city, instinct with foreign life, that goes by the name of Chinatown. Sordid and foul as it appears by daylight, there was a charm and romance to it under the lantern-lights that softened the darkness. Windows and doors were illuminated. Brown, flat-nosed men in loose clothing gathered in groups and discussed their affairs in a strange singsong tongue and high-pitched voices. Here, was the sound of the picking of the Chinese banjo-fiddle; there, we heard a cracked voice singing a melancholy song in the confusion of minor keys that may pass for music among the brown men; there, again, a gong with tin-pan accompaniment assisted to reconcile the Chinese to the long intervals between holidays. Crowds hurried along the streets, loitered at corners, gathered about points of interest, but it seemed as though it was all one man repeated over and over.

"Why, they're all alike!" exclaimed Mrs. Bowser. "How do they ever tell each other apart?"

"Oh, that's aisy enough, ma'am," replied Corson with a twinkle in his eye. "They tie a knot in their pigtails, and that's the way you know 'em."

"Laws! you don't say!" said Mrs. Bowser, much impressed. "I never could tell 'em that way."

"It is a strange resemblance," said Mr. Carter. "Don't you find it almost impossible to distinguish between them?"

"To tell you the truth, sor, no," said Corson. "It's a trick of the eye with you, sor. If you was to be here with 'em for a month or two you'd niver think there was two of 'em alike. There's as much difference betwixt one and another as with any two white men. I was loike you at first. I says to meself that they're as like as two pease. But, now, look at those two mugs there in that door. They're no more alike than you and me, as Mr. Wilton here can tell you, sor."

The difference between the two Chinese failed to impress me, but I was mindful of my reputation as an old resident.

"Oh, yes; a very marked contrast," I said promptly, just as I would have sworn that they were twins if Corson had suggested it.

"Very remarkable!" said Mr. Carter dubiously.

In and out we wound through the oriental city-the fairy-land that stretched away, gay with lanterns and busy with strange crowds, changing at times as we came nearer to a tawdry reality, cheap, dirty, and heavy with odors. Here was a shop where ivory in delicate carvings, bronze work that showed the patient handicraft and grotesque fancy of the oriental artist, lay side by side with porcelains, fine and coarse, decorated with the barbaric taste in form and color that rules the art of the ancient empire. Beyond, were carved cabinets of ebony and sandal-wood, rich brocades and soft silks and the proprietor sang the praises of his wares and reduced his estimate of their value with each step we took toward the door. Next the rich shop was a low den from whose open door poured fumes of tobacco and opium, and in whose misty depths figures of bloused little men huddled around tables and swayed hither and thither. The click of dominoes, the rattling of sticks and counters, and the excited cries of men, rose from the throng.

"They're the biggest gamblers the Ould Nick iver had to his hand," said Corson; "there isn't one of 'em down there that wouldn't bet the coat off his back."

"Dear me, how dreadful!" said Mrs. Bowser. "And do we have to go down into that horrible hole, and how can we ever get out with our lives?"

"We're not going down there, ma'am," interrupted Corson shortly.

"And where next?" asked Luella.

The question was addressed to the policeman, not to me. Except for a formal greeting when we had met, Luella had spoken no word to me during the evening.

"Here's the biggest joss-house in town," said Corson. "We might as well see it now as any time."

"Oh, do let us see those delightfully horrible idols," cried Mrs. Bowser. "But," she added, with a sudden access of alarm at some recollection of the reading of her school-days, "do they cut people's hearts out before the wicked things right in the middle of the city?"

The policeman assured her that the appetite of the joss for gore remained unsatisfied, and led the way into the dimly-lighted building that served as a temple.

I lingered a moment by the door to see that all my party passed in.

"There's Wainwright," whispered Porter, who closed the procession.

"Where?" I asked, a dim remembrance of the mission on which I had sent him in pursuit of the snake-eyed man giving the information a sinister twist.

Porter gave a chirrup, and Wainwright halted at the door.

"He's just passed up the alley here," said Wainwright in a low voice.

"Who? Terrill?" I asked.

"Yes," said Wainwright. "I've kept him in sight all the evening."

"Hasn't he seen you?" asked Porter. "I spied you as soon as you turned the corner."

"Don't know," said Wainwright; "but something's up. There he goes now. I mustn't miss him." And Wainwright darted off.

I looked searchingly in the direction he took, but could see no sign of the snake-eyed enemy.

The presence of Terrill gave me some tremors of anxiety, for I knew that his unscrupulous ferocity would stop at nothing. I feared for the moment that some violence might threaten the party, and that perhaps Luella was in danger. Then I reflected that the presence of Doddridge Knapp's daughter was a protection against an attack from Doddridge Knapp's agents, and I followed the party into the heathen temple without further apprehensions.

The temple was small, and even in the dim, religious light that gave an air of mystery to the ugly figure of the god and the trappings of the place, the whole appeared cheap—a poor representative of the majesty of a religion that claims the devotion of four hundred million human beings.

"That's one of the richest carvings ever brought into this country," said Corson, pointing to a part of the altar mounting. "Tin thousand dollars wouldn't touch one side of it."

"You don't say!" cried Mrs. Bowser, while the rest murmured in the effort to admire the work of art. "And is that stuff burning for a disinfectant?"

She pointed to numerous pieces of punk, such as serve the small boy on the Fourth of July, that were consuming slowly before the ugly joss.

"No, ma'am-not but they needs it all right enough," said Corson, "but that's the haythen way of sayin' your prayers."

This information was so astonishing that Corson was allowed to finish his explanation without further remarks from Mrs. Bowser.

"I'll show you the theater next," said he, as he led the way out of the temple with Mrs. Bowser giving her views of the picturesque heathen in questions that Corson found no break in the conversation long enough to answer. As I lingered for a moment in some depression of spirit, waiting for the others to file out, a voice that thrilled me spoke in my ear.

"Our guide is enjoying a great favor." It was Luella, noticing me for the first time since the expedition had started.

"He has every reason to be delighted," I returned, brightening at the favor I was enjoying.

"Foreign travel is said to be of great value in education," said Luella, taking my arm, "but it's certainly stupid at times."

I suspected that Mr. Carter had not been entirely successful in meeting Miss Knapp's ideas of what an escort should be.

"I didn't suppose you could find anything stupid," I said.

"I am intensely interested," she retorted, "but unfortunately the list of subjects has come to an end."

"You might have begun at the beginning again."

"He did," she whispered, "so I thought it time he tried the guide or Aunt Julia."

"Thank you," I said.

"Thank him, you mean," she said gaily. "Now don't be stupid yourself, so please change the subject. Do you know," she continued without giving me time to speak, "that the only way I can be reconciled to this place and the sights we have seen is to imagine I am in Canton or Peking, thousands of miles from home? Seen there, it is interesting, instructive, natural—a part of their people. As a part of San Francisco it is only vile."

"Ugh!" said I, as a whiff from an underground den floated up on the night air, and Luella caught her handkerchief to her face to get her breath. "I'm not sure that this rose would smell any sweeter by the name of Canton."

"I'm afraid your argument is too practical for me to answer," she laughed. "Yet I'm certain it would be more poetic seven thousand miles away."

"Come this way," said Corson, halting with the party at one of the doors. "I'll show you through some of the opium dens, and that will bring us to the stage door of the theater."

"How close and heavy the air is!" said Luella, as we followed the winding passage in the dim illumination that came from an occasional gas-jet or oil lamp.

"The yellow man is a firm believer in the motto, 'Ventilation is the root of all evil,'" I admitted.

The fumes of tobacco and opium were heavy on the air, and a moment later we came on a cluster of small rooms or dens, fitted with couches and bunks. It needed no description to make the purpose plain. The whole process of intoxication by opium was before me, from the heating of the metal pipe to the final stupor that is the gift and end of the Black Smoke. Here, was a coolie mixing the drug; there, just beyond him, was another, drawing whiffs from the bubbling narcotic through the bamboo handle of his pipe; there, still beyond, was another, lying back unconscious, half-clad, repulsive, a very sorry reality indeed to the gorgeous dreams that are reputed to follow in the train of the seductive pipe.

"Do they really allow them to smoke that dreadful stuff?" asked Mrs. Bowser shrilly. "Why, I should think the governor, or the mayor, or you, Mr. Policeman, would stop the awful thing right off. Now, why don't you?"

"Oh, it's no harm to the haythen," said Corson. "It's death and destruction to the white man, but it's no more to the yellow man than so much tobacco and whiskey. They'll be all right to-morrow. We niver touches 'em unless they takes the whites into their dens. Then we raids 'em. But there's too much of it goin' on, for all that."

"This is depressing," said Luella, with a touch on my arm. "Let's go on."

"Turn to the right there," Corson called out, as we led the way while he was explaining to Mr. Carter the method of smoking.

"Let us get where there is some air," said Luella. "This odor is sickening."

We hastened on, and, turning to the right, soon came on two passages. One led up a stair, hidden by a turn after half a dozen steps. The other stretched fifty or seventy-five feet before us, and an oil lamp on a bracket at the farther end gave a smoky light to the passage and to a mean little court on which it appeared to open.

"We had better wait for the rest," said Luella cautiously.

As she spoke, one of the doors toward the farther end of the passage swung back, and a tall heavy figure came out. My heart gave a great bound, and I felt without realizing it at the moment, that Luella clutched my arm fiercely.

In the dim light the figure was the figure of the Wolf, the head was the head of the Wolf, and though no light shone upon it, the face was the face of the Wolf, livid, distorted with anger, fear and brutal passions.

"Doddridge Knapp!" I exclaimed, and gave a step forward.

It flashed on me that one mystery was explained. I had found out why the Doddridge Knapp of plot and counterplot, and the Doddridge Knapp who was the generous and confidential employer, could dwell in the same body. The King of the Street was a slave of the Black Smoke, and, like many another, went mad under the influence of the subtle drug.

As I moved forward, Luella clung to me and gave a low cry. The Wolf figure threw one malignant look at us and was gone.

"Take me home, oh, take me home!" cried Luella in low suppressed tones, trembling and half-falling. I put my arm about her to support her.

"What is it?" I asked.

She leaned upon me for one moment, and the black walls and gloomy passage became a palace filled with flowers. Then her strength and resolution returned, and she shook herself free.

"Come; let us go back to the others," she said a little unsteadily. "We should not have left them."

"Certainly," I replied. "They ought to be here by this time."

But as we turned, a sudden cry sounded as of an order given. There was a bang of wood and a click of metal, and, as we looked, we saw that unseen hands had closed the way to our return. A barred and iron-bound door was locked in our faces.

CHAPTER XVIII. THE BATTLE IN THE MAZE

For an instant I was overwhelmed with terror and self-reproach. The bolted door before me gave notice of danger as plainly as though the word had been painted upon its front. The dark and lowering walls of the passage in which the Wolf figure of Doddridge Knapp had appeared and disappeared whispered threats. The close air was heavy with the suggestion of peril, and the solitary lamp that gave its dim light from the end of the passage flashed a smoky warning. And I, in my folly and carelessness, had brought Luella Knapp into this place and exposed her to the dangers that encircled me. It was this thought that, for the moment, unnerved me.

"What does this mean?" asked Luella in a matter-of-fact tone.

"It is a poor practical joke, I fear," said I lightly. I took occasion to shift a revolver to my overcoat pocket.

"Well, aren't you going to get me out of here?" she asked with a little suggestion of impatience.

"That is my present intention," I replied, beating a tattoo on the door.

"You'll hurt your fists," she said. "You must find some way besides beating it down."

"I'm trying to bring our friends here," said I. "They should have been with us before now."

"Isn't there another way out?" asked Luella.

"I suspect there are a good many ways out," I replied, "but, unfortunately, I don't know them." And I gave a few resounding kicks on the door.

"Where does this stairway go, I wonder?" said Luella.

"Into the celestial regions, I suppose," I ventured.

Matters were in too serious a position for the jest to be appreciated, and Luella continued: "It can't be the way out. Isn't there another?"

"We might try the passage."

She gave a shudder and shrank toward me.

"No, no," she cried in a low voice. "Try the door again. Somebody must hear you, and it may be opened."

I followed her suggestion with a rain of kicks, emphasized with a shout that made the echoes ring gloomily in the passage.

I heard in reply a sound of voices, and then an answering shout, and the steps of men running.

"Are you there, Mr. Wilton?" cried the voice of Corson through the door.

"Yes, all safe," I answered.

"Well, just hold on a bit, and we'll—"

The rest of his sentence was lost in a suppressed scream from Luella. I turned and darted before her, just in time to face three Chinese ruffians who were hastening down the passage. The nearest of the trio, a tall dark savage with a deep scar across his cheek, was just reaching out his hand to seize Luella when I sprang forward and planted a blow square upon his chin. He fell back heavily, lifted almost off his feet by my impact, and lay like a log on the floor.

The other two ruffians halted irresolute for an instant, and I drew my revolver. In the faint light of the passage I could scarcely see their villainous faces. The countenance of the coolie is not expressive at best, but I could feel, rather than see, the stolid rascality of their appearance. Their wish seemed to be to take me alive if possible. After a moment of hesitation there was a muttered exclamation and one of the desperadoes drew his hand from his blouse.

"Oh!" cried Luella. "He's got a knife!"

Before he could make another movement I fired once, twice, three times. There was a scramble and scuffle in the passageway, and the smoke rolled thick in front, blotting out the scene that had stood in silhouette before us.

Fearful of a rush from the Chinese, I threw one arm about Luella, and, keeping my body between her and possible attack, guided her to the stair that led upward at nearly right angles from the passage. She was trembling and her breath came short, but her spirit had not quailed. She shook herself free as I placed her on the first step.

"Have you killed them?" she asked quietly.

"I hope so," I replied, looking cautiously around the corner to see the results of my fusillade. The smoke had spread into a thin haze through the passage.

"There's one fellow there," I said. "But it's the one I knocked down."

"Can't you see the others?" inquired Luella.

"No more in sight," said I, after a bolder survey. "They've run away."

"Oh, I'm glad," said Luella. "I should have seen them always if you had killed them."

"I shouldn't have minded giving them something to remember," said I, vexed at my poor display of marksmanship, but feeling an innate conviction that I must have hit them.

"What on earth did they attack us for?" exclaimed Luella indignantly. "We hadn't hurt anything."

Before I could reply to Luella's question, a tattoo was beaten upon the door and a muffled shout came from the other side. I stepped down from the stair to listen.

"Are you hurt?" shouted Corson. "What's the matter?"

"No damage," I returned. "I drove them off."

Corson shouted some further words, but they were lost in a sudden murmur of voices and a scuffle of feet that arose behind.

"Look out!" cried Luella peremptorily. "Come back here!"

I have said that the passage opened into a little court, and at the end a lamp gave light to the court and the passage.

As I turned I saw a confusion of men pouring into the open space and heading for the passage. They were evidently Chinese, but in the gleam of the lamp I was sure I saw the evil face and snake-eyes of Tom Terrill. He was wrapped in the Chinese blouse, but I could not be mistaken. Then with a chorus of yells there was the crack of a pistol, and a bullet struck the door close to my ear.

It was all done in an instant. Before the sound of the shot I dropped, and then made a leap for the stair.

"Oh!" cried Luella anxiously; "were you hit?"

"No, I'm all right," I said, "but it was a close shave. The gang means mischief."

"Go up the stairs, and find a way out or a place to hide," said Luella excitedly. "Give me the pistol. They won't hurt me. It's you they're after. Go, now."

Her tone was the tone of the true daughter of the Wolf.

"Thank you, Miss Knapp. I have a pressing engagement here with a lady, and I expect to meet Mr. Corson in a few minutes."

I stooped on an impulse and kissed the back of her gloved hand, and murmured, "I couldn't think of leaving."

"Well, tell me something I can do," she said.

I gave her my smaller revolver. "Hand that to me when I want it," I said. "If I'm killed, get up the stairs and defend yourself with it. Don't fire unless you have to. We are short of ammunition." I had but three shots in the large six-shooter.

"Are they coming?" asked Luella, as the wild tumult of shouts stilled for a moment and a single voice could be heard.

I peered cautiously around the corner.

"There's a gentleman in a billycock hat who's rather anxious to have them lead the way," I said; "but they seem to prefer listening to fighting."

The gentleman whose voice was for war I discovered to be my snake-eyed friend. He seemed to be having difficulty with the language, and was eking out his Pidgin-English with pantomime.

"There!" cried Luella with a start; "what's that?"

A heavy blow shook the walls of the building and sounded through the passage.

"Good!" I said. "If our friends yonder are going to make trouble they must do it at once. Corson's got an ax, and the door will be down first they know."

"Thank Heaven!" whispered Luella. And then she began to tremble.

The blows followed fast upon each other, but suddenly they were drowned in a chorus of yells, and a volley of revolver shots sent the bullets spatting against the door.

"Look out, Miss Knapp," I said. "They're coming. Stand close behind me, and crouch down if they get this far."

I could feel her straighten and brace herself once more behind me as I bent cautiously around the corner.

The band was advancing with a frightful din, but was making more noise than speed. Evidently it had little heart for its job.

I looked into the yelling mob for the snake-eyed agent of Doddridge Knapp, but could not single him out.

I dared wait no longer. Aiming at the foremost I fired twice at the advancing assailants. There were shouts and screams of pain in answer, and the line hesitated. I gave them the remaining cartridge, and, seizing the smaller weapon from Luella, fired as rapidly as I could pull the trigger.

The effect was instantaneous. With a succession of howls and curses the band broke and ran-all save one man, who leaped swiftly forward with a long knife in his hand.

It would have gone hard with me if he had ever reached me, for he was a large and powerful fellow, and my last shot was gone. But in the dark and smoky passage he stumbled over the prostrate body of the first desperado whom I had been fortunate enough to knock down, and fell sprawling at full length almost at my feet.

With one leap I was on his back, and with a blow from the revolver I had quieted him, wrenched the knife from his hand, and had the point resting on his neck.

Luella gave a scream.

"Oh!" she cried, "are you hurt?"

"No," I said lightly, "but I don't think this gentleman is feeling very well. He's likely to have a sore head for a day or two."

"Come back here," said Luella in a peremptory tone. "Those men may come again and shoot you."

"I don't think so," said I. "The door is coming down. But, anyhow, I can't leave our friend here. Lie still!" I growled, giving the captive a gentle prod in the neck with the point of his knife to emphasize my desire to have peace and quiet between us.

I heard him swear under his breath. The words were foreign, but there was no mistaking the sentiment behind them.

"You aren't killing him are you?" inquired Luella anxiously.

"I think it might be a service to the country," I confessed, "but I'll save him for the hangman."

"You needn't speak so regretfully," laughed Luella, with a little return of her former spirit. "But here our people come."

The ax had been plied steadily on the stubborn planks all through the conflict and its sequel. But the iron-bound beams and heavy lock had been built to resist police raids, and the door came down with difficulty.

At last it was shaking and yielding, and almost as Luella spoke it swayed, bent apart, and broke with a crash, and with a babel of shouts Corson, Porter, Barkhouse and Wainwright, with two more policemen, poured through the opening.

"Praise the powers, you're safe!" cried Corson, wringing my hand, while the policemen took the prostrate Chinese in charge. "And is the young lady hurt?"

"No harm done," said Luella. "Mr. Wilton is quite a general."

"I can't think what's got into the scoundrelly highbinders," said Corson apologetically. "It's the first time I ever knew anything of the kind to happen." And he went on to explain that while the Chinese desperado is a devil to fight among his own kind, he does not interfere with the white man.

I called my men aside and spoke sharply.

"You haven't obeyed orders," I said. "You, Porter, and you, Barkhouse, were to keep close by me to-night. You didn't do it, and it's only by good luck that the young lady and I were not killed. You, Wainwright, were to follow Tom Terrill. I saw Terrill just now in a gang of Chinese, and you turn up on the other side of a barred door."

Porter and Barkhouse looked sheepish enough, but Wainwright protested:

"I was following Terrill when he gets into a gang of highbinders, and goes into one of these rooms over here a ways. I waits a while for him, and then starts to look around a bit, and first I knows, I runs up against Porter here hunting for an ax, and crazy as a loon, saying as how you was murdered, and they had got to save you."

"Well, just keep close to me for the rest of the night, and we'll say no more about it. There's no great damage done-nothing but a sore knuckle." I was feeling now the return effects of my blow on the coolie's chin. I felt too much in fault myself to call my attendants very sharply to task. It was through me that Luella had come into danger, and I had to confess that I had failed in prudence and had come near to paying dear for it.

"I don't understand this, Mr. Wilton," said Corson in confidential perplexity. "I don't see why the haythen were after yez."

"I saw—I saw Tom Terrill," said I, stumbling over the name of Doddridge Knapp. I determined to keep the incident of his appearance to myself.

"I don't see how he worked it," said Corson with a shake of the head. "They don't like to stand against a white man. It's a quare tale he must have told 'em, and a big sack he must have promised 'em to bring 'em down on ye. Was it for killin' ye they was tryin', or was they for catchin' yez alive?"

"They were trying to take us alive at first, I think, but the bullets whistled rather close for comfort."

"I was a little shaky myself, when they plunked against the door," said Corson with a smile.

"Oh, Mr. Wilton," said Mrs. Bowser, "it was awful of you-for it was so frightfully improper to get behind that locked door, to say nothing of throwing us all into conniptions with firing guns, and calling for axes, and highbinders, and police, and Heaven knows what all-and what are highbinders, Mr. Wilton? And it's a blessing we have our dear Luella safe with us again. I was near fainting all the time, and it's a mercy I had a smelling bottle."

"Dear Luella" looked distressed, and while Corson was attempting to explain to Mrs. Bowser the nature of the blackmailing bands of the Chinese criminal element, Luella said:

"Please get us out of this. I can't stand it."

I had marveled at her calm amid the excited talk of those about her, but I saw now that it was forced by an effort of her will. She was sadly shaken.

"Take my arm," I said. "Mr. Corson will lead the way." I signed to Porter to go ahead and to Barkhouse and Wainwright to follow me. "It's very close here."

"It's very ridiculous of me," said Luella, with an hysterical laugh, "but I'm a little upset."

"I dare say you're not used to it," I suggested dryly.

Luella gave me a quick glance.

"No, are you? It's not customary in our family," she said with an attempt at gaiety.

I thought of the wolf-figure who had come out of the opium-den, and the face framed in the lantern-flash of the alley, and was silent. Perhaps the thought of the scene of the passage had come to her, too, for she shuddered and quickened her step as though to escape.

"Do you want to go through the theater?" asked Corson.

"No-no," whispered Luella, "get me home at once."

"We have seen enough sights for the evening, I believe," said I.

Mrs. Bowser was volubly regretful, but declined Corson's offer to chaperon her through a night of it.

On the way home Luella spoke not a word, but Mrs. Bowser filled the time with a detailed account of her emotions and sensations while Corson and his men were searching for us and beating down the door. And her tale was still growing when the carriage pulled up before the bronze lions that guarded the house of the Wolf, and I handed the ladies up the steps.

At the door Luella held out her hand impulsively.

"I wish I knew whom to thank-but I do thank him-for my safety-perhaps for my life. Believe me —I am grateful to a brave man."

I felt the warm clasp of her fingers for a moment, and then with a flash of her eyes that set my blood on fire she was gone, and I was staggering down Doddridge Knapp's steps in a tumult of emotions that turned the dark city into the jeweled palaces of the genii peopled with angels.

But there was a bitter in the sweet. "I wish I knew whom to thank." The bitter grew a little more perceptible as her phrases stamped themselves on my brain. I blessed and cursed at once the day that had brought me to her.

CHAPTER XIX. A DEAL IN STOCKS

The wolf-face, seamed with hatred and anger, and hideous with evil passions, that had glowered for a moment out of the smoky frame of the Chinese den, was still haunting me as I forced myself once more to return to the office. Wednesday morning had come, and I was due to meet Doddridge Knapp. But as I unlocked the door, I took some comfort in the reflection that I could hardly be more unwilling to meet the Wolf than he must be to meet me.

I had scarcely settled myself in my chair when I heard the key turn in the lock. The door swung open, and in walked Doddridge Knapp.

I had thought to find at least some trace of the opium debauch through which I had gained the clue to his strange and contradictory acts-some mark of the evil passions that had written their story upon his face at the meeting in the passage. But the face before me was a mask that showed no sign of the experiences through which he had passed. For all that appeared, he might have employed the time since I had left here two days before in studying philosophy and cultivating peace and good-will with his neighbors.

"Ah, Wilton," he said affably, rubbing his hands with a purring growl. "You're ready for a hard day's work, I hope."

"Nothing would please me better," I said cheerfully, my repugnance melting away with the magnetism of his presence. "Is the black flag up today?"

He looked at me in surprise for an instant and then growled, still in good humor:

"'No quarter' is the motto to-day." And I listened closely as the King of the Street gave his orders for the morning.

I marveled at the openness and confidence with which he seemed to treat me. There was no trace nor suggestion in his demeanor to-day of the man who sought my life by night. And I shuddered at the power of the Black Smoke to change the nature of this man to that of a demon. He trusted me with secrets of his campaign that were worth millions to the market.

"You understand now," he said at the end of his orders, "that you are to sell all the Crown Diamond that the market will take, and buy all the Omega that you can get below one hundred."

"I understand."

"We'll feed Decker about as big a dose as he can swallow, I reckon," said the King of the Street grimly.

"One thing," I said, "I'd like to know if I'm the only one operating for you."

The King of the Street drew his bushy brows down over his eyes and scowled at me a moment.

"You're the only one in the big Board," he said at last. "There are men in the other Boards, you understand."

I thought I understood, and sallied forth for the battle. At Doddridge Knapp's suggestion I arranged to do my business through three brokers, and added Lattimer and Hobart to Wallbridge, and Bockstein and Eppner.

Bockstein greeted me affably:

"Velgome to de marget vonce more, Mr. —, Mr. —"

"Wilton," said Eppner, assisting his partner in his high, dry voice, with cold civility. His blue-black eyes regarded me as but a necessary part of the machinery of commerce.

I gave my orders briefly.

"Dot is a larch order," said Bockstein dubiously.

"You don't have to take it," I was about to retort, when Eppner's high-pitched voice interrupted:

"It's all right. The customary margin is enough."

Wallbridge was more enthusiastic.

"You've come just in the nick of time," said the stout little man, swabbing his bald head from force of habit, though the morning was chill. "The market has been drier than a fish-horn and duller than a foggy morning. You saved me from a trip to Los Angeles. I should have been carried off by my wife in another day."

"You have got Gradgrind's idea of a holiday," I laughed.

"Gradgrind, Gradgrind?" said the little man reflectively. "Don't know him. He's not in the market, I reckon. Oh, I'm death on holidays! I come near dying every day the Board doesn't meet. When it shut up shop after the Bank of California went to the wall, I was just getting ready to blow my brains out for want of exercise, when they posted the notice that it was to open again."

I laughed at the stout broker's earnestness, and told him what I wanted done.

"Whew!" he exclaimed, "you're in business this time, sure. Well, this is just in my line."

Lattimer and Hobart, after a polite explanation of their rules in regard to margins, and getting a certified check, became obsequiously anxious to do my bidding.

I distributed the business with such judgment that I felt pretty sure our plans could not in any way be exposed, and took my place at the rail in the Boardroom.

The opening proceedings were comparatively tame. I detected a sad falling-off in the quality and quantity of lung power and muscular activity among the buyers and sellers in the pit.

At the call of Confidence, Lattimer and Hobart began feeding shares to the market. Confidence dropped five points in half a minute, and the pit began to wake up. There was a roar and a growl that showed me the animals were still alive.

The Decker forces were taken by surprise, but with a hasty consultation came gallantly to the rescue of their stock. At the close of the call they had forced it back and one point higher than at the opening.

This, however, was but a skirmish of outposts. The fighting began at the call of Crown Diamond.

It opened at sixty-three. The first bid was hardly made when with a bellow Wallbridge charged on Decker's broker, filled his bid, and offered a thousand shares at sixty-two.

There was an answering roar from a hundred throats and a mob rushed on Wallbridge with the apparent intent of tearing him limb from limb. Wallbridge's offer was snapped up at once, but a few weak-kneed holders of the stock threw small blocks on the market.

These were taken up at once, and Decker's brokers were bidding sixty-five.

At this Eppner gave a blast like a cornet, and, waving his arms frantically, plunged into a small-sized riot. I had entrusted him with five thousand shares of Crown Diamond to be sold for the best price possible, and he was feeding the opposition judiciously. The price wavered for a moment, but rallied and reached sixty-six.

At this I signaled to Wallbridge, and with another bellow he started an opposition riot on the other side of the room from Eppner, and fed Crown Diamond in lumps to the howling forces of the Decker combination.

The battle was raging furiously.

I had no wish to break the price of the stock. I was intent only at selling shares at a good price, but I had convinced the Decker forces that there was a raid on the stock, and they had rallied to protect it at whatever cost.

The price see-sawed between sixty-six and sixty-five, and amid a tumult of yells and shouts I sold twelve thousand shares. At last they were gone, but the offers still continued.

Outsiders had become scared at the persistent selling, and were trying to realize before a break should come, and in spite of Decker's efforts the price ran down to sixty.

There was a final rally of the Decker forces, and the call closed with Crown Diamond at sixty-three.

I was pleased at the result. Doddridge Knapp had intrusted me with the shares with the remark, "I paid fifty for 'em and they're not worth a tinker's dam. I got an inside look at the mine when I was in Virginia City. Feed Decker all he'll take at sixty. He's been fooled on the thing, and I reckon he'll buy a good lot of them at that."

I had sold Doddridge Knapp's entire lot of the stock at an average of over sixty-five, had netted him a profit of fifteen dollars a share, and had, for a second purpose, served the plan of campaign by drawing the enemy's resources to the defense of Crown Diamond and weakening, by so much, his power of operating elsewhere.

By the time Omega was reached I had the plans fully in hand.

The assault on Crown Diamond had caused a nervous feeling all along the line, and under rumors of a bear raid there had been a drop of several points.

Omega felt the results of the nervousness and depression, and opened at seventy-five.

There was a moment's buzz-the quiet of a crowd expectant of great events. Then Wallbridge charged into the throng with a roar. I could not distinguish his words, but I knew that he was carrying out my order to drop five thousand shares on the market. At his cry there was an answering roar, and the scene upon the floor turned to a riot. Men rushed hither and thither, screaming, shouting, waving their arms, pushing, jostling, tearing each other to get into the midst of the throng, whirling about, mobbing first one and then another of the leather-lunged leaders who furnished at each moment fresh centers for the outbreak of disorder. How the market was going, I could only guess. At Wallbridge's onset I saw Lattimer and Eppner make a dive for him and then separate, following other shouting, screaming madmen who pirouetted about the floor and tried to save themselves from a mobbing. I heard seventy shouted from one direction, but could not make out whether it set the price of the stock or not. The din was too confusing for me to follow the course of events.

At last Wallbridge staggered up to the rail, flushed, collarless and panting for breath, with his hat a hopeless wreck.

"We've done it!" he gasped in my ear. "The dogs of war are making the fur fly down here, you bet! Don't you wish you was in it?"

"No, I don't!" I shouted decidedly. "How does it go?"

"I sold down to seventy-one —average seventy-three, I guess-and she's piling in fit to break the floor."

"Did Lattimer and Eppner get your stock?" I could not help asking.

"They got about three thousand of it. Rosenheim got the rest."

I remembered Rosenheim as the agent of Decker, and sighed. But Lattimer and Eppner were busy, and I had hopes.

"Where is it now?" I asked.

"Sixty-nine and a half."

I meditated an instant whether to use my authority to throw another five thousand shares on the market. But I caught sight of Decker opposite, pale, hawklike, just seizing an envelope from a messenger. He tore it open, and though his face changed not a line, I felt by a mysterious instinct that it brought assurance of the aid he sought.

"Buy every share you can get," I said promptly. "Don't get in the way of Lattimer or Eppner. Put on steam, too."

"Two-forty on a turnpike road," said Wallbridge. And, refreshed by a minute of rest, he gave a prolonged bellow and charged frantically for a stout man in a white waistcoat who was doing the maniac dance across the hall.

A moment later the clamor grew louder and the excitement increased. I heard shouts of seventy-five, seventy-eight, eighty and eighty-five. Decker's men had entered into the bidding with energy. The sinews of war had been recruited, and it was a battle for the possession of every block of stock.

Thus far I had followed closely the plan laid down for me by Doddridge Knapp, and the course of the market had agreed with the outlines of his prophecy. But now it was going up faster than he had expected. Yet I could do nothing but buy. I dared not set bounds to the bidding. I dared not stop for an instant to hear how the account of purchases stood, for it might allow Decker to get the stock that my employer would need to give him the control of the mine. I could only grip the railing and wait for the end of the call.

At last it came, and "Omega, one hundred and five and three-quarters" was the closing quotation. I feverishly took the totals of my purchases from the brokers, and gave the checks to bind them. Then I hastily made my way through the excited throngs that blocked the entrance to the Exchange, brought thither by the exciting news of "a boom in Omega," and hurried to the office.

Doddridge Knapp had not yet come, and I consumed myself with impatience for ten minutes till I heard his key in the lock and he entered with a calm smile on his face.

"What luck, Wilton?" was his greeting. The King of the Street, whose millions had been staked in the game, was less excited than I who risked nothing.

I gave him my memoranda, and tried to read his face as he studied them.

"You did a good job with Crown Diamond," he grunted approvingly.

"Thanks," I returned. "I thought it wasn't bad for a stock that was not worth mentioning."

"Um, yes. Decker can light his cigars with it next month."

"A million dollars' worth of cigar-lighters might be called a piece of extravagance," I murmured.

"You'll think so if you ever buy 'em, Wilton," growled the King of the Street feelingly. "And here is seven thousand six hundred shares of Omega bought and five thousand sold. That scheme worked pretty well. We made twenty-six hundred by it. Um-the price went up pretty fast."

The King of the Street looked sourly at the figures before him. "You ought to have got more stock," he growled.

This was a shock to my self-congratulation over my success, and I gave an inquiring "Yes?"

"As I figure it out," he said, "somebody else got seven thousand shares and odd. There were over fifteen thousand shares sold in your Board."

I murmured that I had done my best.

"Yes, yes; I suppose so," said my employer. "But we need more."

"How much?" I asked.

"I've got a little over forty-eight thousand shares," he said slowly, "and I must have near sixty thousand. It looks as though I'd have to fight for them."

"Which will cost you about a million and a half at present rates," I returned.

"I'll give you a million commission, Wilton, if you'll get them for that."

The King of the Street plainly did not underrate the task he had set.

"Well, Decker isn't any better off than you," I said consolingly.

"He's ten or fifteen thousand shares worse off than I am."

"And he's put a fortune into Crown Diamond, and is pretty well loaded with Confidence."

"True, my boy."

"And so," I argued, "he must be nearer the bottom of his sack than you are."

"Very good, Wilton," said the King of the Street with a quizzical look. "But you've left one thing out. You don't happen to know that the directors of the El Dorado Bank had a secret meeting last night and decided to back Decker for all they are worth."

"Rather a rash proceeding," I suggested.

"Well, he had three millions of their money in his scheme, so I reckon they thought the tail might as well follow the hide," explained my employer.

"The only thing to do then is to get a bank yourself," I returned.

Doddridge Knapp's lips closed, and a trace of a frown was on his brows.

"Well, this isn't business," he said. "Now here is what I want," he continued. And he gave directions for the buying at the afternoon session.

"Now, not over one hundred and twenty-five," was his parting injunction. "You may not get much —I don't think you will-though I have a scheme that may bring a reaction."

Doddridge Knapp's scheme for a reaction must have been one of the kind that goes off backward, for Omega jumped skyward on the afternoon call, and closed at one hundred and thirty. Rumors were flying fast that a big bonanza, "bigger than the Consolidated Virginia," had been discovered on the six-hundred-foot level, and the great public was rushing to Pine Street to throw its dollars into the blind pool against Knapp, Decker and the El Dorado bank. And I had been able to get a scant one thousand five hundred shares when the call was over.

"I did better than you," said Doddridge Knapp, when I explained to him the course of the session. "I found a nest of two thousand five hundred, and gathered them in at one hundred and twenty. But that's all right. You've done well enough-as well as I expected."

"And still eight thousand to get," I said.

"Nearly."

"Well, we'll get them in due time, I suppose," I said cheerfully.

"We'll have 'em by Monday noon, or we won't have 'em at all," growled Doddridge Knapp.

"How is that?"

"You seem to have forgotten, young man, that the stock transfer books of the Omega Company close on Monday at two o'clock."

As I had never heard this interesting piece of information before, I could not in strictness be said to have forgotten it.

"Well, we ought to have the stock by that time," I said consolingly.

"We ought," said the King of the Street grimly, pausing in the doorway, "but things don't always happen as they ought."

As I remembered that if things had happened as they ought Doddridge Knapp would be in jail, I gave a hearty assent to the proposition as the door closed behind my retreating employer.

"You really don't mean it," said Luella severely, "and it's very wrong to say what you don't mean."

"In society?" I asked blandly. "I'm afraid you're a heretic, L — — Miss Knapp."

I blushed as I stumbled over her name. She was Luella to me by night and day, but I did not consider myself on a footing to use so thrilling a word in her presence.

"Don't be rude," she said. "Everything has its place in society."

"Even prevarication," I assented.

"Even a polite consideration for the feelings of others," corrected Luella.

"Then you might have some consideration for mine," I said in an injured tone.

"But we're not in society, —not just now, that is to say. We're just friends talking together, and you're not to say what you don't mean just for the sake of pleasing my vanity."

"Well, if we're just friends talking together —" said I, looking up in her face. I was seated on the footstool before her, and it was very entertaining to look at her face, so I stopped at that.

"Yes," said Luella, bending forward in her interest.

"It was the bravest and truest and most womanly girl I ever knew or heard of. It's the kind a man would be glad to die for."

I really couldn't help it. Her hand lay very temptingly near me, and I don't think I knew what I was doing till she said:

"Please let go of my hand."

"But he'd rather live for her," I continued boldly.

"If you don't behave yourself, I'll surrender you to Aunt Julia," said Luella, rising abruptly and slipping to the curtains of the alcove in which we were sitting. She looked very graceful and charming as she stood there with one hand raised to the lace folds.

"Has she recovered?" I asked.

"What a melancholy tone! The poor dear was in bed all Tuesday, but she took advantage of her rest to amplify her emotions."

"She has acquired a subject of conversation, at least."

"To last her for the rest of her life," laughed Luella, turning back. "'Twill be a blood-curdling tale by the time she reaches the East once more. And now do be sensible-no, you sit right where you are-and tell me how it all happened, and what it was about."

I revolved for a moment the plan of a romance that would have, at least, the merit of chaining Miss Knapp's interest. But it was gone as I looked into her serious eyes.

"That's what I should like to know myself," I confessed candidly. Then I added with pardonable mendacity: "I think I must have been taken for somebody else, if it was anything more than a desperate freak of the highbinders."

"Are you sure they had no interest in seeking you?" asked Luella gravely, with a charming tremor in her voice.

Before I could reply, Mrs. Knapp's voice was in my ear, and Mrs. Knapp's figure was in the archway of the alcove.

"Oh, you are here," she said. "I thought I heard your voices. Luella, your father wants to see you a minute. And how do you do, Mr. Wilton?"

I greeted Mrs. Knapp cordially, though I wished that she had delayed her appearance, and looked regretfully after Luella.

"I want to thank you for your heroism the other evening," she said.

"Oh, it was nothing," I answered lightly. "Any one would have done the same."

"Perhaps-but none the less we are all very grateful. If I had only suspected that anything of the kind could have happened, I should never have allowed them to go."

I felt rebelliously glad that she had not suspected.

"I blame myself for it all," I bowed. "It was very careless of me."

"I'm afraid so, after all the warning you have had," said Mrs. Knapp.

"But as it turned out, no harm was done," I said cheerfully.

"I suppose so," said Mrs. Knapp absently. Then she spoke with sudden attention. "Do you think your enemies followed you there?"

I was taken aback with the vision of the Wolf figure in the grimy passage, a fiend in the intoxication of opium, and stammered for a reply.

"My snake-eyed friend made himself a little familiar, I'm afraid," I admitted.

"It is dreadful that these dangers should follow you everywhere," said Mrs. Knapp with feeling. "You must be careful."

"I have developed eyes in the back of my head," I said, smiling at her concern.

"I fear you need more than that. Now tell me how it all happened, just as you saw it. I'm afraid Luella was a little too hysterical to give a true account of it."

I gave her the story of the scene in the passage, with a few judicious emendations. I thought it hardly worth while to mention Doddridge Knapp's appearance, or a few other items that were more precious to me than to anybody else.

When I had done Mrs. Knapp sighed.

"There must be an end of this some day," she said.

"I hope the day isn't far off," I confessed, "unless it should happen to be the day the coroner is called on to take a particular interest in my person."

Mrs. Knapp shuddered.

"Oh no, no-not that way."

Then after a pause, she continued: "Would you not rather attack your dangers at once, and have them over, than to wait for them to seek you?"

I felt a trifle uneasy at this speech. There seemed to be a suggestion in it that I could end the whole matter by marching on my enemies, and coming to decisive battle. I wished I knew what she was hinting at, and how it was to be done, before I answered.

"I haven't felt any particular disposition to hunt them up," I confessed, "but if I could cut off all the heads of the hydra at once, it would be worth while. Anything for peace and quiet, you know."

Mrs. Knapp smiled.

"Well, there is no use challenging your fate. There is no need for you to act, unless the boy is in danger."

"Oh, no, none at all," I replied unblushingly.

"And we'll hope that he will be kept safe until the danger has passed."

I hoped so devoutly, and said as much. And after a few more words, Mrs. Knapp led me, feebly resisting, to Mrs. Bowser.

"Oh, Mr. Wilton," said that charming dame, "my heart goes pit-a-pat when I see you, for it's almost like being among those dreadful highbinders again, and how could you bring the horrid creatures down on our dear Luella, when she might have been captured and sold into slavery under our very eyes."

"Ah, Mrs. Bowser," said I gallantly, "I ought to have known what to expect on bringing such a temptation before our Chinese friends. I do not see how you escaped being carried off."

"Oh, now, Mr. Wilton," exclaimed Mrs. Bowser, retreating behind her fan; "you are really too flattering. I must say, though, that some of them did make dreadful eyes at me, till I felt that I should faint. And do they really hold their slave-market right in the middle of San Francisco? And why doesn't the president break it up, and what is the Emancipation Proclamation for, I should like to know?"

"Madam," I replied, "the slave-market is *sub rosa*, but I advise you to keep out of Chinatown. Some temptations are irresistible."

Mrs. Bowser giggled behind her fan and was too pleased to speak, and I took advantage of the lull to excuse myself and make a dive into the next room where I espied Luella.

"Yes, you may sit down here," she said carelessly. "I want to be amused."

I was not at all certain that I was flattered to be considered amusing; but I was willing to stay on any terms, so we fell into animated conversation on nothing and everything. In the midst of this entertaining situation I discovered that Mrs. Knapp was watching us, and her face showed no easy state of mind. As I caught her eye she moved away, and a minute later Mr. Carter appeared with,—

"Excuse me, Miss Knapp, but your mother would like to see you. She and my wife have some conspiracy on hand."

I was pleased to see that Luella did not take the interruption gratefully, but she surrendered her place to Mr. Carter, who talked about the weather with a fertility of commonplaces that excited my admiration. But as even the weather has its limits as a subject of interest and the hour grew late, I suppressed a yawn and sought the ladies to take my leave.

"Oh, must you go?" said Luella, rising. And, leaving Mrs. Carter to her mother, she walked with me to the hall as though she would speak with me.

But once more alone, with only the hum of voices from the reception-room as company, she fell silent, and I could think of nothing to say.

"It's very good of you to come," she said hesitatingly.

My mind went back to that other evening when I had left the door in humiliation and bitterness of spirit. Perhaps she, too, was thinking of the time.

"It's much better of you to wish me to come," I said with all my heart, taking her hand.

"Come on Saturday," she said at last.

"I'm at your service at any time," I murmured.

"Don't," she said. "That's conventional. If you are to be conventional you're not to come." And she laughed nervously. I looked into her eyes, and then on impulse stooped and kissed the hand I still held.

"It was what I meant," I said.

She snatched her hand away, and as she did so I saw in the dim light that hid the further end of the hall, the figure of the Wolf, massive, dark, threatening, and my mind supplied it with all the fires of passion and hate with which I had twice seen the face inflamed.

Luella's eyes grew large with wonder and alarm as she caught on my face the reflection of the Wolf's coming. But as she turned to look, the figure faded away without sound, and there was only Mrs. Knapp appearing in the doorway; and her alarm turned to amusement.

"Oh, I was afraid you had gone," said Mrs. Knapp. "Would you mind, Luella, looking after the guests a minute?"

Luella bowed me a good night and was gone.

"Oh, Henry," said Mrs. Knapp, "I wanted to ask you about Mr. Knapp. Is your aid absolutely essential to his success?"

"I presume not, thought it would probably embarrass him somewhat if I should take ship for China before morning."

As I held in the bank securities worth nearly three millions of dollars, I believed that I spoke within bounds.

"I suppose it would do no good to try to dissuade him from his plans?"

"It would take a bolder man than I," said I with a smile at the audacity of the idea.

Mrs. Knapp smiled sadly in response.

"Do you think, Henry," she asked hesitatingly, "do you think that Mr. Knapp is quite himself?"

My mind leaped at the recollection of the Wolf figure in the opium-dens. But I choked down the thought, and replied calmly:

"He certainly has a vigorous business head on his shoulders."

"I wish you could tell me about his business affairs," said Mrs. Knapp wistfully. "But I know you won't."

"You wouldn't think much of me if I did," I said boldly.

"It would be right to tell *me*," she said. "But I mustn't keep you standing here. Good night."

I walked down the steps, and joined my waiting guards with a budget of new thoughts and feelings to examine.

The three days that followed were days of storm and stress in the market; a time of steady battle in the Stock Exchange, of feints and sallies on stocks which we did not want, of "wash sales" and bogus bargains, of rumors on rumors and stratagems on stratagems-altogether a harvest season for the Father of Lies.

Doddridge Knapp fought for the control of Omega, and the Decker syndicate fought as stubbornly for the same end. I was forced to admire the fertility of resource displayed by the King of the Street. He was carrying on the fight with the smaller capital, yet by his attack and defense he employed his resources to better result. The weakness of the syndicate lay in its burden of Confidence and Crown Diamond. Doddridge Knapp had sold out his holdings of both at a handsome profit, but, so far from ceasing his sales of these stocks, as I had expected, he had only begun. He suddenly developed into a most pronounced "bear," and sold both stocks for future delivery in great blocks. He was cautious with Confidence, but his assaults on Crown Diamond were ruthless. At every session he sold for future delivery at lower and lower prices, and a large contingent of those "on the Street" joined in the bear movement. Decker and his brokers stood gallantly to the defense of their threatened properties and bought heavily. Yet it was evident that Omega, Crown Diamond and Confidence together made a little heavier burden than even the El Dorado Bank could carry. In spite of their efforts to buy everything that was offered, Crown Diamond "futures" fell to forty, thirty, twenty-five, and even twenty, closing at the afternoon session at twenty and three-fourths.

But the King of the Street was less successful in his manipulation of Omega. Despite his efforts, despite the rumors that were industriously spread about of the "pinching out" of the great veins, the price continued to go up by leaps and bounds. The speculating public as well as Decker and Company were reaching out for the stock, and it was forced up ten and twenty points at a time, closing on Saturday afternoon at three hundred and twenty-five.

"This is merry war," gasped Wallbridge, at the close of the last session. "I wouldn't have missed this for five years of my life. Doddridge Knapp is the boy for making the market hum when he takes the notion. By George, we've had a picnic this week! And last Monday I thought everything was dead, too!"

"Doddridge Knapp!" I exclaimed. "Is he in this deal, too?"

Wallbridge looked at me in a little confusion, and mopped his head with comical abandon. Then he winked a most diabolical wink, and chuckled.

"Of course, a secret's a secret; but when the whole Street's talking about it, you can't exactly call it a close-corporation secret," he explained apologetically.

I assured the stout little broker solemnly that Doddridge Knapp was to know nothing of my dealings.

"I'll do anything for a good customer like you," he gasped. "Lord, if it wasn't for the lying, where would the market be? Dead, sir, dead!" And Wallbridge shook his head merrily over the moral degradation of the business that chained his thoughts by day and his dreams by night.

I joined Doddridge Knapp at the office and confided to him the fact that the cat was out of the bag. The King of the Street looked a little amused at the announcement.

"Good Lord, Wilton! Where are your ears?" he said. "The Street had the whole story on Friday. Decker was sure of it on Wednesday. But I kept under cover long enough to get a good start, and that was as much as I expected."

"How do we stand now?" I asked. I knew that our purchases had not been progressing very well.

"There's five hundred shares to get," said the King of the Street thoughtfully; "five hundred and thirty-six, to be accurate."

"That's not a very promising outlook," I suggested, remembering that we had secured only four hundred shares in the whole day's struggle.

"Well, there'll be an earthquake in the Street if we don't get them, and maybe there'll be one if we do. Decker is likely to dump all his shares on the market the minute we win, and it will be the devil's own job to keep the bottom from falling out if he does."

The King of the Street then gave some brief directions.

"Now," he continued, "you are to be at the Exchange without fail, on Monday morning. I'll be there to give you your orders. Don't be one minute behind hand, or there may be Tophet to pay." And he emphasized his words with an impressive growl that showed the Wolf's fangs.

"I'll be on hand," I replied.

"Well, then, go," he growled; "and see that you come with a clear head on Monday. Keep your thirst until after the game is over."

A few hours later I was at the house of the Wolf, but I forgot to ask for Doddridge Knapp. Luella received me with apparent indifference that contrasted sharply with her parting, and I was piqued. Mrs. Knapp was gracious, and sailed between us before I had received a dozen words.

"Where are your spirits to-night?" she asked railingly. "Have you left them in lower Pine Street?"

"I have a heart for any fate," I returned lightly. "Am I too grave for the occasion?"

"You're always under orders to be cheerful," Luella broke in, "or at least to explain the reason why."

"He can't explain," retorted her mother. "Mr. Knapp won't let him."

It struck me, on watching mother and daughter, that it was they who were grave. Luella gave an occasional flash of brightness, but seemed tired or depressed, while Mrs. Knapp appeared to struggle against some insistent sorrow. But presently we found a subject in which Luella roused her interest, and her bright mind and ready wit drove away the fancy that had first assailed me. Then some caller claimed the attention of Mrs. Knapp, and I was content to monopolize Luella's conversation for the evening. At last I was constrained to go. Mrs. Knapp was still busied in conversation with her visitor, and Luella followed me once more into the hall.

Again her animation left her, and she was silent; and I, on my side, could think of nothing to say. Then her deep gray eyes flashed upon me a look that sent my pulses throbbing, an indefinable, pleading glance that shook my soul.

"Can't you tell me-won't you tell me?" she said in a low tone that was the complement of the silent speech of the eyes.

"I wish I could," I whispered.

"I know it must be right-it is right," she said in the same tone. "But I wish that I might know. Will you not tell me?"

"I will tell you some day," I said brokenly. "Now it is another's, and I can not. But it shall all be yours."

"All?"

"Everything."

In another moment I know not what I should have done, so stirred and tempted was I by her tone and look. But in an instant her manner changed, and she exclaimed in a mocking voice:

"Now I have your promise, so I'll let you go. You'd better not linger, or mama will certainly have some business to talk over with you." And before I could touch her hand she was gone, and her laughing "good night" echoed down the hall.

I was puzzled by these changes of mood, and decided that Luella Knapp was a most unaccountable young woman. And then there dashed over me a sickening realization of what I had done, of what I had promised, and of how impossible it was that I should ever reveal to her the secret I guarded. I cursed the mad folly and crime of her father, for they stood between her and me. Yet under the subtle influence that she cast upon me I felt the bonds of duty relaxed and slipping away. I had now to confess to myself that I loved Luella Knapp. And she? I hoped and feared, and ran over in my mind every incident of my later visits that might tell in what regard I was held-the tones, the words, the manner, that ran from deep interest to indifference. And trying to untangle the skein, I was a good deal startled to feel a touch on my arm as I reached the sidewalk.

"Oh, it's you, Porter, is it?" I exclaimed, on recognizing my retainer. "Is Barkhouse here?"

"Yes, sir. An' here's Wilson with a message for you."

"A message for me! From whom?"

Wilson took me aside, and thrust an envelope into my hand.

"That come to your room-about nine o'clock, I reckon," he said. "Leastways, that's the first we saw of it. An' Mother Borton was there, an' she says she must see you to-night, sure. She wouldn't stay, but says you was to come down there before you goes to bed, sure, if you wants to keep out of trouble."

I looked at the envelope, and in the flickering light from the street-lamp I could make out the address to Henry Wilton. By the handwriting and by the indefinable scent that rose from the paper, I knew it for a message from the Unknown who held for me the secrets of life and death.

CHAPTER XXI. AT THE BIDDING OF THE UNKNOWN

The windows of Borton's shone cheerfully, although it was past midnight. At our cautious approach a signal was given, and with the answering word a man appeared from the obscurity.

"All safe?" I inquired.

"It's all right," said Barkhouse. "There's a dozen men in the bar-room, and I'm not sure there ain't some of the hounds amongst them. But you're to go in the side door, and right up stairs."

"Two of you may keep at the foot of the stairs, just inside the door," I said. "You may stand watch outside, Barkhouse."

There was sound of rude song, and the clink of glass and bottle in the bar and dining-room, as I passed through the side hall. But the door was closed, and I saw nothing of the late revelers. In the upper hallway Mother Borton stood by an open door, silhouetted dark and threatening against the dim flickerings that came from the candle in the room behind her.

I had but opened my mouth to give her word of greeting when she raised a warning claw, and then seizing me, drew me swiftly into the room and closed and locked the door.

"How air ye, dearie?" she said, surveying me with some apparent pride. "You're safe and whole, ain't ye?"

As the candlelight fell on her face, she seemed older and more like a bird of prey than ever. The nose and chin had taken a sharper cast, the lines of her face were deeper drawn with the marks of her evil life, and her breath was strong with the strength of water-front whisky. But her eyes burned bright and keen as ever in their sunken sockets, with the fire of her fevered brain behind them.

"I am safe," I said, "though I had a close shave in Chinatown."

"I heerd of it," said Mother Borton sourly. "I reckon it ain't much good to sit up nights to tell you how to take keer of yourself. It's a wonder you ever growed up. Your mammy must 'a' been mighty keerful about herdin' ye under cover whenever it rained."

"I *was* a little to blame," I admitted, "but your warning was not thrown away. I thought I was well-guarded."

Mother Borton sniffed contemptuously.

"I s'pose you come down here alone?"

"No." And I explained the disposition of my forces.

"That's not so bad," she said. "They could git up here soon enough, I reckon, if there was a row. But I guess you didn't think I sent for ye jest to tell ye you was a fool in Chinatown."

I admitted that I should have expected to wait till morning for such a piece of information.

"Well," said Mother Borton, "that ain't it. Something's up."

"And what might it be?" I inquired. "The moon?"

Mother Borton did not take this flippancy kindly. Her face grew darker and more evil as it was framed in the dancing shadows behind her.

"You can git a knife in ye as easy as winking if I'll jest keep my mouth shut," she cried spitefully.

"Yes," said I repentantly, putting my hand upon her arm. "But you are my very good friend, and will tell me what I ought to know."

The creature's face lighted at my tone and action, and her eyes melted with a new feeling.

"That I will," she said; "that I will, as if you were my own boy."

She seized my hand and held it as she spoke, and looked intently, almost lovingly, on my face. Elsewhere I could have shivered at the thought of her touch. Here, with the bent figure amid the gloomy shadows of the den in which we sat, with the atmosphere of danger heavy about us, I was moved by a glow of kindly feeling.

"I was a-listening to 'em," she continued in a low, earnest tone, glancing around fearfully as if she had the thought that some one else might be listening in turn. "I was a-listening, an' I heerd what they says."

"Who said?" I inquired.

"The ones you knows on," she returned mysteriously.

"What ones?" I persisted, though I supposed she meant to indicate some of my energetic enemies.

Mother Borton paid no attention to my question, and continued:

"I knowed they was a-talking about you, an' they says they would cut your liver out if they found ye there."

"And where is there?" I asked with growing interest.

"That's what I was listening to find out," said Mother Borton. "I couldn't hear much of what they says, but I hears enough to git an idee."

"Well?" I said inquiringly as she hesitated.

She bent forward and hissed rather than whispered:

"They've found out where the boy is!"

"Are you certain?" I asked in sudden alarm.

"Pretty sure," she said, "pretty sure. Now you won't go near the place, will ye, dearie?" she continued anxiously.

"You forget that I haven't the first idea where the boy is hidden," I returned.

"Oh, Lord, yes! I reckon my mind's going," grunted Mother Borton. "But I'm afeard of their knives for ye."

"I wish I could give warning," said I, much disturbed by the information. "The protector of the boy ought to know about this. I'm afraid I have done wrong."

Mother Borton looked at me fixedly.

"Don't you worry, my dear. She'll know about it all right."

Again the feeling stole over me that this woman knew more than she told. But I knew that it was useless to question her directly. I considered a moment, and then decided to trust her with a secret which might surprise her into admitting her knowledge.

"I suspect that she knows already. I got a note to-night," said I, drawing from my pocket the envelope I had received from the Unknown.

Mother Borton seized it, looked for a moment at the firm, delicate hand of the address, and drew out the sheet that it inclosed.

"Read it, dearie," she said, handing it back after a scrutiny. "I can't tell anything but big print."

I suspected that Mother Borton was trying to deceive me, but I repeated the words of the note:

"Send six men to 8 o'clock boat. Come with one in hack to courtyard of the Palace Hotel at 7:40."

Mother Borton's face changed not a whit at the reading, but at the end she nodded. "She knows," she said.

"What does it mean?" I asked. "What is to happen?"

"Don't go, dearie-you won't go, will you?"

"Yes," I said. "I must go."

"Oh," she wailed; "you may be killed. You may never come back."

"Nonsense," said I. "In broad daylight, at the Palace Hotel? I'm much more likely to be killed before I get home to-night."

Her earnestness impressed me, but my resolution was not shaken. Mother Borton rested her head on the table in despair at my obstinacy.

"Well, if you will, you will," she said at last; "and an old woman's warnings are nothing to you. But if you will put your head in the traps, I'll do my best to make it safe after you git it there. You jist sit still, honey." And she took the candle and went to a corner where she seated herself at a stand.

Her shadow grew very large, and her straggling locks sent streamers of blackness dancing on the grimy ceiling. The weird figure, thrown into bold relief by the candle-lighted wall beyond it while all else was in obscurity, gave an uncanny feeling that turned half to dread as I looked upon her. What secret did she hold? What was the danger she feared?

Mother Borton appeared to have some difficulty in arranging her words to her liking. She seemed to be writing, but the pen did not flow smoothly. At last she was done, and, sealing her work in an envelope, she brought the flickering light once more to the table.

"Take that," she said, thrusting the envelope into my hand. "If you find a one-eyed man when you git into trouble, give him that letter I've writ ye, and it may do ye some good. It's the best I can do fer ye. You'd better go now and git some sleep. You may need it."

I thanked Mother Borton and pressed her hand, and she held the candle as I tiptoed down the stairs, joined my waiting guards, and went out into the night.

The fresh, cool air of the early morning hours was grateful after the close and tainted atmosphere of the den we had left, but I had other things to think of than the pleasure of once more filling my lungs.

"Where are Barkhouse and Phillips?" I asked, as we turned our faces toward the west.

Porter gave a low whistle, and, as this failed to bring an answer, followed it with one louder and more prolonged. We listened, but no response came.

"We'd better get out of here," said Wilson. "There's no telling what may happen when they hear that whistle."

"Hist! What's that?" said Porter, drawing me back into a doorway.

There were running steps on the block above us, and I thought a shadow darted from one side of the street to the other.

"There seem to be friends waiting for us," said I. "Just get a good grip of your clubs, boys, and keep your revolvers handy in case they think they have a call to stop us."

"Hold on," said Porter. "There's a gang of 'em there. I see a dozen of 'em, and if we're the ones they're after we had better cut for it."

"I believe you are right," said I, peering into the darkness. I could see a confused mass, but whether of men or boxes I could only guess.

"We'll go up here, and you can cut around the other way," said Porter. "There's no need for you to risk it."

"There's no need for any one to risk it. We'll cut together."

"This way then," said Wilson. "I know this part of town better than you do. Run on your toes." And he darted past Borton's, and plunged into an alley that led toward the north. Porter and I followed, as quietly as possible, through the dark and noisome cut-off to Pacific Street. Wilson turned toward the bay, and crossing the street at the next corner followed the main thoroughfare to Broadway.

"I guess we're all right now," he gasped, as we turned again to the west, "but we'd best keep to the middle of the street."

And a little later we were in sight of the house of mystery which fronted, forbidding and gloomy as ever, on Montgomery Street.

"Where's Barkhouse?" I asked of Trent, who was on guard.

"He hasn't come in, sir. Phillips got here a bit ago, and I think he has something to report."

As Phillips had been sent scouting with Barkhouse I thought it likely, and called him to my room.

"No, sir, I didn't see Bob for nigh on an hour before I came back. Not after we got to Borton's."

"I left him just outside the door," I said.

"Then you seen him after I did. I was following two fellows down to the Den, you know, and that was the last I seen of Bob."

I understood that the Den was one of the meeting-places of the enemy.

"Did you find anything there?"

“Not a thing. The two fellows went in, but they didn’t come out. Another gang of three comes along and goes in, but none of ’em shows up again, and I reckoned they’d gone to bed; so I takes it as a hint and comes up here.”

“I suppose it would have done no good to wait.”

“You don’t think Bob’s been took, do you?”

I did feel uneasy over the absence of the stalwart scout, and but for the orders I had received for the morning I should have had my forces out to find him, or get a hostage in exchange. But as it was, I dissembled my fears and made some reassuring reply.

At the earliest light of the morning I was once more astir, but half-refreshed by my short and broken rest, and made my dispositions for the day. I ordered Porter, Fitzhugh, Brown, Wilson, Lockhart and Abrams to wait for me at the Oakland Ferry. Trent, who was still weak from his wound, I put in charge of the home-guard, with Owens, Phillips and Larson as his companions, and gave instructions to look for Barkhouse, in case he did not return. Wainright I took with me, and hailing a hack drove to the Palace Hotel.

There was a rattle of wagons and a bustle of departing guests as we drove into the courtyard of the famous hostelry. The eight-o’clock boat was to carry the passengers for the east-bound overland train, and the outgoing travelers were filling the place with noise and confusion.

I stepped out of the hack, and looked about me anxiously. Was I to meet the Unknown? or was I to take orders from some emissary of my hidden employer? No answering eye met mine as I searched the place with eager glance. Neither woman nor man of all the hurrying crowd had a thought for me.

The hotel carriages rattled away, and comparative quiet once more fell on the court. I looked impatiently about. Was there some mistake? Had the plans been changed? But as I glanced at the clock that ticked the seconds in the office of the hotel I saw that I had been early, and that it was even now but twenty minutes to the hour.

The minute-hand had not swept past the figure VIII when the door opened, there was a hurried step, and two women stood before me, leading a child between them. Both women were closely veiled, and the child was muffled and swathed till its features could not be seen.

One of the women was young, the other older-perhaps middle-aged. Both were tall and well-made. I looked eagerly upon them, for one of them must be the Unknown, the hidden employer whose task had carried Henry Wilton to his death, who held my life in her hands, and who fought the desperate battle with the power and hatred of Doddridge Knapp.

I was conscious of some disappointment, I could not say why. But neither of the women filled the outline of the shadowy picture my fancy had drawn of the Unknown. Neither gave impression of the force and decision with which my fancy had endowed the woman who had challenged the resources and defied the vengeance of the Wolf. So much I took to my thoughts in the flash of an eye as they approached. It was to the younger that I turned as the more likely to have the spirit of contest, but it was the older who spoke.

“Here is your charge, Mr. Wilton,” she said in a low, agitated voice. As she spoke, I felt the faint suggestion of the peculiar perfume that had greeted me from the brief letters of the Unknown.

“I am ready for orders,” I said with a bow.

It was apparently a mere business matter between us. I had fancied somehow that there had been a bond of friendship, as much as of financial interest, between Henry Wilton and his employer, and felt the sense of disappointment once more.

“Your orders are in this envelope,” said the Unknown, hurriedly thrusting a paper into my hand. “Drive for the boat, and read them on the way. You have no time to lose.”

The younger woman placed the child in the hack.

“Climb in, Wainwright,” said I, eying the youngster unfavorably. “Will he travel with us, ma’am? He’s rather young.”

“He’ll go all right,” said the elder woman with some agitation. “He knows that he must. But treat him carefully. Now good-by.”

"Oakland Ferry, driver," I cried, as I stepped into the hack and slammed the door. And in a moment we were dashing out into New Montgomery Street, and with a turn were on Market Street, rolling over the rough cobbles toward the bay.

CHAPTER XXII. TRAILED

"Did you see him?" asked Wainwright, as the hack lurched into Market Street and straightened its course for the ferry.

"Who?"

"Tom Terrill. He was behind that big pillar near the arch there. I saw him just as the old lady spoke to you, but before I catches your eye, he cuts and runs."

I felt of my revolver at this bit of news, and was consoled to have the touch of it under my hand.

"I didn't see him," I said. "Keep the child between us, and shoot anybody who tries to stop us or to climb into the hack. I must read my orders."

"All right, sir," said Wainwright, making the child comfortable between us.

I tore open the envelope and drew forth the scented paper with its familiar, firm, yet delicate handwriting, and read the words:

"Take the train with your men for Livermore. Await orders at the hotel. Protect the boy at all hazards."

Inclosed in the sheet were gold-notes to the value of five hundred dollars—a thoughtful detail for which I was grateful at the outset of such an expedition. I thrust the money into my pocket and pondered upon the letter, wondering where Livermore might be. My knowledge of the geography of California was exceedingly scant. I knew that Oakland lay across the bay and that Brooklyn lay close by, a part of Oakland. I remembered a dinner at Sacramento, and knew Los Angeles on the map. Further than this my ideas were of the most hazy character, and Livermore was nowhere to be found in my geographical memory.

I had some thought of questioning Wainwright, who was busy trying to make friends with the child, but reflecting that I might be supposed to know all about it I was silent. Wainwright's efforts to get the child to speak were without success. The little thing might from its size have been five years old, but it was dumb-frightened, as I supposed, by the strangeness of the situation, and would speak no word.

This, then, was the mysterious boy whose fate was linked so closely with my own; about whose body battled the hirelings of Doddridge Knapp and of my unknown employer; for whom murder had been done, and for whom perhaps many now living were to give up their lives.

Who was he? Whence had he come? What interests were bound up in his life? Why was his body the focus of plot and counterplot, and its possession disputed with a fierce earnestness that stopped at no crime? Perhaps, could he be got to talk, the key of the mystery might be put in my hands. Out of the mouth of the babe I might learn the secret that had racked my brain for days and weeks.

And why was he put thus in my charge? What was I to do with him? Whither was I to carry him? I reproached myself that I had not stopped the Unknown to ask more questions, to get more light on the duties that were expected of me. But the hack on a sudden pulled up, and I saw that we were before the long, low, ugly wooden building that sat square across Market Street as the gateway to San Francisco through which the tide of travel must pass to and from the Golden City.

"Look out on both sides, Wainwright," I cautioned. "You carry the boy and I'll shoot if there's any trouble. See that you keep him safe."

There were nearly ten minutes before the boat left, but the hurry for tickets, the rush to check baggage, the shouts of hackmen and expressmen, the rattle and confusion of the coming and departing street-cars that centered at the ferry, made us inconspicuous among the throng as we stepped out of the hack.

"Here Fitzhugh, Brown," I said, catching sight of two of my retainers, "get close about. Have you seen anything—*any* signs of the enemy?"

"I haven't," said Fitzhugh, "but Abrams thought he saw Dotty Ferguson over by the Fair Wind saloon there. Said he cut up Clay Street before the rest of us caught sight of him-so maybe Abrams was off his nut."

"Quite likely," I admitted as we turned the jutting corner of the building and came under shelter by the ticket office. "But keep a close watch."

The other four retainers were in the passageway, and I called to the ticket-seller for the tickets to Livermore. By the price I decided that Livermore must be somewhere within fifty miles, and marshaling my troop about the boy, marched into the waiting-room, past the door-keeper, through the sheds, and on to the ferry boat.

I saw no signs of the enemy, and breathed freer as the last belated passenger leaped aboard, the folding gang-plank was raised, and the steamer, with a prolonged blast of the whistle, slid out into the yellow-green waters of the bay.

The morning had dawned pleasant, but the sky was now becoming overcast. The wind came fresh and strong from the south. The white-capped waves were beginning to toss and fret the shallow waters, and the air gave promise of storm. We could see men busy making all things snug on the vessels that swung uneasily to their anchors in the harbor, and tugs were rushing about, puffing noisily over nothing, or here and there towing some vessel to a better position to meet the rising gale. The panorama of the bay, with the smoke-laden city, grim and dark behind, the forest of masts lining its shore, the yellow-green waters, dotted here and there with ships tossing sharply above the white-capped waves that chased each other toward the north, the cloud squadrons flying up in scattered array from the south, and the Alameda hills lying somber and dark under the gray canopy of the eastern sky in front, had a charm that took my mind for the time from the mysterious enterprise that lay before me.

"Keep together, boys," I cautioned my retainers as I recalled the situation. "Has any one seen signs of the other gang?"

There was a general murmur in the negative.

"Well, Abrams, will you slip around and see if any of them got aboard? There's no such thing as being comfortable until we are sure."

In the hurry and excitement of preparation and departure, the orders I had given and received, and the work that filled every moment, I had been conscious of the uneasy burden of a task forgotten. I had surely neglected something. Yet for my life I could not see that we lacked anything. I had my seven retainers, the boy was safe with us, I had my purse, we were well-armed, and every man had his ticket to Livermore. But at last the cause of my troubles came to my mind.

"Great Scott!" I thought. "It's Doddridge Knapp. That little engagement in the stock-market is casting its shadow before."

It seemed likely indeed that the demands of my warring employers would clash here as well as in the conflict over the boy.

Yet with all the vengeful feeling that filled my heart as I looked on the child and called up the memory of my murdered friend, I could but feel a pang of regret at the prospect that Doddridge Knapp's fortune should be placed in hazard through any unfaithfulness of mine. He had trusted me with his plans and his money. And the haunting thought that his fortune was staked on the venture, and that his ruin might follow, with the possible beggary of Luella and Mrs. Knapp, should I fail him at tomorrow's crisis, weighed on my spirits.

My uncomfortable reflections were broken by the clanging engine-bells and the forward movement of the passengers as the steamboat passed into the slip at Long Wharf.

"Stand together, boys," I cautioned my men. "Keep back of the crowd. Wainwright will take the boy, and the rest of you see that nobody gets near him."

"All right," said Wainwright, lifting the child in his arms. "It will take a good man to get him away from me."

"Where's Abrams?" I asked, noting that only six of my men were at hand.

"You sent him forward," said Lockhart.

"Not for all day."

"Well, he hasn't been seen since you told him to find out who's aboard."

I was a little vexed at the seeming neglect of my retainer, and as we had come down the rear stairs to avoid the crowd and marched through the driveway on the lower deck, I cast a glance into the bar-room with the expectation of finding him engaged in the gentle art of fortifying his courage. But no sign of the missing man met my eye.

"It's no use to wait for him," I growled. "But the next man that takes French leave had better look somewhere else for a job, for by the great horn spoon, he's no man of mine."

We marched off the boat in the rear of the crowd, I in no pleasant humor, and the men silent in reflection of my displeasure. And with some difficulty we found seats together in a forward coach. I arranged my men in three seats on one side of the car and two on the other, Wainwright taking the center of the three with the boy, guarded thus front and rear, while I sat opposite and one seat behind, where I could observe any attempt at interference, with Lockhart in front of me. I judged that any one who tried to attack the position would have a lively five minutes on his hands.

The train was the east-bound overland, and it seemed hours before the baggage was taken aboard and the signal given to start. I grew uneasy, but as my watch assured me that only ten minutes had passed when the engine gave the first gentle pull at the train, I suspected that I was losing the gift of patience. The train had not gathered headway before a man bent beside me, and Abrams' voice spoke softly in my ear.

"There are two of 'em aboard."

"Yes? Where did you find them?" I asked.

"In the stoke hole. I hid behind a bench till every one had gone and saw 'em crawl out. They bribed a fireman or deck-hand or some one to keep 'em under cover. They got off the boat at the last minute, and I sneaked after 'em."

"And they're on the train?"

"Yes, three cars back,—next to the sleepers. Shall we chuck 'em overboard as soon as we get out of Oakland?"

"Not unless we are attacked," I returned. "Just sit down by the rear door and give the signal if they come this way. There'll be no trouble if they are only two."

My precautions were not called to a test, and we reached Livermore at near eleven o'clock, without further incident than a report from Abrams that the spies of the enemy got off the train at every station and watched for our landing. Yet when we stood on the platform of the bare little station at Livermore and saw the yellow cars crawling away on their eastward journey, we looked in vain for the men who had tracked us.

"Fooled, by thunder!" said Fitzhugh with a laugh in which the others joined. "They're off for Sacramento."

"They'll have to earn their money to find us there," said Abrams.

The gray day had become grayer, and the wind blew fresh in our faces with the smell of rain heavy upon it, as we sought the hotel. It was a bare country place, yet trees grew by the hotel and there were vines climbing about its side, and it looked as though we might be comfortable for a day, should we have to stay there so long.

"Plenty of room," said the landlord rubbing his hands.

"Are there any letters here for Henry Wilton?" I inquired, bethinking me that orders might have been sent me already.

"No, sir."

"Nor telegrams?"

"O Lord, no, sir. We don't have telegrams here unless somebody's dead."

"You may give me Mr. Wilton's mail if any comes," I said.

The landlord led the way up the stairs, and beguiled me by informing me what a fine house he had and how hard the times were.

"We wish a large room, you know, where we can be together," I said, "and sleeping-rooms adjoining."

"Here's just the place for you," said the landlord, taking the way to the end of the upper hall and throwing open a double door. "This is the up-stairs parlor, but I can let you have it. There's this large bedroom opening off it, —the corner bedroom, sir, —and this small one here at this side opens into the parlor and the hall. Perhaps you would like this other one, too."

He seemed ready and anxious to rent us the whole house.

"This is enough for our comfort," I assured him.

"There'll be a fire here in a minute," said the landlord, regarding the miserable little stove with an eye of satisfaction that I attributed to its economical proportions.

"This is good enough," said Lockhart, looking about approvingly at the prim horsehair furniture that gave an awesome dignity to the parlor.

"Beats our quarters below all hollow," said Fitzhugh. "And no need to have your gun where you can grab it when the first man says boo!"

"Don't get that idea into your head," said I. "Just be ready for anything that comes. We're not out of the woods yet, by a long way."

"They've gone on to Sacramento," laughed Fitzhugh; and the others nodded in sympathy.

"Indeed?" I said. "How many of you could have missed seeing a party of nine get off at a way-station on this line?"

There was silence.

"If there's any one here who thinks he would have missed us when he was set to look for us, just let him speak up," I continued with good-humored raillery.

"I guess you're right," said Fitzhugh. "They couldn't well have missed seeing us."

"Exactly. And they're not off for Sacramento, and not far from Livermore."

"Well, they're only two," said Lockhart.

"How long will it take to get a dozen more up here?" I asked.

"There's a train to Niles about noon," said one of the men. "They could get over from there in an hour or two more by hard riding."

"The Los Angeles train comes through about dark," said another.

"I think, gentlemen," said I politely, "that we'd best look out for our defenses. There's likely to be a stormy evening, I should judge."

"Well," growled Wainwright, "we can look out for ourselves as well as the next fellow."

"If there's bloody crowns going round, the other gang will get its share," said Fitzhugh. And the men about me nodded.

I was cheered to see that they needed nobody to do their fighting, however advisable it might be to do their thinking by deputy.

"Very good," I said. "Now I'll just look about the town a bit. You may come with me, if you please, Fitzhugh."

"Yes, sir."

"And Abrams and Lockhart may go scouting if they like."

Abrams and Lockhart thought they would like.

"Better keep together," I continued. "What's the earliest time any one could get here?"

"Two o'clock-if they drove over."

"I'll be around here by that time. You, Abrams, can look out for the road and see who comes into town."

"All right, sir," said Abrams. "There won't anybody get in here without I catch sight of him."

Lockhart nodded his assent to the boast, and after cautioning the men who were left behind we sallied forth.

The town was a straggling, not unpleasing country place. The business street was depressing with its stores closed and its saloons open. A few loafers hung about the doors of the dram-shops, but the moist breath of the south wind eddying about with its burden of dust and dead leaves made indoors a more comfortable location, and through the blue haze of tobacco smoke we could see men gathered inside. Compared with the dens I had found about my lodgings in the city, the saloons were orderly; but nevertheless they offended my New England sense of the fitness of things. In the city I had scarcely known that there was a Sunday. But here I was reminded, and felt that something was amiss.

In the residence streets I was better pleased. Man had done little, but nature was prodigal to make up for his omissions. The buildings were poor and flimsy, but in the middle of December the flowers bloomed, vines were green, bushes sent forth their leaves, and the beauty of the scene even under the leaden skies and rising gale made it a delight to the eye.

"Not much of a place," said Fitzhugh, looking disdainfully at the buildings. "Hello! Here's Dick Thatcher. How are you, Dick? It's a year of Sundays that I haven't seen you. This is-er —a friend of mine, Thatcher, —you needn't mention that you've seen us." And Fitzhugh stumbled painfully over the recollection that we were incognito, and became silent in confusion.

"We needn't be strangers to Mr. Thatcher," I laughed. "My name is Wilton. Of course you won't mention our business."

"Oh, no, Mr. Wilton," said Thatcher, impressed, and shifting the quid of tobacco in his lantern jaws. "Of course not."

"And you needn't say anything of our being here at all," I continued. "It might spoil the trade."

"Mum's the word," said Thatcher. "I'll not let a soul know till you say 'Let 'er go.' O Lord! I hope the trade goes through. We want a lot more capital here."

Mr. Thatcher began to scratch his head and to expectorate tobacco-juice copiously, and I suspected he was wondering what the secret might be that he was not to betray. So I made haste to say:

"Is this stable yours?"

"Yes, sir," said Thatcher eagerly. "I've been running it nigh on two years now."

"Pretty good business, eh, Dick?" said Fitzhugh, looking critically about.

"Nothin' to brag on," said Thatcher disparagingly. "You don't make a fortune running a livery stable in these parts-times are too hard."

And then Mr. Thatcher unbent, and between periods of vigorous mastication at his cud, introduced us to his horses and eagerly explained the advantages that his stable possessed over any other this side of Oakland.

"Very good," I said. "We may want something in your line later. We can find you here at any time, I suppose."

"O Lord, yes. I live here days and sleep here nights. But if you want to take a look at the property before it gets a wetting you'll have to be pretty spry."

My suggestion of a trade had misled the worthy stableman into the impression that I was considering the purchase of real estate.

"I'll see about it," I said.

"There's a big rain coming on, sure," he said warningly, as we turned back to the hotel.

It was a little after one o'clock, but as we approached our quarters Lockhart came running toward me.

"What is it?" I asked, as he panted, out of breath.

"There's a special train just come in," he said; "an engine and one car. It's at the station now."

"So? Did any of our friends come on it?"

"Abrams has gone down to find out."

"Come along then," said I. "We'll see what is to be seen."

"Don't!" cried Fitzhugh, catching my arm. "They might get you."

"Nonsense," said I, shaking off his grasp. "Have your revolver ready, and follow me."

CHAPTER XXIII. A PIECE OF STRATEGY

A few idlers were on the platform of the station as we approached with much apparent unconcern, our hands in our overcoat pockets where the weapons lay.

"Where's the train?" I asked, looking at the bare track.

"Yonder," grunted a native, pointing his thumb lazily up the road where the engine lay by the watering tank, slaking its thirst.

"Well, just let me and Lockhart walk ahead," said Fitzhugh gruffly, as we started along the track. "I shouldn't have the first idea what we was here for if you was to be knocked over."

Fitzhugh could not be much more in the dark on this point than I, but I let him have his way. If some one was to be shot, I was ready to resign my claim to the distinction in favor of the first comer.

There were perhaps a score of people about the car.

"There's Abrams," said Lockhart.

"There's no danger, then," said Fitzhugh with a grin. "See, he's beckoning to us."

We hastened forward eagerly.

"What is it?" I asked.

"There's no one here," said Abrams, with a puzzled look.

"Well, this car didn't come alone," I returned. "Have you asked the engineer?"

"Yes."

"And the fireman?"

"Yes."

"And they say—"

"That it's against the rules to talk."

"Nonsense; I'll see them myself." And I went forward to the engine.

The engineer was as close-mouthed as though words were going at a dollar apiece and the market bounding upward. He declined dinner, could not be induced to come and take a drink, and all that could be got out of him was that he was going back to Niles, where he would stop until he got orders from the superintendent.

When I tried to question the fireman, the engineer recovered his tongue, and had so many orders to be attended to that my words were lost in a rattle of coal and clang of iron.

And the engine, having drunk its fill, changed its labored breathing to a hissing and swishing of steam that sent the hot vapor far on both sides, and then gathering speed, puffed its swift way back the road by which it had come, leaving the car deserted on a siding.

"Here's a go!" cried Fitzhugh. "A regular puzzler!"

"Guess it's none of the gang, after all," said Lockhart.

Abrams shook his head.

"Don't you fool yourself," he said. "They've landed below here, and maybe they're in town while we've got our mouths open, fly-catching around an empty car."

"Good boy, Abrams," I said. "My opinion exactly."

"And what's to be done, then?" he asked anxiously.

"For the first thing, to visit the telegraph office at once."

The operator was just locking his little room in the station as we came up.

"No, sir, no telegrams," he said; "none for anybody."

"This is a new way of running trains," I said with a show of indifference, nodding toward the empty car.

"Oh, there was a party came up," said the agent; "a dozen fellows or more. Bill said they took a fancy to get off a mile or more down here, and as they were an ugly-looking crew he didn't say anything to stop them."

"I don't see what they can be doing up in this part of the country," I returned innocently.

"I guess they know their business-anyway, it's none of mine," said the agent. "Do you go in here, sir? Well, it will save you from a wetting."

We had been walking toward the hotel, and the chatty agent left us under its veranda just as the light drops began to patter down in the dust of the road, and to dim the outlines of the distant hills.

"I reckon that's the gang," said Fitzhugh.

"I told you so," said Abrams. "I knew it was one of Tom Terrill's sneaky tricks."

"Shall we take a look for 'em?" asked Lockhart.

"There's no need," I replied.

The home guard of our party received the news calmly.

Wainwright had established a *modus vivendi* with his young charge, and I saw that he managed to get a word out of him now and then. I had to abandon the theory that the boy was dumb, but I suspected that it was fear rather than discretion that bridled his tongue.

"Do you think the gang have got into town?" asked one.

"They'll have wet jackets if they are on the road," I returned, looking at the rain outside.

"Hadn't we better find out?" inquired Wainwright.

"Are you in a hurry?" I asked in turn. "The landlord has promised to send up a good dinner in a few minutes."

"But you see —"

"Yes, I see," I interrupted. "I see this-that they are here, that there are a dozen or more of them, and that they are ready for any deviltry. What more can we find out by roaming over the country?"

Wainwright nodded his agreement with me.

"And then," I continued, "they won't try to do anything until after dark-not before the middle of the night, I should say-or until the townspeople have gone to bed."

"You're right, sir," said Abrams. "A dark night and a clear field suits that gang best."

"Well, here's the dinner," said I; "so you can make yourselves easy. Porter, you may keep an eye on the stairway, and Brown may watch from the windows. The rest of us will fall to."

In the midst of the meal Porter came in.

"Darby Meeker's in the office below," he announced.

"Very good," I said. "Just take Fitzhugh and Wilson with you, and ask Mr. Meeker to join us."

The men looked blank. Porter was the first to speak.

"You don't mean —"

"I mean to bring him up here," I said blandly, rising from the table. "I suppose, though, it's my place as host to do the honors."

"No-no," came in chorus from the men.

"Come on, Porter-Fitzhugh-Wilson," I said; and then added sharply, "sit down, the rest of you! We don't need a regiment to ask a man to dinner."

The others sank back into their seats, and the three I had named followed me meekly down the hall and stairs.

I had never had the pleasure of meeting Mr. Meeker face to face, but I doubted not that I should be able to pick him out. I was right. I knew him the moment I saw him. He was tall and broad of shoulder, long of arm, shifty of eye, and his square jaw was covered with a stubby red beard. His color heightened as we walked into the office and cut off the two doors of retreat.

"An unexpected pleasure," I said, giving him good day.

His hand slipped to the side pocket of his sack coat, and then back again, and he made a remark in an undertone that I fear was not intended for a pleasant greeting.

"There's a little dinner of a few friends going on up stairs," I said politely. "Won't you join us?"

Meeker scowled a moment with evident surprise.

"No, I won't," he growled.

"But it is a sad case for a man to dine alone," I said smoothly. "You will be very welcome."

"No, sir," said he, looking furtively at my men drawing near, between him and the doors.

"But I insist," I said politely. Then I added in a lower tone meant for him alone: "Resist, you hound, and I'll have you carried up by your four legs."

His face was working with fear and passion. He looked at the blocked way with the eye of a baited animal.

"I'll be damned first!" he cried. And seizing a chair he whirled around, dashed it through a window, and leaped through the jagged panes before I could spring forward to stop him.

"Round in front, men!" I cried, motioning my followers to sally through the door. "Bring him back!" And an instant later I leaped through the window after the flying enemy.

There was a fall of six feet, and as I landed on a pile of broken glass, a bit shaken, with the rain beating on my head, it was a few seconds before I recovered my wits. When I looked, no one was in sight. I heard the men running on the porch of the hotel, so the enemy was not to be sought that way. I set off full speed for the other corner, fifty yards away, half suspecting an ambush. But at the turn I stopped. The rain-soaked street was empty for a block before me. Far down the next block a plodding figure under an umbrella bent to the gusts of the wind and tried to ward off the driving spray of the storm. But Darby Meeker had disappeared as though the earth had swallowed him up.

"Where is he?" cried Porter, the first of my men to reach my side.

I shrugged my shoulders. "I haven't seen him."

"He didn't come our way-that I'll swear," panted Fitzhugh.

"He was out of sight before I got my feet," said I. "They must have a hiding-place close by."

"He must have jumped the fence here," said Wilson, pointing to a cottage just beyond the hotel's back yard. "I'll see about it." And he vaulted the pickets and looked about the place.

He was back in a minute with a shake of the head.

"Well, it's no great matter," I said. "We can get along without another guest for the afternoon. Now get under cover, boys, or you'll be soaked through."

The landlord met us with an air half-anxious, half-angry.

"I'd like to know who's to pay for this!" he cried. "There's a sash and four panes of glass gone to smithereens."

"The gentleman who just went out will be glad to pay for it, if you'll call it to his attention," I said blandly.

"I'll have the law on him!" shouted the landlord, getting red in the face. "And if he's a friend of yours you'd better settle for him, or it will be the worse for him."

"I'm afraid he isn't a friend of mine," I said dubiously. "He didn't appear to take that view of it."

"That's so," admitted the landlord. "But I don't know his name, and somebody's got to settle for that glass."

I obliged the landlord with Mr. Meeker's name, and with the bestowal of this poor satisfaction returned to the interrupted meal.

"Well, I reckon he wouldn't have been very pleasant company if you'd got him," said one of the men consolingly, when we had told our tale of the search for a guest.

"I suspect he would be less disagreeable in here than out with his gang," I returned dryly, and turned the subject. I did not care to discuss my plan to get a hostage now that it had failed.

The gray day plashed slowly toward nightfall. The rain fell by fits and starts, now with a sudden dash, now gently as though it were only of half a mind to fall at all. But the wind blew strong, and the clouds that drove up from the far south were dark enough to have borne threats of a coming deluge.

As the time wore on I suspected that my men grew uneasy, wondering what we were there for, and why I did not make some move. Then I reflected that this could not be. It was I who was wondering. The men were accustomed to let me do their thinking for them, and could be troubled no more here than in San Francisco. But what was I expected to do? Where could my orders be? Had they gone astray? Had the plans of the Unknown come to disaster through the difficulty of getting the telegraph on Sunday? The office here was closed. The Unknown, being a woman, I ungallantly reflected, would have neglected to take so small a circumstance into consideration, and she might even now be besieging the telegraph office in San Francisco in a vain effort to get word to Livermore.

On this thought I bestirred myself, and after much trouble had speech with the young man who combined in his person the offices of telegraph operator, station master, ticket seller, freight agent and baggage handler for the place. He objected to opening the office "out of office hours."

"There might be inducements discovered that would make it worth your while, I suppose?" I said, jingling some silver carelessly in my pocket.

He smiled.

"Well, I don't care if I do," he replied. "Whatever you think is fair, of course."

It was more than I thought fair, but the agent thawed into friendship at once, and expressed his readiness to "call San Francisco" till he got an answer if it took till dark.

I might have saved my trouble and my coin. San Francisco replied with some emphasis that there was nothing for me, and never had been, and who was I, anyhow?

There was nothing to be done. I must possess my soul in patience in the belief that the Unknown knew what she was about and that I should get my orders in due time-probably after nightfall, when darkness would cover any necessary movement.

But if I could shift the worry and responsibility of the present situation on the Unknown, there was another trouble that loomed larger and more perplexing before my mind with each passing hour. If the mission of to-day were prolonged into the morrow, what was to become of the Omega deal, and where would Doddridge Knapp's plans of fortune be found? I smiled to think that I should concern myself with this question when I knew that Doddridge Knapp's men were waiting and watching for my first movement with orders that probably did not stop at murder itself. Yet my trouble of mind increased with the passing time as I vainly endeavored to devise some plan to meet the difficulty that had been made for me.

But as I saw no way to straighten out this tangle, I turned my attention to the boy in the hope of getting from him some information that might throw light on the situation.

"He's as shy as a young quail," said Wainwright, when my advances were received in stubborn silence.

"You seem to be getting along pretty well with him," I suggested.

"Yes, sir; he'll talk a bit with me, but he's as close-mouthed a chap as you'll find in the state, sir, unless it's one of them deef and dummies."

I made another unsuccessful attempt to cultivate the acquaintance of my charge.

"You've got a day's job before you if you get him to open his head," said Wainwright, amused at the failure of my efforts as an infant-charmer.

"What has he been talking about?" I inquired, somewhat disgusted.

"The train," chuckled Wainwright. "Blamed if I think he's seen anything else since he started."

"The train?"

"Yes; the one we come on. He's been talking about it, and wondering what I'd do with it and without it till I reckon we've covered pretty near everything that could happen to a fellow with a train or without one."

"Is that the only subject of interest?"

"Well, he did go so far as to say that the milk was different here, and that he wanted a kind of cake we didn't get at dinner."

I attacked the young man on his weak point, and got some brief answers in reply to my remarks on the attractiveness of locomotives and the virtues of cars. But as any venture away from the important subject was met with the silence of the clam, I had at last to give up with a wild desire to shake the young man until some more satisfactory idea should come uppermost.

As darkness came on, the apprehensions of danger which had made no impression on me by daylight, began to settle strongly on my spirits. The wind that dashed the rain-drops in gusts on the panes seemed to whistle a warning, and the splash of the water outside was as the muttering of a tale of melancholy in an unknown tongue.

I concealed my fears and depressions from the men, and with the lighting of the lamps made my dispositions to meet any attack that might come. I had satisfied myself that the rear bedroom, that faced the south, could not be entered from the outside without the aid of ladders. The parlor showed a sheer drop to the street on the west, and I felt assured we were safe on that side. But the front windows of the parlor, and the front bedroom which joined it, opened on the veranda roof in common with a dozen other rooms. Inside, the hallway, perhaps eight feet wide and twenty-five feet long, offered the only approach to our rooms from the stairs. The situation was not good for defense, and at the thought I had a mind even then to seek other quarters.

It was too late for such a move, however, and I decided to make the best of the position. I placed the boy in the south bedroom, which could be reached only through the parlor. With him I placed Wainwright and Fitzhugh, the two strongest men of the party. The north bedroom, opening on the hallway, the veranda roof and the parlor, looked to be the weakest part of my position, but I thought it might be used to advantage as a post of observation. The windows were guarded with shutters of no great strength. We closed and secured those of the parlor and the inner bedroom as well as possible. Those of the north bedroom I left open. By leaving the room dark it would be easy for a sentinel to get warning of an assault by way of the veranda roof. I stationed Porter in the hall, and Abrams in the dark bedroom, while Lockhart, Wilson, Brown and I held the parlor and made ourselves comfortable until the time should come to relieve the men on guard.

One by one the lights that could be seen here and there through the town disappeared, the sounds from the streets and the other parts of the house came more infrequently and at last were smothered in silence, and only darkness and the storm remained.

I thrust open the door to the bedroom to see that the boy and his guards were safe, and this done I turned down the light, threw myself on the floor before the door that protected my charge, and mused over the strange events that had crowded so swiftly upon me.

Subtle warnings of danger floated over my senses between sleeping and waking, and each time I dropped into a doze I awoke with a start, to see only the dimly-lighted forms of my men before me, and to hear only the sweep and whistle of the wind outside and the dash of water against the shutters. Thrice I had been aroused thus, when, on the borderland between dreams and waking, a voice reached my ear.

"S-s-t! What was that?"

I sprang up, wide-awake, revolver in hand. It was Lockhart who spoke. We all strained our ears to listen. There was nothing to be heard but the moan of the wind and the dash of water.

"What was it?" I whispered.

"I don't know."

"I heard nothing."

"It was a coo-hoo—like the call of an owl, but—"

"But you thought it was a man?" Lockhart nodded. Brown and Wilson had not heard it.

"Was it inside or outside?"

"It was out here, I thought," said Lockhart doubtfully, pointing to the street that ran by the side of the hotel.

I opened the door to the dark bedroom in which Abrams kept watch. It swung noiselessly to my cautious touch. For a moment I could see nothing of my henchman, but the window was open. Then, in the obscurity, I thought I discovered his body lying half-way across the window-sill. I waited for him to finish his observations on the weather, but as he made no move I was struck with the fear that he had met foul play and touched him lightly.

In a flash he had turned on me, and I felt the muzzle of a revolver pressing against my side.

"If you wouldn't mind turning that gun the other way, it would suit me just as well," I said.

"Oh, it's you, is it?" said Abrams with a gulp. "I thought Darby Meeker and his gang was at my back, sure."

"Did you hear anything?" I asked.

"Yes; there was a call out here a bit ago. And there's half a dozen men or more out there now-right at the corner."

"Are you sure?"

"Yes; I was a-listening to 'em when you give me such a start."

"What were they saying?"

"I couldn't hear a word."

"Give warning at the first move to get into the house. Blaze away with your gun if anybody tries to climb on to the porch."

Porter had heard nothing, but was wide awake, watching by the light of the lamp that hung at the head of the stairway. And after a caution to vigilance I returned to my chair.

For half an hour I listened closely. The men were open-eyed but silent. The storm kept up its mournful murmur, but no sound that I could attribute to man came to my straining ears.

Suddenly there was a cry from the hall.

"Who's there?" It was Porter's voice.

An instant later there was a crash of glass, an explosion seemed to shake the house, and there was a rush of many feet.

I leaped to the door and flung it open, Lockhart, Wilson and Brown crowding close behind me. A body of men filled the hallway, and Porter was struggling in the hands of three ruffians. His revolver, whose shot we had heard, had been knocked from his hand and lay on the floor.

The sudden appearance of four more weapons in the open doorway startled the enemy into pausing for a moment. I sprang forward and gave the nearest of Porter's assailants a blow that sent him staggering into the midst of his band, and with a wrench Porter tore himself loose from the other two and was with us again.

"What does this mean?" I cried angrily to the invaders. "What are you here for?"

There were perhaps a dozen of them altogether, and in the midst of the band I saw the evil face and snake-eyes of Tom Terrill. At the sight of his repulsive features I could scarce refrain from sending a bullet in his direction.

Darby Meeker growled an answer.

"You know what we're here for."

"You have broken into a respectable house like a band of robbers," I cried. "What do you want?"

"You know what we want, Mr. Wilton," was the surly answer. "Give us the boy and we won't touch you."

"And if not?"

There was silence for a few moments.

"What are you waiting for?" growled a voice from beyond the turn of the hall.

At the sound I thrilled to the inmost fiber. Was it not the growl of the Wolf? Could I be mistaken in those tones? I listened eagerly for another word that might put it beyond doubt.

"Well, are you going to give him up?" asked the hoarse voice of Meeker.

"There has got to be some better reason for it than your demand," I suggested.

"Well, we've got reasons enough here. Stand ready, boys."

"Look out!" I said to my men, with a glance behind. As I turned I saw without noting it that Wainwright and Fitzhugh had come out of the boy's room to take a hand in the impending trouble. Lockhart and Wilson slipped in front of me.

"Get back and look after the boy," whispered the former. "We can hold 'em here."

"Move ahead there!" shouted a fierce voice that again thrilled the ear and heart with the growl of the Wolf. "What are you afraid of?"

"Stand fast, boys," I said to my men. "Wainwright, keep close to the bedroom." Then I shouted defiance to the enemy. "The first man that moves forward gets killed! There are eight revolvers here."

Then I saw that Wainwright had come forward, despite my bidding, eager to take his share of the onslaught. And by some freak of the spirit of the perverse the boy, who had shown himself so timid during the day, had now slipped out of his room and climbed upon a chair to see what the excitement was about, as though danger and death were the last things in the world with which he had to reckon.

I caught a glimpse of his form out of the tail of my eye as he mounted the chair in his night-dress. I turned with an exclamation to Wainwright and was leaping to cover him from a possible bullet, when there was a roar of rage and the voice of Terrill rang through the hall:

"Tricked again!" he cried with a dreadful oath. "It's the wrong boy!"

CHAPTER XXIV. ON THE ROAD

The wrong boy!

For a moment I could not understand nor believe; and when the meaning of the words came to me, I groped in mental darkness, unable to come in touch with the significant facts by which I was surrounded. The solid earth had fallen from under me, and I struggled vainly to get footing in my new position.

But there was no time for speculation. Half in a daze I heard a roar of curses, orders, a crash of glass as the lamp was extinguished, and over all came the prolonged growl of a wolf-voice, hoarse and shaken with anger. There was a vision of a wolf-head rising above the outline of faces a few yards away, dark, distorted, fierce, with eyes that blazed threats, and in an instant I found myself in the center of a struggling, shouting, swearing mass of savage men, fighting with naught but the instinct of blind rage. Shots were fired, but for the most part it was a hand-to-hand struggle. The clearest picture that comes to me out of the confused tangle is that of Wainwright handling his pistol like a bowie knife, and trying to perform a surgical operation extensive enough to let a joke into Darby Meeker's skull.

I doubt not that I was as crazy as the rest. The berserker rage was on me, and I struck right and left. But in my madness there was one idea strong in my mind. It was to reach the evil face and snake-eyes of Tom Terrill, and stamp the life out of him. With desperate rage I shouldered and fought till his white face with its venomous hatred was next to mine, till the fingers of my left hand gripped his throat, and my right hand tried to beat out his brains with a six-shooter.

"Damn you!" he gasped, striking fiercely at me. "I've been waiting for you!"

I tightened my grip and spoke no word. He writhed and turned, striving to free himself. I had knocked his revolver from his hand, and he tried in vain to reach it. My grip was strong with the strength of madness, and the white face before me grew whiter except where a smear of blood closed the left eye and trickled down over the cheek beneath. A trace of fear stole into the venomous anger of the one eye that was unobscured, as he strove without success to guard himself from my blows. But he gave a sudden thrust, and with a sinuous writhe he was free, while I was carried back by the rush of men with the vague impression that something was amiss with me. Then a great light flamed up before me in which the struggling, shouting mob, the close hall and room, and the universe itself melted away, and I was alone.

The next impression that came to me was that of a voice from an immeasurable distance.

"He's coming to," it said; and then beside it I heard a strange wailing cry.

"What is it?" I asked, trying to sit up. My voice seemed to come from miles away, and to belong to some other man.

"That's it, you're all right," said the voice encouragingly, and about the half of Niagara fell on my face.

I sat up and beheld the room whirling about, the walls, the furniture, and the people dancing madly together to a strange wailing sound that carried me back to the dens of Chinatown. Then the mists before my eyes cleared away, and I found that I was on the floor of the inner bedroom and Wainwright had emptied a water-jug over me. The light of a small kerosene lamp gave a gloomy illumination to the place. Lockhart and Fitzhugh leaned against the door, and Wilson bent with Wainwright over me. The boy was sitting on the bed, crying shrilly over the melancholy situation.

I tried to stagger to my feet.

"Wait a bit," said Wainwright. "You'll get your head in a minute."

I felt acutely conscious already that I had my head. It seemed a very large head that had suffered from an internal explosion.

"What is it?" I asked, gathering my scattered wits. "What has happened?"

"We've been licked," said Wainwright regretfully. "The rest of the boys got took, but we got in here. Fitz and me seen the nasty knock you got, and dragged you back, and when we got you here the parlor was full of the hounds, and Porter and Abrams and Brown was missing. We found you was cut, and we've tried to fix you up."

I looked at my bandaged arm, and put one more count in the indictment against Terrill. He had tried to stab me over the heart at the time he had wrenched free, but he had merely slashed my arm. It was not a severe wound, but it gave me pain.

"Only a scratch," said Wainwright.

I envied the philosophic calm with which he regarded it.

"It'll heal," I returned shortly. "Where is the other gang? Are they gone?"

"No; there's half a dozen of 'em out in the parlor, I reckon."

"You'd better tell him," said Fitzhugh, shifting an unpleasant task.

"Well," said Wainwright, "we heard orders given to shoot the first man that comes out before morning, but before all to kill you if you sticks your nose outside before sun-up."

The amiable intentions of the victors set me to thinking. If it was important to keep me here till morning, it must be important to me to get out. There was no duty to keep me here, for I need fear no attack on the boy who was with us. I looked at my watch, and found it was near one o'clock.

"Tie those blankets together," I ordered, as soon as I was able to get my feet.

The men obeyed me in silence, while Wainwright vainly tried to quiet the child. I was satisfied to have him cry, for the more noise he made the less our movements would be heard. I had a plan that I thought might be carried out.

While the others were at work, I cautiously raised the window and peered through the shutters. The rain was falling briskly, and the wind still blew a gale. I thought I distinguished the dark figure of a man on guard within a few feet of the building, and my heart sank.

"How many are in the parlor, Wilson?" I asked.

Wilson applied his eye to the keyhole.

"Can't see anybody but that one-eyed fellow, Broderick, but there might be more."

A flash of memory came to me, and I felt in my pocket for Mother Borton's mysterious scrawl. "Give that to a one-eyed man," she had said. It was a forlorn hope, but worth the trying.

"Hand this to Broderick," I said, "as soon as you can do it without any one's seeing you."

Wilson did not like the task, but he took the envelope and silently brought the door ajar. His first investigations were evidently reassuring, for he soon had half his body outside.

"He's got it," he said on reappearing.

A little later there was a gentle tap at the door, and the head of the one-eyed man was thrust in.

"It's as much as my life's worth," he whispered. "What do you want me to do?"

"How many men are in the street below here?"

"There's one; but more are in call."

"Well, I want him got out of the way."

"That's easy," said Broderick, with a diabolical wink of his one eye. "I'll have him change places with me."

"Good! How many men are here?"

"You don't need to know that. There's enough to bury you."

"Have Meeker and Terrill gone?"

"Tom? He's in the next room here, and can count it a mercy of the saints if he gits out in a week. Meeker's gone with the old man. Well, I can't stay a-gabbin' any longer, or I'll be caught, and then the divil himsilf couldn't save me."

I shuddered at the thought of the "old man," and the shadow of Doddridge Knapp weighed on my spirits.

"Are you ready for an excursion, Fitzhugh?" I whispered.

He nodded assent.

"Well, we'll be out of here in a minute or two. Take that overcoat. I've got one. Now tie that blanket to the bedpost. No, it won't be long enough. You'll have to hold it for us, boys."

I heard the change of guards below, and, giving directions to Wainwright, with funds to settle our account with the house, I blew out the lamp, quietly swung open the shutter and leaned over the sill.

"Hold on to the blanket, boys. Follow me, Fitz," I whispered, and climbed out. The strain on my injured arm as I swung off gave me a burning pain, but I repressed the groan that came into my throat. I half-expected a bullet to bring me to the ground in a hurry, for I was not over-trustful of the good faith of Mother Borton's friend. But I got to the ground in safety, and was relieved when Fitzhugh stood beside me, and the improvised rope was drawn up.

"Where now?" whispered Fitzhugh.

"To the stable."

As we slipped along to the corner a man stepped out before us.

"Don't shoot," he said; "it's me,—Broderick. Tell Mother Borton I wouldn't have done it for anybody but her."

"I'm obliged to you just the same," I said. "And here's a bit of drink money. Now, where are my men?"

"Don't know. In the lockup, I reckon."

"How is that?"

"Why, you see, Meeker tells the fellows here he has a warrant for you,—that you're the gang of burglars that's wanted for the Parrott murder. And he had to show the constable and the landlord and some others the warrant, too."

"How many were hurt?"

"Six or seven. Two of your fellows looked pretty bad when they was carried out."

We turned down a by-street, but as soon as the guard had disappeared we retraced our steps and hastened to the Thatcher stables.

The rain was whipped into our faces as we bent against the wind, and the whish and roar of the gale among the trees, and the rattle of loose boards and tins, as they were tossed and shaken behind the houses, gave a melancholy accompaniment to our hasty march.

"Hist!" said Fitzhugh in my ear. "Is that some one following us?"

I drew him into a corner, and peered back into the darkness.

"I can see no one."

"I thought I heard a man running."

"Wait a minute. If there is any one after us he must lose us right here."

We listened in silence. Only the plash of water and the voice of the storm came to our ears.

"Well, if they are looking for us they have gone the other way. Come along," I said.

We nearly missed the stable in the darkness, and it was several minutes before we roused Thatcher to a state in which he could put together the two ideas that we wanted to get in, and that it was his place to get up and let us in.

"Horses to-night?" he gasped, throwing up his hands. "Holy Moses! I couldn't think of letting the worst plug of the lot out in this storm."

"Well, I want your best."

"You'll have to do it, Dick," said Fitzhugh with a few words of explanation. "He'll make it all right for you."

"Where are you going?" said Thatcher.

"Oakland."

He threw up his hands once more.

"Great Scott! you can't do it. The horses can't travel fifty miles at night and in this weather. You'd best wait for the morning train. The express will be through here before five."

I hesitated a moment, but the chances of being stopped were too great.

"I must go," I said decidedly. "I can't wait here."

"I have it," said Thatcher. "By hard riding you can get to Niles in time to catch the freight as it goes up from San Jose. It will get you down in time for the first boat, if that's what you want."

"Good! How far is it?"

"We call it eighteen miles,—it's a little over that by the road. There's only one nasty bit. That's in the canyon."

"I think we shall need the pleasure of your company," I said.

The stableman was moved by a conflict of feelings. He was much indisposed to a twenty-mile ride in the storm and darkness; yet he was plainly unwilling to trust his horses unless he went with them. I offered him a liberal price for the service.

"It's a bad job, but if you must, you must," he groaned. And he soon had three horses under the saddle.

I eyed the beasts with some disfavor. They were evidently half-mustang, and I thought undersized for such a journey. But I was to learn before the night was out the virtues of strength and endurance that lie in the blood of the Indian horse.

"Hist! What's that?" said Fitzhugh, extinguishing the light.

The voices of the storm and the uneasy champing of the horses were the only sounds that rewarded a minute's listening.

"We must chance it," said I, after looking cautiously into the darkness, and finding no signs of a foe.

And in a moment more we were galloping down the street, the hoof-beats scarcely sounding in the softened earth of the roadway. Not a word was spoken after the start as we turned through the side streets to avoid the approaches to the hotel. I looked and listened intently, expecting each bunch of deeper darkness in the streets to start into life with shouts of men and crack of revolvers in an effort to stay our flight. Thatcher led the way, and Fitzhugh rode by my side.

"Look there!" cried Fitzhugh in my ear. "There's some one running to the hotel!"

I looked, and thought I could see a form moving through the blackness. The hotel could just be distinguished two blocks away. It might well be a scout of the enemy hastening to give the alarm.

"Never mind," I said. "We've got the start."

Thatcher suddenly turned to the west, and in another minute we were on the open highway, with the steady beat of the horses' hoofs splashing a wild rhythm on the muddy road.

The wind, which had been behind us, now whipped the rain into our faces from the left, half blinding us as the gusts sent the spray into our eyes, then tugged fiercely at coats and hats as if nothing could be so pleasing to the powers of the air as to send our raiment in a witch's flight through the clouds.

With the town once behind us, I felt my spirits rise with every stroke of the horse's hoofs beneath me. The rain and the wind were friends rather than foes. Yet my arm pained me sharply, and I was forced to carry the reins in the whip hand.

Here the road was broader, and we rode three abreast, silent, watchful, each busy with his own thoughts, and all alert for the signs of chase behind. Thrice my heart beat fast with the sound in my ears of galloping pursuers. Thrice I laughed to think that the patter of falling drops on the roadway should deceive my sense of sound. Here the track narrowed, and Thatcher shot ahead, flinging mud and water from his horse's heels fair upon us. There it broadened once more, and our willing beasts pressed forward and galloped beside the stableman's till the hoofs beat in unison.

"There!" said Thatcher, suddenly pulling his horse up to a walk. "We're five miles out, and they've got a big piece to make up if they're on our track. We'll breathe the horses a bit."

The beasts were panting a little, but chafed at the bits as we walked them, and tossed their heads uneasily to the pelting of the storm.

"Hark!" I cried. "Did you hear that?" I was almost certain that the sound of a faint halloo came from behind us. I was not alone in the thought.

"The dern fools!" said Fitzhugh. "They want a long chase, I guess, to go through the country yelling like a pack of wild Injuns."

"I reckon 'twas an owl," said Thatcher; "but we might as well be moving. We needn't take no chances while we've got a good set of heels under us. Get up, boys."

The willing brutes shot forward into the darkness at the word, and tossed the rain-drops from their ears with many an angry nod.

Of the latter part of the journey I have but a confused remembrance. I had counted myself a good rider in former days, but I had not mounted a horse for years. I had slept but little in forty-eight hours, and, worst of all, my arm pained me more and more. With the fatigue and the jar of the steady gallop, it seemed to swell until it was the body and I the poor appendage to it. My head ached from the blow it had got, and in a stupor of dull pain I covered the weary miles. But for the comfortable Mexican saddle I fear I should have sunk under the fatigue and distress of the journey and left friends and enemies to find their way out of the maze as best they might.

I have a dim recollection of splashing over miles of level road, drenched with water and buffeted by gusts of wind that faced us more and more, with the monotonous beat of hoofs ever in my ears, and the monotonous stride of the horse beneath me ever racking my tired muscles. Then we slackened pace in a road that wound in sharp descent through a gap in the hills, with the rush and roar of a torrent beneath and beside us, the wind sweeping with wild blasts through the trees that lined the way and covered the hillside and seeming to change the direction of its attack at every moment.

"We'll make it, I reckon," said Thatcher, at last. "It's only two miles farther, and the train hasn't gone up yet."

The horses by this time were well-blown. The road was heavy, and we had pressed them hard. Yet they struggled with spirit as they panted, and answered to the whip when we called on them for the last stretch as we once more found a level road.

There was no sign of life about the station as we drew our panting, steaming horses to a halt before it, and no train was in sight. The rain dripping heavily from the eaves was the only sound that came from it, and a dull glow from an engine that lay alone on a siding was the only light that was to be seen.

"What's the time?" asked Thatcher. "We must have made a quick trip."

"Twenty minutes past three," said I, striking a match under my coat to see my watch-face.

"Immortal snakes!" cried Thatcher. "I'm an idiot. This is Sunday night."

I failed to see the connection of these startling discoveries, but I had spirit enough to argue the case. "It's Monday morning, now."

"Well, it's the same thing. The freight doesn't run to-night."

I awoke to some interest at this announcement.

"Why, it's got to run, or we must take to saddle again for the rest of the way."

"These horses can't go five miles more at that gait, let alone twenty-five," protested Thatcher.

"Well, then, we must get other horses here."

"Come," said Fitzhugh; "what's the use of that when there's an engine on the siding doing nothing?"

"Just the idea. Find the man in charge."

But there did not appear to be any man in charge. The engineer and fireman were gone, and the watchman had been driven to cover by the foul weather.

We looked the iron horse over enviously.

"Why, this is the engine that came up with the special this noon," said Fitzhugh. "I remember the number."

"Good! We are ahead of the enemy, then. They haven't had a chance to get the wire, and we beat them on the road. We must find the engineer and get it ourselves."

"I've got an idea," said Fitzhugh. "It's this: why not take the machine without asking? I was a fireman once, and I can run it pretty well."

I thought a moment on the risk, but the need was greater.

"Just the thing. Take the money for the horses to your friend there. I'll open the switch."

In a few minutes Fitzhugh was back.

"I told him," he chuckled. "He says it's a jail offense, but it's the only thing we can do."

"It may be a case of life and death," I said. "Pull out."

"There's mighty little steam here-hardly enough to move her," said Fitzhugh from the cab, stirring the fire.

But as he put his hand to the lever she did move easily on to the main track, and rested while I reset the switch.

Then I climbed back into the cab, and sank down before the warm blaze in a stupor of faintness as the engine glided smoothly and swiftly down the track.

CHAPTER XXV. A FLUTTER IN THE MARKET

The gray pall of the storm hung over San Francisco. The dim light of the morning scarcely penetrated into the hallways as we climbed the stairs that led to our lodgings, leaving behind us the trail of dripping garments. I heaved a sigh of relief as Trent opened the door, and we once more faced the pleasing prospect of warmth, dry clothing and friends.

We had made the run from Niles without incident, and had left the engine on a siding at Brooklyn without being observed. If the railroad company still has curiosity, after all these years, to know how that engine got from Niles to Brooklyn, I trust that the words I have just written may be taken as an explanation and apology.

"Where's Barkhouse?" I asked, becoming comfortable once more with dry clothes, a warm room and a fresh bandage on my arm.

"He hasn't shown up, sir," said Trent. "Owens and Larson went out to look for him toward evening yesterday, but there wasn't a sign of him."

"Try again to-day. You may pick up news at Borton's or some of the water-front saloons."

"Oh, there was a letter for you," said Trent. "I near forgot."

I snatched the envelope, for the address was in the hand of the Unknown. The sheet within bore the words:

"Where is the boy? Have you removed him? Send the key to Richmond. Let me know when you return, for I must see you as soon as it is safe."

I read the note three or four times, and each time I was more bewildered than before. I had left the boy in Livermore, but certainly he was not the one she meant. He was the "wrong boy," and my employer must be well aware that I had taken him at her orders. Or could that expedition be a jest of the enemy to divert my attention? I dismissed this theory as soon as it suggested itself.

But where was the "right boy"? I had for a moment a sinking feeling of terror in the thought that the enemy had captured him. Mother Borton's warning that they had found his place of hiding returned to confirm this thought. But in an instant I remembered that the enemy had followed me in force to Livermore in chase of the wrong boy, and had attacked me in pure chagrin at the trick that had been played on them. That showed me beyond question that they had not obtained possession of the right boy. And the "key" that I was to send to Richmond, what was that?

The closing portion of the note set my heart beating fast. At last I was to have the opportunity to meet my mysterious employer face to face. But what explanation was I to make? What reception would I meet when she learned that Henry Wilton had given up his life in her service, and that I, who had taken his place, could tell nothing of the things she wished to know?

I wrote a brief note to Richmond stating that I had no key, inclosed the Unknown's note, with the remark that I had returned, and gave it to Owens to deliver. I was in some anxiety lest he might not know where Richmond was to be found. But he took the note without question, and I lay down with orders that I was to be called in time to reach the opening session of the stock market, and in a moment was fast asleep.

The Stock Exchange was a boiling and bubbling mass of excited men as I reached it. Pine Street, wet and sloppy, was lined with a mob of umbrellas that sheltered anxious speculators of small degree, and the great building was thronged with the larger dealers-with millionaires and brokers, with men who were on their way to fortune, and those who had been millionaires and now were desperately struggling against the odds of fate as they saw their wealth swept away in the gamblers' whirlpool.

I shouldered my way through the crowd into the buzzing Board-room as the session opened. Excitement thrilled the air, but the opening was listless. All knew that the struggle over Omega was to be settled that day, and that Doddridge Knapp or George Decker was to find ruin at the end of the call, and all were eager to hasten the decisive moment.

Wallbridge came panting before me, his round, bald head bobbing with excitement.

"Ready for the fray, eh? Oh, it's worth money to see this. Talk of your theaters now, eh? Got any orders?"

"Not yet," I returned, hardly sharing the little man's enjoyment of the scene. The size of the stakes made me tremble.

I could see nothing of Doddridge Knapp, and the uneasy feeling that he was at Livermore came over me. What was my duty in case he did not appear? Had he left his fortune at the mercy of the market to follow his lawless schemes? Had he been caught in his own trap, and was he now to be ruined as the result of his own acts? For a moment I felt a vengeful hope that he might have come to grief. But when I remembered that it was Luella who must suffer with him, I determined to make an effort to save the deal, even without authority, if the money or credit for buying the remaining shares was to be had.

I might have spared my worry. The call had not proceeded far, when the massive form of Doddridge Knapp appeared at the railing. The strong wolf-marks of the face were stronger than ever as he watched the scene on the floor. I looked in vain for a trace upon him of last night's work. If he had been at Livermore, he showed no sign of the passions or anxieties that had filled the dark hours.

He nodded carelessly for me to come to him as he caught my eye.

"You have the stock?"

"All safe."

"And the proxies?"

"Just as you ordered."

The King of the Street looked at me sharply.

"I told you to keep sober till this deal was over," he growled.

"You are obeyed," I said. "I have not touched a drop."

"Well, you look as though you had taken a romp with the devil," he said.

"I have," I returned with a meaning look.

His eyes fell before my steady gaze, and he turned them on the noisy throng before us.

"Any orders?" I asked at last.

"Be where I can call you the minute I want you," he replied.

"Now, my boy," he continued after a minute, "you are going to see what hasn't been seen in the Boards for years, and I reckon you'll never see it again."

"What is it?" I asked politely. I was prepared for almost any kind of fire-works in that arena.

Doddridge Knapp made no reply, but raised his hand as if to command silence, and a moment later the call of Omega was heard. And, for a marvel, a strange stillness did fall on the throng.

At the word of call I saw Doddridge Knapp step down to the floor of the pit, calm, self-possessed, his shoulders squared and his look as proud and forceful as that of a monarch who ruled by the might of his sword, while a grim smile played about his stern mouth.

The silence of the moment that followed was almost painful. In that place it seemed the most unnatural of prodigies. Brokers, speculators and spectators were as surprised as I, and a long-drawn "Ah-h!" followed by a buzzing as of a great swarm of bees greeted his appearance. The stillness and the buzzing seemed to take an hour, but it could not have been as much as a minute when the voice of Doddridge Knapp rang like a trumpet through the Boardroom.

"Five hundred for Omega!"

This was a wild jump from the three hundred and twenty-five that was marked against the stock at the close on Saturday, but I supposed the King of the Street knew what he was about.

At the bid of Doddridge Knapp a few cries rose here and there, and he was at once the center of a group of gesticulating brokers. Then I saw Decker, pale, eager, alert, standing by the rail across the room, signaling orders to men who howled bids and plunged wildly into the crowd that surrounded his rival.

The bids and offers came back and forth with shouts and barks, yet they made but a murmur compared to the whirlwind of sound that had arisen from the pit at the former struggles I had witnessed. There seemed but few blocks of the stock on the market. Yet the air was electric with the tense strain of thousands of minds eager to catch the faintest indication of the final result, and I found it more exciting than the wildest days of clamor and struggle.

"This is great," chuckled Wallbridge, taking post before me. "There hasn't been anything like it since Decker captured Chollar in the election of seventy-three. You don't remember that, I guess?"

"I wasn't in the market then," I admitted.

"Lord! Just to hear that!" cried the stout little man, mopping his glistening head frantically and quivering with nervous excitement. "Doddridge Knapp bids fifteen hundred for the stock and only gets five shares. Oh, why ain't I a chance to get into this?"

I heard a confused roar, above which rose the fierce tones of Doddridge Knapp.

"How many shares has he got to-day?" I asked.

"Not forty yet."

"And the others?"

"There's been about two thousand sold."

I gripped the rail in nervous tension. The battle seemed to be going against the King of the Street.

"Oh!" gasped Wallbridge, trembling with excitement. "Did you hear that? There! It's seventeen hundred-now it's seventeen-fifty! Whew!"

I echoed the exclamation.

"Oh, why haven't I got ten thousand shares?" he groaned.

"Who is getting them?"

"Knapp got the last lot. O-oh, look there! Did you ever see the like of that?"

I looked. Decker, hatless, with hair disheveled, had leaped the rail and was hurrying into the throng that surrounded Doddridge Knapp.

"There was never two of 'em on the floor before," cried Wallbridge.

At Decker's appearance the brokers opened a lane to him, the cries fell, and there was an instant of silence, as the kings of the market thus came face to face.

I shall never forget the sight. Doddridge Knapp, massive, calm, forceful, surveyed his opponent with unruffled composure. He was dressed in a light gray-brown suit that made him seem larger than ever. Decker was nervous, disheveled, his dress of black setting off the pallor of his face, till it seemed as white as his shirt bosom, as he fronted the King of the Street.

The foes faced each other, watchful as two wrestlers looking to seize an opening, and the Board-room held its breath. Then the crowd of brokers closed in again and the clamor rose once more.

I could not make out the progress of the contest, but the trained ear of Wallbridge interpreted the explosions of inarticulate sound.

"Phew! listen to that! Two thousand, twenty-one hundred, twenty-one fifty. Great snakes! See her jump!" he cried. "Decker's getting it."

My heart sank. Doddridge Knapp must have smothered his brain once more in the Black Smoke, and was now paying the price of indulgence. And his plans of wealth were a sacrifice to the wild and criminal scheme into which he had entered in his contest against the Unknown. I saw the wreck of fortune engulf Mrs. Knapp and Luella, and groaned in spirit. Then a flash of hope shot through me. Luella Knapp, the heiress to millions, was beyond my dreams, but Luella Knapp, the daughter of a ruined speculator, would not be too high a prize for a poor man to set his eyes upon.

The clang of the gong recalled me from the reverie that had shut out the details of the scene before me.

"There! Did you hear that?" groaned Wall-bridge. "Omega closes at two thousand six hundred and Decker takes every trick. Oh, why didn't you have me on the floor out there? By the great horn spoon, I'd 'a' had every share of that stock, and wouldn't 'a' paid more than half as much for it, neither."

I sighed and turned, sick at heart, to meet the King of the Street as he shouldered his way from the floor.

There was not a trace of his misfortune to be read in his face. But Decker, the victor, moved away like a man oppressed, pale, staggering, half-fainting, as though the nervous strain had brought him to the edge of collapse.

Doddridge Knapp made his way to the doors and signed me to follow him, but spoke no word until we stood beside the columns that guard the entrance.

The rain fell in a drizzle, but anxious crowds lined the streets, dodged into doorways for shelter, or boldly moved across the walks and the cobbled roadway under the protection of bobbing umbrellas. The news of the unprecedented jump in Omega in which the price had doubled thrice in a few minutes, had flown from mouth to mouth, and excitement was at fever heat.

"That was warm work," said Doddridge Knapp after a moment's halt.

"I was very sorry to have it turn out so," I said.

A grim smile passed over his face.

"I wasn't," he growled good-humoredly. "I thought it was rather neatly done."

I looked at him in surprise.

"Oh, I forgot that I hadn't seen you," he continued. "And like enough I shouldn't have told you if I had. The truth is, I found a block of four thousand shares on Saturday night, and made a combination with them."

"Then the mine is yours?"

"The directors will be."

"But you were buying shares this morning."

"A mere optical illusion, Wilton. I was in fact a seller, for I had shares to spare."

"It was a very good imitation."

"I don't wonder you were taken in, my boy. Decker was fooled to the tune of about a million dollars this morning. I thought it was rather neat for a clean-up."

I thought so, too, and the King of the Street smiled at my exclamations over his cleverness. But my congratulations were cut short as a small dark man pressed his way to the corner where we stood, and whispered in Doddridge Knapp's ear.

"Was he sure?" asked the King of the Street.

"Those were his exact words."

"When was this?"

"Not five minutes ago."

"Run to Caswell's. Tell him to wait for me."

The messenger darted off and we followed briskly. Caswell, I found, was an attorney, and we were led at once to the inner office.

"Come in with me," said my employer. "I expect I shall need you, and it will save explanations."

The lawyer was a tall, thin man, with chalky, expressionless features, but his eyes gave life to his face with their keen, almost brilliant, vision.

"Decker's playing the joker," said the King of the Street. "I've beaten him in the market, but he's going to make a last play with the directors. There's a meeting called for twelve-thirty. They are going to give him a two years' contract for milling, and they talk of declaring twenty thousand shares of my stock invalid."

"How many directors have you got?"

"Two-Barber and myself. Decker thinks he has Barber."

"Then you want an injunction?"

"Yes."

The lawyer looked at his watch.

"The meeting is at twelve-thirty. H'm. You'll have to hold them for half an hour-maybe an hour."

"Make it half an hour," growled Doddridge Knapp. "Just remember that time is worth a thousand dollars a second till that injunction is served."

He went out without another word, and there was a commotion of clerks as we left.

"How's your nerve, Wilton?" inquired the King of the Street calmly. "Are you ready for some hot work?"

"Quite ready."

"Have you a revolver about you?"

"Yes."

"Very good. I don't want you to kill any one, but it may come in handy as an evidence of your good intentions."

He led the way to California Street below Sansome, where we climbed a flight of stairs and went down a hall to a glass door that bore the gilt and painted letters, "Omega Mining Co., J. D. Storey, Pres't."

"There's five minutes to spare," said my employer. "He may be alone."

A stout, florid man, with red side-whiskers and a general air of good living, sat by an overshadowing desk in the handsome office, and looked sourly at us as we entered. He was not alone, for a young man could be seen in a side room that was lettered "Secretary's Office."

"Ah, Mr. Knapp," he said, bowing deferentially to the millionaire, and rubbing his fat red hands. "Can I do anything for you to-day?"

"I reckon so, Storey. Let me introduce you to Mr. Wilton, one of our coming directors."

I had an inward start at this information, and Mr. Storey regarded me unfavorably. We professed ourselves charmed to see each other.

"I suppose it was an oversight that you didn't send me a notice of the directors' meeting," said Doddridge Knapp.

Mr. Storey turned very red, and the King of the Street said in an undertone: "Just lock that door, Wilton."

"It must have been sent by mail," stammered Storey. "Hi, there! young man, what are you doing?" he exclaimed, jumping to his feet as I turned the key in the lock. "Open that door again!"

"No you don't, Storey," came the fierce growl from the throat of the Wolf. "Your game is up."

"The devil it is!" cried Storey, making a dash past Doddridge Knapp and coming with a rush straight for me.

"Stop him!" roared my employer.

I sprang forward and grappled Mr. Storey, but I found him rather a large contract, for I had to favor my left arm. Then he suddenly turned limp and rolled to the floor, his head thumping noisily on a corner of the desk.

Doddridge Knapp coolly laid a hard rubber ruler down on the desk, and I recognized the source of Mr. Storey's discomfiture.

"I reckon he's safe for a bit," he growled. "Hullo, what's this?"

I noted a very pale young man in the doorway of the secretary's office, apparently doubtful whether he should attempt to raise an alarm or hide.

"You go back in your room and mind your own business, Dodson," said the King of the Street. "Go!" he growled fiercely, as the young man still hesitated. "You know I can make or break you."

The young man disappeared, and I closed and locked the door on him.

"There they come," said I, as steps sounded in the hall.

"Stand by the door and keep them out," whispered my employer. "I'll see that Storey doesn't get up. Keep still now. Every minute we gain is worth ten thousand dollars."

I took station by the door as the knob was tried. More steps were heard, and the knob was tried again. Then the door was shaken and picturesque comments were made on the dilatory president.

Doddridge Knapp looked grim, but serene, as he sat on the desk with his foot on the prostrate Storey. I breathed softly, and listened to the rising complaints from without.

There were thumps and kicks on the door, and at last a voice roared:

"What are you waiting for? Break it in."

A crash followed, and the ground-glass upper section of the door fell in fragments.

"I beg your pardon, gentlemen," I said, as a man put his hand through the opening. "This revolver is loaded, and the first man to come through there will get a little cold lead in him."

There was a pause and then a storm of oaths.

"Get in there!" cried Decker's voice from the rear. "What are you afraid of?"

"He's got a gun."

"Well, get in, three or four of you at once. He can't shoot you all."

This spirited advice did not seem to find favor with the front-rank men, and the enemy retired for consultation. At last a messenger came forward.

"What do you want?" he asked.

"I want you to keep out."

"Who is he?" asked Decker's voice.

"There's another one there," cried another voice. "Why, it's Doddridge Knapp!"

Decker made use of some language not intended for publication, and there was whispering for a few minutes, followed by silence.

I looked at Doddridge Knapp, sitting grim and unmoved, counting the minutes till the injunction should come. Suddenly a man bounded through the broken upper section of the door, tossed by his companions, and I found myself in a grapple before I could raise my revolver.

We went down on the floor together, and I had a confused notion that the door swung open and four or five others rushed into the room.

I squirmed free from my opponent, and sprang to my feet in time to see the whole pack around Doddridge Knapp.

The King of the Street sat calm and forceful with a revolver in his hand, and all had halted, fearing to go farther.

"Don't come too close, gentlemen," growled the Wolf.

Then I saw one of the men raise a six-shooter to aim at the defiant figure that faced them. I gave a spring and with one blow laid the man on the floor. There was a flash of fire as he fell, and a deafening noise was in my ears. Men all about me were striking at me. I scarcely felt their blows as I warded them off and returned them, for I was half-mad with the desperate sense of conflict against odds. But at last I felt myself seized in an iron grip, and in a moment was seated beside Doddridge Knapp on the desk.

"The time is up," he said. "There's the sheriff and Caswell with the writ."

"I congratulate you," I answered, my head still swimming, noting that the enemy had drawn back at the coming of reinforcements.

"Good heavens, man, you're hurt!" he cried, pointing to my left sleeve where a blood stain was spreading. The wound I had received in the night conflict at Livermore had reopened in the struggle.

"It's nothing," said I. "Just a scratch."

"Here! get a doctor!" cried the King of the Street. "Gentlemen, the directors' meeting is postponed, by order of court."

CHAPTER XXVI. A VISION OF THE NIGHT

"You are a very imprudent person," said Luella, smiling, yet with a most charming trace of anxiety under the smile.

"What have I been doing now?" I asked.

"That is what you are to tell me. Papa told us a little about your saving his life and his plans this morning, but he was so very short about it. Let me know the whole story from your own mouth. Was this the arm that was hurt?"

I started to give a brief description of my morning's adventure, but there was something in my listener's face that called forth detail after detail, and her eyes kindled as I told the tale of the battle that won Omega in the stock Board, and the fight that rescued the fruits of victory in the office of the company.

"There is something fine in it, after all," she said when I was through. "There is something left of the spirit of the old adventurers and the knights. Oh, I wish I were a man! No, I don't either. I'd rather be the daughter of a man—a real man-and I know I am that."

I thought of the Doddridge Knapp that she did not know, and a pang of pity and sorrow wrenched my heart.

She saw the look, and misinterpreted it.

"You do not think, do you," she said softly, "that I don't appreciate your part in it? Indeed I do." I took her hand, and she let it lie a moment before she drew it away.

"I think I am more than repaid," I said.

"Oh, yes," said she, changing her tone to one of complete indifference. "Papa said he had made you a director."

"Yes," I said, taking my cue from her manner. "I have the happiness to share the honor with three other dummies. Your father makes the fifth."

"How absurd!" laughed Luella. "Do you want to provoke me?"

"Oh, of course, I mean that your father does the thinking, and—"

"And you punch the head he points out to you, I suppose," said Luella sarcastically.

"Exactly," I said. "And—"

"Don't mind me, Henry," interrupted the voice of Mrs. Knapp.

"But I must," said I, giving her greeting. "What service do you require?"

"Tell me what you have been doing."

"I have just been telling Miss Luella."

"And what, may I ask?"

"I was explaining this morning's troubles."

"Oh, I heard a little of them from Mr. Knapp. Have you had any more of your adventures at Borton's and other dreadful places?"

I glanced at Luella. She was leaning forward, her chin resting on her hand, and her eyes were fixed on me with close attention. "I should like to hear of them, too," she said.

I considered a moment, and then, as I could see no reason for keeping silent, I gave a somewhat abridged account of my Livermore trip, omitting reference to the strange vagaries of the Doddridge Knapp who traveled by night.

I had reason to be flattered by the attention of my audience. Both women leaned forward with wide-open eyes, and followed every word with eager interest.

"That was a dreadful danger you escaped," said Mrs. Knapp with a shudder. "I am thankful, indeed, to see you with us with no greater hurt."

Luella said nothing, but the look she gave me set my heart dancing in a way that all Mrs. Knapp's praise could not.

"I do hope this dreadful business will end soon," said Mrs. Knapp. "Do you think this might be the last of it?"

"No," said I, remembering the note I had received from the Unknown on my return, "there's much more to be done."

"I hope you are ready for it," said Mrs. Knapp, with a troubled look upon her face.

"As ready as I ever shall be, I suppose," I replied. "If the guardian angel who has pulled me through this far will hold on to his job, I'll do my part."

Mrs. Knapp raised a melancholy smile, but it disappeared at once, and she seemed to muse in silence, with no very pleasant thought on her mind. Twice or thrice I thought she wished to speak to me, but if so she changed her mind.

I ventured a few observations that were intended to be jocose, but she answered in the monosyllables of preoccupation, and I turned to Luella.

She gave back flashes of brightness, but I saw on her face the shadow of her mother's melancholy, and I rose at an early hour to take my leave.

"I wonder at you," said Luella softly, as we stood alone for a moment.

"You have little cause."

"What you have done is much. You have conquered difficulties."

I looked in her calm eyes, and my soul came to the surface.

"I wish you might be proud of me," I said.

"I—I am proud of such a friend-except—" She hesitated.

"Always an 'except,'" I said half-bitterly.

"But you have promised to tell me—"

"Some day. As soon as I may." Under her magnetic influence, I should have told her then had she urged me. And not until I was once more outside the house did I recall how impossible it was that I could ever tell her.

"What shall I do? What shall I do?" was the refrain that ran through my brain insistently, as the battle between love and duty rose and swelled. And I was sorely tempted to tell the Unknown to look elsewhere for assistance, and to bury the memory of my dead friend and the feud with Doddridge Knapp in a common grave.

"Here's some one to see you, sir," said Owens, as I reached the walk, and joined the guards I had left to wait for me. The rain had ceased, but the wind, which had fallen during the day, was freshening once more from the south.

"Yes, sor, you're wanted at Mother Borton's in a hurry," said another voice, and a man stepped forward. "There's the divil to pay!"

I recognized the one-eyed man who had done me the service that enabled me to escape from Livermore.

"Ah, Broderick, what's the matter?"

"I didn't get no orders, sor, so I don't know, but there was the divil's own shindy in the height of progression when I left. And Mother Borton says I was to come hot-foot for you, and tell you to come with your men if ye valued your sowl."

"Is she in danger?"

"I reckon the thought was heavy on her mind, for her face was white with the terror of it."

We hastened forward, but at the next corner a passing hack stood ready for passengers, and we rolled down the street, the horses' hoofs outstripped by my anxiety and apprehensions.

One of the men was sent to bring out such of my force as had returned, and I, with the two others, hurried on to Borton's.

There was none of the sounds of riot I had expected to hear as we drew up before it. The lantern blinked outside with its invitation to manifold cheer within. Lights streamed through the window and the half-opened door, and quiet and order reigned.

As I stepped to the walk, I found the explanation of the change in the person of a policeman, who stood at the door.

"Holy St. Peter! the cops is on!" whispered Broderick.

I failed to share his trepidation in the presence of the representative of law and order, and stepped up to the policeman.

"Has there been trouble here, officer?" I asked.

"Oh, is it you, sor?" said Corson's hearty voice. "I was wondering about ye. Well, there has been a bit of a row here, and there's a power of broken heads to be mended. There's wan man cut to pieces, and good riddance, for it's Black Dick. I'm thinking it's the morgue they'll be taking him to, though it was for the receiving hospital they started with him. It was a dandy row, and it was siventeen arrists we made."

"Where is Mother Borton?"

"The ould she-divil's done for this time, I'm a-thinking. Whist, I forgot she was a friend of yours, sor."

"Where is she-at the receiving hospital? What is the matter with her?"

"Aisy, aisy, sor. It may be nothing. She's up stairs. A bit of a cut, they say. Here, Shaughnessy, look out for this door! I'll take ye up, sor."

We mounted the creaking stairs in the light of the smoky lamp that stood on the bracket, and Corson opened a door for me.

A flickering candle played fantastic tricks with the furniture, sent shadows dancing over the dingy walls, and gave a weird touch to the two figures that bent over the bed in the corner. The figures straightened up at our entrance, and I knew them for the doctor and his assistant.

"A friend of the lady, sor," whispered Corson.

The doctor looked at me in some surprise, but merely bowed.

"Is she badly hurt?" I asked.

"I've seen worse," he answered in a low voice, "but—" and he completed the sentence by shrugging his shoulders, as though he had small hopes for his patient.

Mother Borton turned her head on the pillow, and her gaunt face lighted up at the sight of me. Her eyes shone with a strange light of their own, like the eyes of a night-bird, and there was a fierce eagerness in her look.

"Eh, dearie, I knew you would come," she cried.

The doctor pushed his way to the bedside.

"I must insist that the patient be quiet," he said with authority.

"Be quiet?" cried Mother Borton. "Is it for the likes of you that I'd be quiet? You white-washed tombstone raiser, you body-snatcher, do you think you're the man to tell me to hold my tongue when I want to talk to a gentleman?"

"Hush!" I said soothingly. "He means right by you."

"You must lie quiet, or I'll not be responsible for the consequences," said the doctor firmly.

At these well-meant words Mother Borton raised herself on her elbow, and directed a stream of profanity in the direction of the doctor that sent chills chasing each other down my spine, and seemed for a minute to dim the candle that gave its flickering gloom to the room.

"I'll talk as I please," cried Mother Borton. "It's my last wish, and I'll have it. You tell me I'll live an hour or two longer if I'm quiet, but I'll die as I've lived, a-doin' as I please, and have my say as long as I've got breath to talk. Go out, now-all of you but this man. Go!"

Mother Borton had raised herself upon one elbow; her face, flushed and framed in her gray and tangled hair, was working with anger; and her eyes were almost lurid as she sent fierce glances at one after another of the men about her. She pointed a skinny finger at the door, and each man as she cast her look upon him went out without a word.

"Shut the door, honey," she said quietly, lying down once more with a satisfied smile. "That's it. Now me and you can talk cozy-like."

"You'd better not talk. Perhaps you will feel more like it to-morrow."

"There won't be any to-morrow for me," growled Mother Borton. "I've seen enough of 'em carved to know when I've got the dose myself. Curse that knife!" and she groaned at a twinge of pain.

"Who did it?"

"Black Dick-curse his soul. And he's roasting in hell for it this minute," cried Mother Borton savagely.

"Hush!" I said. "You mustn't excite yourself. Can't I get you a minister or a priest?"

Mother Borton spat out another string of oaths.

"Priest or minister! Not for me! Not one has passed my door in all the time I've lived, and he'll not do it to-night. What could he tell me that I don't know already? I've been on the road to hell for fifty years, and do you think the devil will let go his grip for a man that don't know me? No, dearie; your face is better for me than priest or minister, and I want you to close my eyes and see that I'm buried decent. Maybe you'll remember Mother Borton for something more than a vile old woman when she's gone."

"That I shall," I exclaimed, touched by her tone, and taking the hand that she reached out to mine. "I'll do anything you want, but don't talk of dying. There's many a year left in you yet."

"There's maybe an hour left in me. But we must hurry. Tell me about your trouble-at Livermore, was it?"

I gave her a brief account of the expedition and its outcome. Mother Borton listened eagerly, giving an occasional grunt of approval.

"Well, honey; I was some good to ye, after all," was her comment.

"Indeed, yes."

"And you had a closer shave for your life than you think," she continued. "Tom Terrill swore he'd kill ye, and it's one of the miracles, sure, that he didn't."

"Well, Mother Borton, Tom Terrill's laid up in Livermore with a broken head, and I'm safe here with you, ready to serve you in any way that a man may."

"Safe-safe?" mused Mother Borton, an absent look coming over her skinny features, as though her mind wandered. Then she turned to me impressively. "You'll never be safe till you change your work and your name. You've shut your ears to my words while I'm alive, but maybe you'll think of 'em when I'm in my coffin. I tell you now, my boy, there's murder and death before you. Do you hear? Murder and death."

She sank back on her pillow and gazed at me with a wearied light in her eyes and a sibyl look on her face.

"I think I understand," I said gently. "I have faced them and I ought to know them."

"Then you'll-you'll quit your job-you'll be yourself?"

"I can not. I must go on."

"And why?"

"My friend-his work-his murderer."

"Have you got the man who murdered Henry Wilton?"

"No."

"Have you got a man who will give a word against-against-you know who?"

"I have not a scrap of evidence against any one but the testimony of my own eyes," I was compelled to confess.

"And you can't use it-you dare not use it. Now I'll tell you, dearie, I know the man as killed Henry Wilton."

"Who was it?" I cried, startled into eagerness.

"It was Black Dick-the cursed scoundrel that's done for me. Oh!" she groaned in pain.

"Maybe Black Dick struck the blow, but I know the man that stood behind him, and paid him, and protected him, and I'll see him on the gallows before I die."

"Hush," cried Mother Borton trembling. "If he should hear you! Your throat will be cut yet, dearie, and I'm to blame. Drop it, dearie, drop it. The boy is nothing to you. Leave him go. Take your own name and get away. This is no place for you. When I'm gone there will be no one to warn ye. You'll be killed. You'll be killed."

Then she moaned, but whether from pain of body or mind I could not guess.

"Never you fear. I'll take care of myself," I said cheerily.

She looked at me mournfully. "I am killed for ye, dearie."

I started, shocked at this news.

"There," she continued slowly, "I didn't mean to let you know. But they thought I had told ye."

"Then I have two reasons instead of one for holding to my task," I said solemnly. "I have two friends to avenge."

"You'll make the third yourself," groaned Mother Borton, "unless they put a knife into Barkhouse, first, and then you'll be the fourth belike."

"Barkhouse-do you know where he is?"

"He's in the Den-on Davis Street, you know. I was near forgetting to tell ye. Send your men to get him to-night, for he's hurt and like to die. They may have to fight. No, —don't leave me now."

"I wasn't going to leave you."

Mother Borton put her hand to her throat as though she choked, and was silent for a moment. Then she continued:

"I'll be to blame if I don't tell you —I *must* tell you. Are you listening?"

Her voice came thick and strange, and her eyes wandered anxiously about, searching the heavy shadows with a look of growing fear.

The candle burned down till it guttered and flickered in its pool of melted tallow, and the shadows it threw upon wall and ceiling seemed instinct with an impish life of their own, as though they were dark spirits from the pit come to mock the final hours of the life that was ebbing away before me.

"I am listening," I replied.

"You must know-you must-know, —I must tell you. The boy-the woman is —"

On a sudden Mother Borton sat bolt upright in bed, and a shriek, so long, so shrill, so freighted with terror, came from her lips that I shrank from her and trembled, faint with the horror of the place.

"They come-there, they come!" she cried, and throwing up her arms she fell back on the bed.

The candle shot up into flame, sputtered an instant, and was gone. And I was alone with the darkness and the dead.

CHAPTER XXVII. A LINK IN THE CHAIN

I sprang to my feet. The darkness was instinct with nameless terrors. The air was filled with nameless shapes. A spiritual horror surrounded me, and I felt that I must reach the light or cry out. But before I had covered the distance to the door, it was flung open and Corson stood on the threshold; and at the sight of him my courage returned and my shaken nerves grew firm. At the darkness he wavered and cried:

"What's the matter here?"

"She is dead."

"Rest her sowl! It's a fearsome dark hole to be in, sor."

I shuddered as I stood beside him, and brought the lamp from the bracket in the hall.

Mother Borton lay back staring affrightedly at the mystic beings who had come for her, but settled into peace as I closed her eyes and composed her limbs.

"She was a rare old bird," said Corson when I had done, "but there was some good in her, after all."

"She has been a good friend to me," I said, and we called a servant from below and left the gruesome room to his guardianship.

"And now, there's another little job to be done. There's one of my men a prisoner down on Davis Street. I must get him out."

"I'm with you, sor," said Corson heartily. "I'm hopin' there's some heads to be cracked."

I had not counted on the policeman's aid, but I was thankful to accept the honest offer. In the restaurant I found five of my men, and with this force I thought that I might safely attempt an assault on the Den.

The Den was a low, two-story building of brick, with a warehouse below, and the quarters of the enemy, approached by a narrow stairway, above.

"Step quietly," I cautioned my men, as we neared the dark and forbidding entrance. "Keep close to the shadow of the buildings. Our best chance is in a surprise."

There was no guard at the door that stood open to the street, and we halted a moment before it to make sure of our plans.

"It's a bad hole," whispered Corson.

"A fine place for an ambush," I returned dubiously.

"Well, there's no help for it," said the policeman. "Come on!" And drawing his club and revolver he stole noiselessly up the stairs.

I felt my way up step by step, one hand against the wall and my shoes scraping cautiously for a resting-place, while my men followed in single file with the same silent care.

But in spite of this precaution, we were not two-thirds the way up the flight before a voice shot out of the darkness.

"Who's there?"

We stopped and held our breath. There was a minute of silence, but it was broken by the creak of a board as one of the men shifted his weight.

"There's some one here!" cried the voice above us. "Halt, or I'll shoot! Peterson! Conn! Come quick!"

There was no more need for silence, and Corson and I reached the landing just as a door opened that let the light stream from within. Two men had sprung to the doorway, and another could be seen faintly outlined in the dark hall.

"Holy Mother! it's the cops!" came in an awe-stricken voice at the sight of Corson's star.

"Right, my hearty!" cried Corson, making a rush for the man, who darted down the hall in an effort to escape. The two men jumped back into the room and tried to close the door, but I was upon them before they could swing it shut. Four of my men had followed me close, and with a few blows given and taken, the two were prisoners.

"Tie them fast," I ordered, and hastened to see how Corson fared.

I met the worthy policeman in the hall, blown but exultant. Owens was following him, and between them they half-dragged, half-carried the man who had given the alarm.

"He made a fight for it," puffed Corson, "but I got in wan good lick at him and he wilted. You'll surrinder next time when I tell ye, won't ye, me buck?"

"Aren't there any more about?" I asked. "There were more than three left in the gang."

"If there had been more of us, you'd never have got in," growled one of the prisoners.

"Where's Barkhouse?" I asked.

"Find him!" was the defiant reply.

We began the search, opening one room after another. Some were sleeping-rooms, some the meeting-rooms, while the one we had first entered appeared to be the guard-room.

"Hello! What's this?" exclaimed Corson, tapping an iron door, such as closes a warehouse against fire.

"It's locked, sure enough," said Owens, after trial.

"It must be the place we are looking for," I said. "Search those men for keys."

The search was without result.

"It's a sledge we must get," said Owens, starting to look about for one.

"Hould on," said Corson, "I was near forgetting. I've got a master-key that fits most of these locks. It's handy for closing up a warehouse when some clerk with his wits a-wandering forgits his job. So like enough it's good at unlocking."

It needed a little coaxing, but the bolt at last slid back and the heavy doors swung open. The room was furnished with a large table, a big desk, and a dozen chairs, which sprang out of the darkness as I struck a match and lit the gas. It was evidently the council-room of the enemy.

"This is illigant," said the policeman, looking around with approval; "but your man isn't here, I'd say."

"Well, it looks as though there might be something here of interest," I replied, seizing eagerly upon the papers that lay scattered about upon the desk. "Look in the other rooms while I run through these."

A rude diagram on the topmost paper caught my eye. It represented a road branching thrice. On the third branch was a cross, and then at intervals four crosses, as if to mark some features of the landscape. Underneath was written:

"From B—follow 1 1-2 m. Take third road—3 or 5."

The paper bore date of that day, and I guessed that it was meant to show the way to the supposed hiding-place of the boy.

Then, as I looked again, the words and lines touched a cord of memory. Something I had seen or known before was vaguely suggested. I groped in the obscurity for a moment, vainly reaching for the phantom that danced just beyond the grasp of my mental fingers.

There was no time to lose in speculating, and I turned to the work that pressed before us. But as I thrust the papers into my pocket to resume the search for Barkhouse, the elusive memory flashed on me. The diagram of the enemy recalled the single slip of paper I had found in the pocket of Henry Wilton's coat on the fatal night of my arrival. I had kept it always with me, for it was the sole memorandum left by him of the business that had brought him to his death. I brought it out, very badly creased and rumpled from much carrying, but still quite as legible as on the night I had first seen it.

Placed side by side with the map I had before me, the resemblance was less close than I had thought. Yet all the main features were the same. There was the road branching thrice; a cross in both marked the junction of the third road as though it gave sign of a building or some natural landmark; and the other features were indicated in the same order. No-there was a difference in this point; there were five crosses on the third road in the enemy's diagram, while there were but four in mine.

In the matter of description the enemy had the advantage, slight as it was.

"Third road-cockeyed barn-iron cow," and the confused jumble of drunken letters and figures that Henry had written—I could make nothing of these.

"From B—follow 1 1-2 m. Take third road—3 or 5"—this was at least half-intelligible.

Then it came on me like a blow,—was this the mysterious "key" that the Unknown had demanded of me in her letter of this morning? I turned sick at heart at the thought that my ignorance and inattention had put the boy in jeopardy. The enemy had perhaps a clue to the hiding-place that the Unknown did not possess. The desertion of these headquarters swelled my fears. Though Terrill, disabled by wounds, was groaning with pain and rage at Livermore, and the night's arrests at Borton's had reduced the numbers of the band, Darby Meeker was still on the active list. And Doddridge Knapp? He was free now to follow his desperate plot to its end without risking his schemes of fortune. The absence of Meeker, the date of to-day upon the map, suggesting that it had but just come into the hands of the enemy, and the lack of a garrison in the Den, raised the apprehension that fresh mischief was afoot.

I was roused from my reverie of fears by confused shouts from down the hall, and sprang hastily to the door, with the thought that the forces of the enemy were upon us.

"Here he is! they've found him," cried an excited voice.

"Yes, sir! here he comes!"

It was truly the stalwart guard; but two days had made a sad change in him. With head bound in a bloody rag, and face of a waxy yellow hue, he staggered limply out of one of the rear rooms between Corson and Owens.

"Brace up, me boy! You're worth ten dead men," said the policeman encouragingly. "That's right! you'll be yourself in a jiffy."

Barkhouse was soon propped up on the lounge in the guard-room, and with a few sips of whisky and a fresh bandage began to look like a more hopeful case.

"'Twas a nasty cut," said one of the men sympathetically.

"How did you get it?" I asked.

"I don't rightly know," said Barkhouse faintly. "'Twas the night you went to Mother Borton's last week. After I leaves you, I walks down a piece towards the bay, and as I gets about to Drumm Street, I guess, a fellow comes along as I takes to be a sailor half-loaded. 'Hello, mate,' he says, a-trying to steady himself, 'what time did you say it was?' 'I didn't say,' says I, for I was too fly to take out my watch, even if it is a nickel-plater, for how could he tell what it was in the dark? and it's good for a dozen drinks at any water-front saloon. 'Well, what do you make it?' he says; and as I was trying to reckon whether it was nearer twelve or one o'clock, he lurches up agin' me and grabs my arms as if to steady himself. Then three or four fellows jumps from behind a lot of packing-boxes there, and grabs me. I makes a fight for it, and gives one yell, and the next I knows I was in a dark room here with the sorest head in San Francisco. An' I reckon I've been here about six days, and another would have finished me."

Barkhouse's "six days" estimate provoked a smile.

"If you could get paid on your time reckoning," remarked Owens in a humorous tone, "you'd be well off, Bob. 'Twas night before last you got took in."

Barkhouse looked incredulous, but I nodded my support of Owens' remarkable statement.

"However, you'll be paid on your own reckoning, and better, too," I said; and he was thereby consoled.

"Now, we must get out of here," I continued. "Take turns by twos in helping Barkhouse. We had better not risk staying here."

"Right," said Corson, "and now we'll just take these three beauties along to the station."

"On what charge?" growled the man addressed as Conn.

"Disturbing the peace-you've disturbed ours for sure-resisting an officer, vulgar language, keeping a disorderly house, carrying a pistol without a permit, and anything else I can think up between here and the station-house. If that doesn't satisfy ye, I'll put ye down for assault and robbery on Barkhouse's story, and ye may look out for a charge of murder before ye git out."

The men swore at this cheerful prospect, but as their hands were bound behind them, and Corson walked with his club in one hand and his pistol in the other, they took up the march at command, and the rest of us slowly followed.

CHAPTER XXVIII. THE CHASE IN THE STORM

When we reached the entrance to our quarters on Montgomery Street the rain had once more begun to fall, gently now, but the gusts of damp wind from the south promised more and worse to follow.

"Hello!" cried the first man, starting back. "What's this?"

The line stopped, and I moved forward.

"What is it?" I asked.

"A message for you, Mr. Wilton," said a voice suddenly from the recess of the doorway.

"Give it to me," I said.

A slip of paper was thrust into my hand, and I passed up the stairs.

"I'll wait for you," said the messenger, and at the first gas-jet that burned at the head of the stairs I stopped to read the address.

It was in the hand of the Unknown, and my fatigue and indifference were gone in a moment. I trembled as I tore open the envelope, and read:

"Follow the bearer of this note at 12:30. Come alone and armed. It is important."

There was no signature.

If this meant anything it meant that I was to meet the Unknown, and perhaps to search the heart of the mystery. I had been heavy with fatigue and drowsy with want of sleep, but at this thought the energies of life were once more fresh within me.

With my new-found knowledge it might be more important than even the Unknown was aware, that we should meet. To me, the map, the absence of Darby Meeker and his men, the mysterious hints of murder and death that had come from the lips of Mother Borton, were but vaguely suggestive. But to the Unknown, with her full knowledge of the objects sought by the enemy and the motives that animated their ceaseless pursuit, the darkness might be luminous, the obscurity clear.

The men had waited a minute for me as I read the note.

"Go to your rooms and get some rest," I said. "I am called away. Trent will be in charge, and I will send word to him if I need any of you."

They looked at me in blank protest.

"You're not going alone, sir?" cried Owens in a tone of alarm.

"Oh, no. But I shall not need a guard." I hoped heartily that I did not.

The men shook their heads doubtfully, and I continued:

"Corson will be down from the Central Station in fifteen or twenty minutes. Just tell him that I've been sent for, and to come to-morrow if he can make it in his way."

And bidding them good night I ran hastily down the stairs before any of the men could frame his protest into words.

"Are you ready, sir?" asked the messenger.

"It is close on half-past twelve," I answered. "Where is she?"

"It's not far," said my guide evasively.

I understood the danger of speech, and did not press for an answer.

We plunged down Montgomery Street in the teeth of the wind that dashed the spray in our faces at one moment, lulled an instant the better to deceive the unwary, and then leaped at us from behind corners with the impetuous rush of some great animal that turned to vapor as it reached us. The street was dark except for the newspaper offices, which glowed bright with lights on both sides of the way, busy with the only signs of life that the storm and the midnight hour had left.

With the lighted buildings behind us we turned down California Street. Half-way down the block, in front of the Merchants' Exchange, stood a hack. At the sight my heart beat fast and my breath came quick. Here, perhaps, was the person about whom centered so many of my hopes and fears, in whose service I had faced death, and whose words might serve to make plain the secret springs of the mystery.

As we neared the hack my guide gave a short, suppressed whistle, and passing before me, flung open the door to the vehicle and motioned me to enter. I glanced about with some lack of confidence oppressing my spirits. But I had gone too far to retreat, and stepped into the hack. Instead of following, the guide closed the door gently; I heard him mount the seat by the driver, and in a moment we were in motion.

Was I alone? I had expected to find the Unknown, but the dark interior gave no sign of a companion. Then the magnetic suggestion of the presence of another came to my spirit, and a faint perfume put all my senses on the alert. It was the scent that had come to me with the letters of the Unknown. A slight movement made me certain that some one sat in the farther corner of the carriage.

Was it the Unknown or some agent? And if it proved to be the Unknown, was she the lady I had met in cold business greeting in the courtyard of the Palace Hotel? I waited impatiently for the first street-lamp to throw a gleam of light into the carriage. But when it came I was little the wiser. I could see faintly the outlines of a figure shrouded in black that leaned in the corner, motionless save for the swaying and pitching of the hack as it rolled swiftly down the street.

The situation became a little embarrassing. Was it my place to speak first? I wondered. At last I could endure the silence no longer.

"Quite an unpleasant evening," I remarked politely.

There was a rustle of movement, the sound of a short gasp, and a soft, mournful voice broke on my ear.

"Mr. Dudley-can you forgive me?"

The astonishment I felt to hear my own name once more-the name that seemed now to belong to a former state of existence-was swallowed up as the magnetic tones carried their revelation to my mind.

I was stricken dumb for a moment at the discovery they had brought. Then I gasped:

"Mrs. Knapp!"

"Yes, Mrs. Knapp," she said with a mournful laugh. "Did you never suspect?"

I was lost in wonder and confusion, and even yet could not understand.

"What brings you out in this storm?" I asked, completely mystified. "I thought I was to meet another person."

"Indeed?" said Mrs. Knapp with a spark of animation. "Well, I am the other person."

I was paralyzed in mind and nerve for a moment with the astonishment of the disclosure. Even yet I could not believe.

"You!" I exclaimed at last. "Are you the protector of the boy? The employer —" Then I stopped, the tangle in my mind beginning to straighten out.

"I am she," said Mrs. Knapp gently.

"Then," I cried, "who is he? what is he? what is the whole dreadful affair about? and what —"

Mrs. Knapp interrupted me.

"First tell me what has become of Henry Wilton?" she said with sorrow in her voice.

The dreadful scene in the alley flashed before my mind.

"He is dead."

"Dead! And how?"

"Murdered."

"I feared so —I was certain, or he would have let me know. You have much to tell me. But first, did he leave no papers in your hands?"

I brought out the slip that bore the blind diagram and the blinder description that accompanied it. Nothing could be made of it in the darkness, so I described it as well as I could.

"We are on the right track," said Mrs. Knapp. "Oh, why didn't I have that yesterday? But here-we are at the wharf."

The hack had stopped, and a hand was fumbling at the door.

The darkness, the dash of water, the wind whistling about the crazy wooden buildings and through the rigging of ships, made the water-front vocal with the shouting of the storm demons as we alighted.

My guide was before us, and we followed him down the pier, struggling against the gusts.

"Do we cross the bay?" I asked, as Mrs. Knapp clung to my arm. "It's not safe for you in a small boat."

"There's a tug waiting for us," Mrs. Knapp explained.

A moment later we saw its lights, and the fire of its engine-room shot a cheerful glow into the storm. The little vessel swung uneasily at its berth as we made our way aboard, and with shouts of men and clang of bells it was soon tossing on the dark waters of the bay. Out from the shelter of the wharves the wind buffeted us wildly, and the black waves were threshed into phosphorescent foam against the sides of the tug, while their crests, self-luminous, stretched away in changing lines of faint, ghostly fire.

The cabin of the tug was fitted with a shelf table, and over it swung a lamp of brass that gave a dim light to the little room. Mrs. Knapp seated herself here, as the boat pitched and tossed and trembled at the strokes of the waves and quivered to the throbbing of the screw, spread out the paper I had given her, and studied the diagram and the jumble of letters with anxious attention.

"It is the same," she said at last; "in part, at least."

"The same as what?" I asked.

"As the one I got word of to-night, you know," she replied.

"No —I didn't know."

"Of course not," said Mrs. Knapp. "But you might have guessed that I got my summons after you left, this evening. I should have spoken to you then if I had known. I was near coming to an explanation, as it was."

"There are a good many things I haven't guessed," I confessed.

"But," she continued, returning to the map, "this gives a different place. I was to go to the cross-road here,"—indicating the mark at the last branch.

"I'm glad to hear that," said I, taking out the diagram I had found in the citadel of the enemy. "This seems to point to a different place, too, and I really hope that the gentleman who drew this map is a good way off from the truth."

"Where did you get this?" exclaimed Mrs. Knapp.

I described the circumstances in as few words as I could command.

"They are ahead of us," she said in alarm.

"They have started first, I suppose," was my suggestion.

"And they have the right road."

"Then our only hope is that they may not know the right place."

"God grant it," said Mrs. Knapp.

She was silent for a few minutes, and I saw that her eyes were filled with tears.

I was moved by her signs of feeling. I thought they were for the boy and was about to ask what would happen to him in case he was found by the enemy, when she said:

"Now tell me about Henry Wilton-how he died and when."

Again the vision of my first dreadful night in San Francisco rose before me, the cries for help from my murdered friend rang in my ears, and the scene in the alley and the figure in the morgue burned before my eyes.

I told the tale as it had happened, and as I told it I read in the face before me the varying emotions of alarm, horror and grief that were stirred by its incidents.

But one thing I could not tell her. The wolf-face I had seen in the lantern flash in the alley I could not name nor describe to the wife of Doddridge Knapp. Yet at the thought the dark mystery grew darker, yet, and I began to doubt what my eyes had seen, and my ears had heard.

Mrs. Knapp bowed her head in deep, gloomy thought.

"I feared it, yet he would not listen to my warnings," she murmured. "He would work his own way." Then she looked me suddenly straight in the face.

"And why did you take his place, his name? Why did you try to do his work when you had seen the dreadful end to which it had brought him?"

I confessed that it was half through the insistence of Detective Coogan that I was Henry Wilton, half through the course of events that seemed to make it the easiest road to reach the vengeance that I had vowed to bring the murderer of my friend.

"You are bent on avenging him?" asked Mrs. Knapp thoughtfully.

"I have promised it."

"You shall have the chance. Strange thought!" she said gloomily, "that the dead hand of Henry Wilton may reach out from beyond the grave and strike at his slayer when he least expects it."

I was more than ever mystified at these words. I had not expected her to take so philosophically to the idea of hanging Doddridge Knapp, and I thought it best to hold my tongue.

"I have marveled at you," said Mrs. Knapp after a pause. "I marvel at you yet. You have carried off your part well."

"Not well enough, it seems, to deceive you," I said, a little bitterly.

"You should not have expected to deceive me," said Mrs. Knapp. "But you can imagine the shock I had when I saw that it was not Henry Wilton who had come among us that first night when I called you from Mr. Knapp's room."

"You certainly succeeded in concealing any surprise you may have felt," I said. "You are a better actor than I."

Mrs. Knapp smiled.

"It was more than surprise-it was consternation," she said. "I had been anxious at receiving no word from Henry. I suppose you got my notes. And when I saw you I was torn with doubts, wondering whether anything had happened to Henry, whether he had sent you in his stead as a practical joke, whether you knew much or little or nothing of our affairs-in short, I was overwhelmed."

"I didn't suppose I was quite so poor an impostor," I said apologetically, with a qualm at the word. "Though I did get some hint of it," I added, with a painful recollection of the candid statement of opinion I had received from the daughter of the house.

"Oh, you did very well," said Mrs. Knapp kindly, "but no one could have been successful in that house. Luella was quite outraged over it, but I managed to quiet her."

"I hope Miss Knapp has not retained the unfavorable impressions of-er—" I stammered in much confusion.

Mrs. Knapp gave me a keen glance.

"You know she has not," she said.

I felt the subconscious impression somehow that after all Mrs. Knapp would have been better pleased if Luella had kept nearer to her first impressions of me.

"Well," continued Mrs. Knapp, "when I saw you and guessed that something had happened to Henry Wilton, and found that you knew little of what was going on, I changed the plan of campaign. I did not know that you were one to be trusted, but I saw that you could be used to keep the others on a false scent, for you deceived everybody but us."

"There was one other," I said.

"Mother Borton?" inquired Mrs. Knapp. "Yes, I learned that she knew you. But to every one else in the city you were Henry Wilton. I feared, though, you would make some mistake that would betray you and spoil my plans. But you have succeeded marvelously."

Mrs. Knapp paused a moment and then continued slowly. "It was cruel of me. I knew that it was sending you to face death. But I was alarmed, angry at the imposition, and felt that you had brought it on yourself. Can you forgive me?"

"I have nothing to forgive," I said.

"I would have spoken when I found you for what you are," said Mrs. Knapp, "but I thought until the Livermore trip that you could serve me best as you were doing."

"It was blind work," I said.

"It was blind enough for you, not for me. I was deceived in one thing, however; I thought that you had no papers-nothing from Henry that could help or hurt. The first night you came to us I had Henry's room thoroughly searched."

"Oh, I was indebted to you for that attention," I exclaimed. "I gave our friends of the other house the credit."

Mrs. Knapp smiled again.

"I thought it necessary. It was the chance that you did not sleep there that night that kept this paper out of my hands weeks ago."

"I have always kept it with me," I said.

"I did not need it till Sunday," continued Mrs. Knapp. "I have been worried much at the situation of the boy, but I did not dare go near him. Henry and I decided that his hiding-place was not safe. We had talked of moving him a few days before you came. When I found that Henry had disappeared I was anxious to make the change, but I could not venture to attempt it until the others were out of town, for I knew I was watched. Then I was assured from Mother Borton that they did not know where the boy was hidden, and I let the matter rest. But a few days ago-on Saturday-she sent me word that she thought they had found the place. Then it came to me to send you to Livermore with the other boy-oh, I hope no harm came to the little fellow," she exclaimed anxiously.

"He's safe at my rooms in charge of Wainwright," I said. "He got back on the morning train, and can be had for the asking."

"Oh, I'm so glad," said Mrs. Knapp. "I was afraid something would happen to him, but I had to take desperate chances. Well, you see my plan succeeded. They all followed you. But when I went to the hiding-place the boy was gone. Henry had moved him weeks ago, and had died before he could tell me. Then I thought you might know more than you had told me-that Henry Wilton might have got you to help him when he made the change, and I wrote to you."

"And the key," I said, remembering the expression of the note, "Did you mean this diagram?"

"No," said Mrs. Knapp. "I meant the key to our cipher code. I was looking over Henry's letters for some hint of a hiding-place and could not find the key to the cipher. I thought you might have been given one. I found mine this afternoon, though, and there was no need of it, so it didn't matter after all."

The pitching and tossing of the boat had ceased for some minutes, and at this point the captain of the tug opened the cabin.

"Excuse me," he said apologetically, uncertain whether to address Mrs. Knapp or me, and including us both in the question, "but where did you want to land?"

"At Broadway," said Mrs. Knapp.

"Then you're there," said the captain.

And, a minute later, with clang of bells and groan of engine we were at the wharf and were helped ashore.

On this side of the bay the wind had fallen, and there were signs of a break in the clouds. The darkness of the hour was dimly broken by the rays from the lines of street-lamps that stretched at intervals on both sides of Broadway, making the gloom of the place and hour even more oppressive.

"Tell the captain to wait here for us with fires up," said Mrs. Knapp. "The carriage should be somewhere around here," she continued, peering anxiously about as we reached the foot of the wharf.

The low buildings by the railroad track were but piles of blackness, and about them I could see nothing.

"This way," said a familiar voice, and a man stepped from the shadow.

"Dicky Nahl!" I exclaimed.

"Mr. Wilton!" mimicked Dicky. "But it's just as well not to speak so loud. Here you are. I put the hack's lights out just to escape unpleasant remark. We had better be moving, for it's a stiffish drive of six or seven miles. If you'll get in, I'll keep the seat with the driver and tell him the way to go."

Mrs. Knapp entered the carriage, and called to me to follow her.

I remembered Mother Borton's warnings and my doubts of Dicky Nahl.

"You're certain you know where you are going?" I asked him in an undertone.

"No, I'm not," said Dicky frankly. "I've found a man who says he knows. We are to meet him. We'll get there between three and four o'clock. He won't say another word to anybody but her or you. I guess he knows what he is about."

"Well, keep your eyes open. Meeker's gang is ahead of us. Is the driver reliable?"

"Right as a judge," said Dicky cheerfully, "Now, if you'll get in with madam we won't be wasting time here."

I stepped into the carriage. Dicky Nahl closed the door softly and climbed on the seat by the driver, and in a moment we were rolling up Broadway in the gloomy stillness of the early morning hour.

CHAPTER XXIX. THE HEART OF THE MYSTERY

In the tumult of conflicting thoughts that assailed me as we entered on the last stage of our journey, the idea of the perils that might lie ahead fixed my attention for the moment, and I began to feel alarm for the safety of my companion.

"Mrs. Knapp," I said; "there is no need for you to take this journey. You had better stop in Oakland for the rest of the night."

"I must go," she replied.

"There is danger," I argued. "You should not expose yourself to the chances of a brush with the enemy. It is a wet, cold ride, and there may be bullets flying at the end of it."

Mrs. Knapp gave a shudder, but she spoke firmly.

"I could not rest—I could not stay away. It may be important that I should be there-it will be important if we find the boy. You do not know him. Mr. Nahl does not know him."

"None of my men seems to know him," I interrupted; "that is, if one may judge by the way they were all taken in on the boy you sent to Livermore."

"I think none of them ever saw his face, though some of them were with Henry Wilton when he first took the boy, and afterward."

"The enemy seem to know him," said I, remembering the scene at Livermore.

"Terrill knows him. I think none of the other agents could be certain of his face, unless it is Mr. Meeker. But truly, I must go."

"You are very brave," I said, admiring her spirit, though I was loath to have the responsibility of her safety on my hands.

"Without you I should not dare to go, I fear," she made answer, "I need a strong arm to lean on, you see."

"You may wish later that you had chosen a cavalier with two strong arms to his equipment. I fear I shouldn't do so well in a hand-to-hand encounter as I should have done before I met Mr. Terrill last night."

"Oh, I hope it will not come to that," said Mrs. Knapp cheerfully, though there was a little tremor in her voice.

"What if they have seized the boy?"

Mrs. Knapp was silent for a little, as if this contingency had not entered her plans.

"We must follow him and save him, even if we have to raise the whole county to do it." Her voice was firm and resolute.

"What would happen to the boy if he were taken?" I found courage to ask.

"He would not live a month," she replied.

"Would he be murdered?"

"I don't know how the end would come. But I know he would die."

I was in the shadow of the mystery. A hundred questions rose to my lips; but behind them all frowned the grim wolf-visage of Doddridge Knapp, and I could not find the courage that could make me speak to them.

"Mrs. Knapp," I said, "you have called me by my name. I had almost forgotten that I had ever borne it. I have lived more in the last month than in the twenty-five years that I remember before it, and I have almost come to think that the old name belongs to some one else. May I ask how you got hold of it?"

"It was simple enough. Henry had told me about you. I remembered that you were coming from the same town he had come from. I telegraphed to an agent in Boston. He went up to your place, made his inquiries and telegraphed me. I suppose you will be pleased to know," she continued with a droll affectation of malice in her voice, "that he mailed me your full history as gathered from the town pump. It is at the house now."

"I trust it is nothing so very disreputable," I said modestly, raking my memory hastily for any likely account of youthful escapades.

"There was one rather serious bit," said Mrs. Knapp gravely. "There was an orchard—"

"There was more than one," I admitted.

Mrs. Knapp broke into a laugh.

"I might have expected it. I knew the account was too good to be true. You'll have to get Luella's permission if you want to read the charges in full, though. She has taken possession of the document."

Luella knew! At first I was disappointed, then relieved. Something of the promised explanation was taken off my mind.

"I tried to get something out of Mother Borton concerning you," continued Mrs. Knapp. "I even went so far as to see her once."

"I don't think you got any more out of her than she wanted to tell."

"Indeed I did not. I was afraid Mr. Richmond had not gone about it the right way. You know Mr. Richmond acted as my agent with her?"

"No, I didn't know. She was as close-mouthed with me as with you, I think."

"Well, I saw her. I wanted to get what information she had of you and of Henry."

"She had a good deal of it, if she wanted to give it up."

"So I supposed. But she was too clever for me. She spoke well of you, but not a word could I get from her about Henry. Yet she gave me the idea that she knew much."

"I should think she might. I had told her the whole story."

"She is a strange woman."

"She was able to hold her tongue."

"A strange gift, you mean to say, I suppose," laughed Mrs. Knapp.

"She was quite as successful in concealing from me the fact that she had ever had word with you, though I suspected that she knew more than she told."

"She is used to keeping secrets, I suppose," replied Mrs. Knapp. "But I must reward her well for what she has done."

"She is beyond fear or reward."

"Dead?" cried Mrs. Knapp in a shocked voice. "And how?"

"She died, I fear, because she befriended me." And then I told her the story of Mother Borton's end.

"Poor creature!" said Mrs. Knapp sadly. "Yet perhaps it is better so. She has died in doing a good act."

"She was a good friend to me," I said. "I should have been in the morgue before her, I fear, but for her good will."

Mrs. Knapp was silent for a minute.

"I hope we are at the end of the tale of death," she said at last. "It is dreadful that insane greed and malice should spread their evil so far about. Two lives have been sacrificed already, and perhaps it is only the beginning. Yet I believe —I am sure —I have done right."

"I am sure of that," I said, and then was silent as her words called up the image of the Wolf, dark, forbidding, glowing with the fires of hate-the Wolf of the lantern-flash in the alley and the dens of Chinatown-and the mystery seemed deeper than ever. The carriage had been rolling along swiftly. Despite the rain the streets were smooth and hard, and we made rapid progress. We had crossed a bridge, and with many turns made a course toward the southeast. Now the ground became softer, and progress was slow. An interminable array of trees lined the way on both sides, and to my impatient imagination stretched for miles before us. Then the road became better, and the horses trotted briskly forward again, their hoofs pattering dully on the softened ground.

"All the better," I thought. "It's as good as a muffler if any one is listening for us."

"Here's the place," came the voice of Dicky, giving directions to the driver; and the carriage slackened pace and stopped. Looking out I saw that we were at a division of the road where a two-story house faced both of the branching ways.

"You'd better come out," said Dicky at the door, addressing his remark to me. "He was to meet us here."

"Be careful," cautioned Mrs. Knapp.

The night had turned colder, or I was chilled by the inaction of the ride. The sky was clearing, and stars were to be seen. By the outline of the hills we had made to the south. The horses steamed and breathed heavily in the keen air.

I kept my hand on the revolver that lay in my overcoat pocket, and walked with Dicky on to the porch. It was a common roadside saloon, and at this hour it appeared wholly deserted. Even the dog, without which I knew no roadside saloon could exist, was as silent as its owners.

"Here's a go!" said Dicky. "He was to meet us, sure. What time have you got?"

I struck a match in a corner and looked at my watch by its flare.

"Five minutes to three."

"Whew!" he whispered, "we're regularly done. I thought he had a bad eye when I was bargaining with him."

I wondered if Dicky had a hand in the trick, if trick it should prove to be.

"He may be up stairs," I suggested.

Dicky groaned. "It's like advertising with a band wagon to rout 'em out at this time of the night," he whispered.

"The enemy have been along here ahead of us," I said. "They may have picked him up."

"That's like enough," said Dicky ruefully. "But if they've got him, we might as well take the back tracks for town and hunt up a sheriff or two, or send for the boys to come over."

"It's too late to do that," said I decidedly. "We must go on at once."

"Well," said Dicky dubiously, "I think I know where the fellow would have taken us. I trailed him this afternoon, and I'll lay two to one that I can pick out the right road."

"Is this the third road from Brooklyn?" I asked pointing to the track that led to the left.

"I reckon so," said Dicky. "I haven't kept count, but I recollect only two before it."

"All right. Up with you then!"

Dicky obediently mounted to the seat beside the driver.

"I shall ride outside," I said to Mrs. Knapp. "I may be needed."

"I suppose you are right," she replied with somewhat of protest in her voice, and I closed the door, and climbed up. It was close quarters for three, but at the word the horses, refreshed by the brief rest, rolled the carriage up the road that led to the hills.

Half a mile farther we passed a house, and within a quarter of a mile another.

"We are on the right road," was my thought as I compared these in my mind with the crosses on the diagram.

About half a mile farther, a small cluster of buildings loomed up, dark and obscure, by the roadside.

"This is the place," I said confidently, motioning the driver to pull up. I remembered that Henry Wilton's map had stopped at the third cross from the parting of the roads.

"No, it isn't," said Dicky eagerly. "It's two or three miles farther on. I trailed the fellow myself to the next house, and that's a good two miles at least."

I had leaped to the ground, and opened the door of the carriage.

"We are at the fourth place," I said.

"And the cockeyed barn?" inquired Mrs. Knapp, peering out.

I was struck silent by this, and looked blankly at the dark forbidding structure that fronted on the road.

"You're right," said Mrs. Knapp with a laugh. "Can't you make out that funny little window at the end there?"

I looked more closely at the building. In the dim light of the stars, the coat of whitewash that covered it made it possible to trace the outlines of a window in the gable that fronted the road. Some freak of the builder had turned it a quarter of the way around, giving it a comical suggestion of a man with a droop to his eye.

"And the iron cow?" I asked.

"Stupid! a pump, of course," replied Mrs. Knapp with another laugh. "Now see if there is a lane here by the barn."

A narrow roadway, just wide enough for a single wagon, joined the main road at the corner of the building.

"Then drive up it quietly," was Mrs. Knapp's direction.

Just beyond the barn I made out the figure of the pump in a conspicuous place by the roadside, and felt more confident that we were on the right road.

The lane was now wrapped in Egyptian darkness. Trees lined both sides of the narrow way. Their branches brushed our faces as we passed, and their tops seemed to meet above us till even the faint light of the stars scarcely glimmered through. The hoofs of the horses splashed in the mud, and the rather clumsy carriage dragged heavily and slowly forward.

"I'd give five dollars to light my lamps," growled the driver. We were traveling by the instinct of the horses.

"If your life is worth more than five dollars, you'd better keep them dark," I said.

The driver swore in an undertone as the hack lurched and groaned in a boggy series of ruts, and a branch whipped him in the face. I was forced to give a grunt myself, as another slapped my sore arm and sent a sharp twinge of pain shooting from the wound till it tingled in my toes. Dicky, protected between us, chuckled softly. I reflected savagely that nothing spoils a man for company like a mistaken sense of humor.

Suddenly the horses stopped so short that we were almost pitched out.

"Hello! what's this?" I cried, drawing my revolver, fearful of an ambush.

"It's a fence," said the driver.

"There must be a gate," I said, jumping down quickly.

Mrs. Knapp rapped on the carriage door and I opened it.

"Have you come to the bars?" she asked presently.

"I guess so. We've come against something like a fence."

"Well, then," she replied, "when we get through, take the road to the left. That will bring us to the house."

"You are certain?"

"That is what Henry wrote in the cipher beneath the map. The house must be only a few hundred yards away."

The bars were there, and I lifted the wet and soggy boards with an anxious heart. Were we, after all, so near the hiding-place? And what were we to find?

I mounted the seat again, and we drove forward. The road was scarcely distinguishable, but the horses followed it without hesitation as it led behind a tall hedge and among scattered oaks.

My heart beat fast. What if the enemy were before us?

"Have you got your revolver handy?" I whispered to Dicky.

"Two of 'em," he chuckled. "There's a double dose for the man that wants it."

On a sudden turn the house loomed up before us, and a wild clamor of dogs broke the stillness of the night.

"I hope they are tied," I said, with a poor attempt to conceal my misgivings.

"We'll have a lively time in a quarter of a minute if they aren't," laughed Dicky, as he followed me.

But the baying and barking came no nearer, and I helped Mrs. Knapp out of the carriage. She looked at the house closely.

"This is the place," she said, in an unmistakable tone of decision. "We must be quick. I wish something would quiet those dogs; they will bring the whole country out."

It seemed an hour before we could raise any one, but it may not have been three minutes before a voice came from behind the door.

"Who's there?"

"It is L. M. K.," said Mrs. Knapp; then she added three words of gibberish that I took to be the passwords used to identify the friends of the boy.

At the words there was the sound of bolts shooting back, and the heavy door opened enough to admit us. As we passed in, it was closed once more and the bolts shot home.

Before us stood a short, heavy-set man, holding a candle. His face, which was stamped with much of the bulldog look in it, was smooth-shaven except for a bristling brown mustache. He looked inquiringly at us.

"Is he here-the boy?" cried Mrs. Knapp, her voice choked with anxiety. "Yes," said the man. "Do we move again?" He seemed to feel no surprise at the situation, and I inferred that it was not the first time he had changed quarters on a sudden at the darkest hour of the night.

"At once," said Mrs. Knapp, in her tone of decision.

"It will take ten minutes to get ready," said the man. "Come this way."

I was left standing alone by the door in the darkness, with a burden lifted from my mind. We had come in time. The single slip of paper left by Henry Wilton had been the means, through a strange combination of events, to point the way to the unknown hiding-place of the boy. He was still safe, and the enemy were on a false trail. I should not have to reproach myself with the sacrifice of the child.

Yet my mind was far from easy. The enemy might have been misled, but if they had followed the road marked out in the diagram I had brought from their den, they were too close for comfort. I listened for any sound from the outside. The dogs had quieted down. Twice I thought I heard hoof-beats, and there was a chorus of barks from the rear of the house. But it was only the horses that had brought us hither, stamping impatiently as they waited.

In a few minutes the wavering light of the candle reappeared. Mrs. Knapp was carrying a bundle that I took to be the boy, and the man brought a valise and a blanket.

"It's all right," said Mrs. Knapp. "No —I can carry him —I want to carry him."

The man opened the door, then closed and locked it as I helped Mrs. Knapp into the carriage.

"Have you got him safe?" asked Dicky incredulously. "Well, I'll have to say that you know more than I thought you did." And the relief and satisfaction in his tone were so evident that I gladly repented of my suspicions of the light-hearted Dicky.

"Have you heard anything?" I asked him anxiously.

"I thought I heard a yell over here through the woods. We had better get out of here."

"Don't wait a second," said the man. "The south road comes over this other way. If you've heard anybody there, they will be here in five minutes. I'll follow you on a horse."

With an injunction to haste, I stepped after Mrs. Knapp into the carriage, the door was shut, Dicky mounted the seat, and we rolled down the road on the return journey.

"Oh, how thankful I am!" cried Mrs. Knapp. "There is a weight of anxiety off my mind. Can you imagine what I have been fearing in the last month?"

"I had thought a little about that myself," I confessed. "But we are not yet out of the woods, I am afraid."

"Hark! what's that?" said Mrs. Knapp apprehensively.

The carriage was now making its way through the bad stretch in the lane, and there was little noise in its progress.

"I heard nothing," I said, putting down the window to listen. "What was it?"

"I thought it was a shout."

There was no noise but the steady splash of horses' hoofs in the mud, and the sloppy, shearing sound of the wheels as they cut through the wet soil.

As we bumped and groaned again through the ruts, however, there arose in the distance behind us the fierce barking of dogs, their voices raised in anger and alarm.

There was a faint halloo, and a wilder barking followed. Then my ear caught the splashing of galloping hoofs behind, and in a moment the man of the house rode beside us.

"They've come," he said, "or, anyhow, somebody's come. I let the dogs loose, and they will have a lively time for a while."

At his words there was another chorus of barks and shouts. Then a shot rang out, and a fusillade followed with a mournful wail that died away into silence.

"Good Lord! they've shot the dogs," cried the man hotly. "I've a mind to go back and pepper some of 'em."

"No," said Mrs. Knapp, "we may need you. Let us hurry!"

A few yards more brought us to the main road, and once on the firm ground the horses trotted briskly forward, while the horseman dropped behind, the better to observe and give the alarm.

"We were just in time," said Mrs. Knapp, trembling.

"Let us be thankful for so much," said I cheerfully.

"They will follow us," said Mrs. Knapp, with conviction in her tone.

"Not before they have broken into the house. That will keep them for some time, I think."

"Is there no sign of pursuit?"

I leaned out of the window. Only the deadened sound of the hoofs of our own horses, the deadened roll of our own carriage wheels, were audible in the stillness of the night. Then I thought I heard yells and faint hoof-beats in the distance, but again there was silence except for the muffled noise we made in our progress.

"Can't we drive faster?" asked Mrs. Knapp, when I made my report.

"I wouldn't spoil these horses for five hundred dollars," growled the driver when I passed him the injunction to hasten.

"It's a thousand dollars for you if you get to the wharf ahead of the others," cried Mrs. Knapp.

"And you'll have a bullet in your hide if you don't keep out of gunshot of them," I added.

The double inducement to haste had its effect, and we could feel the swifter motion of the vehicle under us, and see the more rapid passage of the trees and fences that lined the way.

The wild ride appeared to last for ages. The fast trot of the horses was a funeral pace to the flight of my excited and anxious imagination. What if we should be overtaken? The hack would offer no protection from bullets, and Mrs. Knapp and the boy could scarcely escape injury if it came to a close encounter. But whenever I looked back there was only the single horseman galloping behind us, and the only sound to be heard was that of our own progress.

At last the houses began to pass more frequently. Now the road was broken by cross streets. Gas-lamps appeared, flickering faint and yellow in the morning air, as though the long night vigil had robbed them of their vitality. We were once more within city limits, and I felt a loosening of the tense nerves of anxiety. The panting horses never slackened pace. We swept over a long bridge, and plunged down a shaded street, and the figure of the horseman was the only sign of life behind us. Of a sudden there sounded a long roll, as of a great drum beating the reveille for an army of giants. The horseman quickened his pace and galloped furiously beside us.

"They're crossing the bridge," he shouted.

"Whip up!" I cried to the driver. "They are only four blocks behind us."

"Are they in sight?" asked Mrs. Knapp.

"I can not see them," I replied, "and it may not be the ones we fear. It is near daybreak, and we are not the only ones astir."

I peered out, but a rising mist from the lagoon and the bay hindered the vision, and the sound of the rolling drum had ceased.

The hack swung around a few corners, and then halted.

"Here we are!" cried Dicky Nahl at the door. "You get aboard the tug and push off. Jake and I will run up to the foot of the wharf. If they come, we can keep 'em off long enough for you to get aboard." Dicky had a revolver in each hand, and the determined ring of his voice, so different from his usual light bantering tone, gave me assurance of his sincerity. With the horseman he hastened to the entrance of the wharf, where the two loomed through the mist like shadow-men.

The tug was where it lay when we left, and at my hail the captain and his crew of three were astir. It was a moment's work to get Mrs. Knapp and her charge aboard.

"Come on!" I cried to Dicky and his companion. And as the lines were cast off they made a running jump on to the deck of the tug boat, and the vessel backed out into the stream.

As the wharf faded away into the mist that hung over the waters I thought I saw shapes of men and horses rushing frantically to the edge, and a massive figure waving its arms like a madman, and shouting impotent curses into the air. But with the distance, the uncertain light, and the curtain of mist that was thickening between us, my eyes might have deceived me, and I omitted to mention my suspicions to Mrs. Knapp.

When the mist and darkness had blotted out shore, wharves and shipping, the tug moved at half-speed down the channel. I persuaded the captain that there was no need to sound the whistle, but he declined gruffly to increase his speed.

"I might as well be shot as run my boat ashore," he growled, with a few emphatic seamanlike adjectives that appeared to belong to nothing in particular. "And any one that doesn't like my way of running a boat can get out and walk."

I did not know of any particular reason for arguing the question, so I joined Mrs. Knapp.

"Thank God, we are safe!" she said, with a sigh of relief.

"We shall be in the city in half an hour, if that is safety," I said.

"It will be safety for a few days. Then we can devise a new plan. I have a strong arm to lean on again."

"I think if you would tell me who the boy is, and why the danger threatens him, I might help you more wisely."

"Perhaps you are right," said Mrs. Knapp thoughtfully. "You shall know before it is necessary to make our next plans."

And then the boy called for her attention and I returned to the deck.

The light of the morning was growing. Vessels were moving. The whistles of the ferry-boats, as they gave warning of their way through the mist, rose shrill on the air. The waters were still, a faint ripple showing in strange contrast to the scene of last night.

"There's a steamer behind us," said Dicky Nahl, with a worried look as I joined him. "I've been listening to it for five minutes."

"It's a tug," said the captain. "She was lying on the other side of the wharf last night."

"Good heavens!" I cried. "Put on full steam, then, or we shall be run down in the bay. It's the gang we are trying to get away from."

The captain looked at me suspiciously for a moment, and was inclined to resent my interference. Then he shrugged his shoulders as though it was none of his business whether we were lunatics or not so long as we paid for the privilege, and rang the engine bell for full speed ahead.

We had just come out of the Oakland Creek channel and the mist suddenly thinned before us. It left the bay and the city fair and wholesome in the gray light, as though the storm had washed the grime and foulness from air and earth and renewed the freshness of life. The clear outline of the hills was scarcely broken by smoke. The ever-changing beauties of the most beautiful of bays took on the faint suggestion of a livelier tint, the herald of the coming sun. We had come but a few hundred yards into the clear air when out of the mist bank behind us shot another tug, the smoke streaming from the funnel, the steam puffing noisily from the escapes and the engine straining to increase the speed.

At the exclamation that broke from us, our captain for the first time showed interest in the speed of his boat, and whistled angrily down to his engineer.

"We can beat *her*" he said, with a contemptuous accent on the "her."

"That's your business," I returned, and walked aft to where Mrs. Knapp was standing, half-way up the steps from the cabin.

"There is Darby Meeker," I said, getting sight of him on the pursuing tug.

"Can they catch us?" inquired Mrs. Knapp, the lines tightening about her mouth.

"I think not-the captain says not. I should say that we were holding our own now."

At this moment a tall, massive figure stepped from the pilot-house of the pursuing tug and shook its fists at us. At the sight of the man my heart stood still. The huge bulk, the wolf-face, just distinguishable, distorted, dark with rage and passion, stopped the blood, and I felt a faintness as of dropping from a height. With a gasp, life and voice came back to me.

"Doddridge Knapp!" I cried.

Mrs. Knapp looked at me in alarm, and grasped the rail.

"No! no!" she exclaimed. "A thousand times no! That is Elijah Lane!"

I gazed at her in wonder. Not Doddridge Knapp! Had my eyes played me false?

"Do you not understand?" she said in a low, intense tone. "He is Elijah Lane, the father of the boy. An evil, wicked man-mad-truly mad. He would kill the boy. He killed the mother of the boy. I know, but it is not a case for proof-not a case that the law can touch. And he hates the boy-and me!"

I began to grasp the truth, and recovered speech.

"But why does he want to kill him? And would not the law punish the crime?"

"You do not understand. The boy inherits a great fortune from his mother. Mr. Knapp and I are left trustees by the mother's will. If he had control of the boy, the boy would die; but it would be from cruelty, disease, neglect. It would not be murder in the eye of the law. But I know what would happen. Oh, see the wretch! How he hates me!"

I was stunned with the words I had heard. They made much plain that had puzzled me, yet they left much more in darkness; and I looked blankly at the figure on the other tug. It was truly a strange sight. The man was beside himself with rage, shouting, gesticulating and leaping about the deck in transports of passion. He showed every mark of a maniac.

Suddenly he drew a revolver and sent shot after shot in our direction. We were far beyond the reach of a pistol bullet, but Mrs. Knapp screamed and dodged.

"How he hates me!" she cried again.

When the last shot was gone from his revolver the man flung the weapon in frenzy, as though he could hope to strike us thus.

Then a strange thing happened. Whether due to the effort he had made in the throw, or to a lurch of the tug in the waves we left behind us, or to a stumble over some obstruction, I could not say. But we saw the man suddenly pitch forward over the low bulwarks of the tug into the waters of the bay.

Mrs. Knapp gave a scream and covered her eyes.

"Stop the boat!" I shouted. "Back her!"

The other tug had checked its headway at the same time, and there was a line of six or seven men along its side.

"There he is!" cried one.

The captain laid our tug across the tidal stream that swept us strongly toward Goat Island. Then he steamed slowly toward the other tug.

"He's gone," said Dicky.

The other tug seemed anxious to keep away from us, as in distrust of our good intentions. I scanned the waters carefully, but the drowning man had gone down.

Then, rising not twenty feet away, floating for a moment on the surface of the water, I saw plainly for the first time, the very caricature of the face of Doddridge Knapp. The strong wolf-features which in the King of the Street were eloquent of power, intellect and sagacity, were here marked with the record of passion, hatred and evil life. I marveled now that I had ever traced a likeness between them.

"Give me that hook!" I cried, leaning over the side of the tug. "Go ahead a little."

One of the men threw a rope. It passed too far, and drifted swiftly behind.

I made a wild reach with the hook, but it was too short. Just as I thought I should succeed, the face gave a convulsive twitch, as if in a parting outburst of hate and wrath, and the body sank out of sight. We waited for a few minutes, but there was no further sign. The other tug that had hovered near us turned about and made for the Oakland shore. I signed to the captain to take his course for the city.

The men talked in subdued tones, and I stood half-bewildered, with a bursting sense of relief, by Mrs. Knapp. At last she took her hands from before her eyes, and the first rays of the sun that cleared the tops of the Alameda Hills touched her calm, solemn, hopeful face.

"A new day has dawned," she said. "Let us give thanks to God."

CHAPTER XXX. THE END OF THE JOURNEY

For a few minutes we were silent. Water and land and sky started into new glories at the touch of the rising sun. The many-hilled city took on the hues of a fairy picture, and the windows gleamed with the magic fires that were flashed back in greeting to the god of day. The few cotton-ball clouds that lingered about the mountain-tops, sole stragglers of the army that had trooped up from the south at the blast of the rain-wind, turned from pink to white. The green-gray waters of the bay rippled lightly in the tide as the tug sent the miniature surges trailing in diverging lines from its bow. The curtain of mist that hid the Alameda shore rose and lightened at the touch of the warm rays. The white sails of the high-masted ships scattered through the bay, drooped in graceful festoons as they turned to the sun to rid them of the rain-water that clung to their folds. The ferry-boats, moving with mock majesty, furnished the signs of life to the silent panorama.

It seemed scarcely possible that this was the raging, tossing water we had crossed last night. And the fiery scene of passion and death we had just witnessed was so foreign to its calm beauties, that I could believe it had happened elsewhere in some dream of long ago.

I was roused by the voice of Mrs. Knapp, who sat at the head of the cabin stairs, looking absently over the water.

"I have not dealt frankly with you," she said. "Perhaps it is better that you should know, as you know so much already. I feel that I may rely on your discretion."

"I think I can keep a secret," I replied, concealing my curiosity.

"I should not tell you if I did not have full confidence." Then she was silent for a minute. "That man," she continued at last, with a shudder in her voice, "that man was Mr. Knapp's brother."

I suppressed an exclamation, and she continued:

"They have little in common, even in looks. I wonder you thought for a moment that he was Mr. Knapp. Few people who know them both have traced a resemblance."

"Perhaps those who do not know them would be more likely to find the common points," I suggested. "Members of a family see only the difference that marks one of them from another. The stranger at first sees the family type in all and notes the differences later."

"Yes," said Mrs. Knapp. "It's like picking out the Chinamen. At first they are all alike. We see only the race type. Afterward, we see the many and marked differences."

"I think," said I, leading back to the main subject, "that the remarkable circumstances under which I had seen Mr. Lane had a good deal to do with the illusion. This morning, for the first time, I saw his face under full light and close at hand."

Mrs. Knapp nodded. Then she continued:

"Mr. Knapp and his brother parted thirty years ago in Ohio. The brother-the man who has just gone-was younger than Mr. Knapp, though he looked older. He was wild in his youth. When he left home it was in the night, and for some offense that would have brought him within reach of the law. Mr. Knapp never told me what it was and I never asked. For fifteen years nothing was heard of him. Mr. Knapp and I married, we had come to San Francisco, and he was already a rising man in the city. One day this man came. He had drifted to the coast in some lawless enterprise, and by chance found his brother."

Mrs. Knapp paused.

"And at once began to live off of him, I suppose," I threw in as an encouragement to proceed.

"Not exactly," said Mrs. Knapp. "He confessed some of his rascality to Mr. Knapp, but pleaded that he was anxious to reform. Mr. Knapp agreed to help him, but made the condition that he should take another name, and should never allow the relationship to be known. Mr. Lane —I can not call him by his true name-was ready to agree to the conditions. I think he was very glad indeed to conceal himself under an assumed name, and hide from the memory of his earlier years."

"Had his crimes then been so great?" I asked, as Mrs. Knapp again ceased to speak.

"He had been a wicked, wicked man," said Mrs. Knapp. "The full tale of his villainy I never knew, but he had been a negro stealer, —one of those who captured free negroes or the darkies from Kentucky and Missouri in the days before the war, and sold them down the river. He had been the leader of a wild band in Arkansas and Texas, who made their living by robbing travelers and stealing horses. He had been near death a hundred times, yet he had escaped unhurt. Mr. Knapp helped him. He prospered in business, bought a ranch, and turned farmer. To all appearances, he had reformed completely. No one would suspect in the Sonoma rancher the daring leader of the outlaws in Texas."

"I could believe anything of him," I said grimly.

"You have had a taste of his quality," said Mrs. Knapp. "Well, it was seven years ago that he married. His wife was much younger than he, —a lovely girl, and her parents were rich. How he got her I do not see. It was his gift of the tongue, I suppose, for he could talk well. She was not happy with him, but was better contented when, two years later, her boy came. Mr. Lane was often from home, but I do not think she regretted the neglect with which he treated her. He was not a man who made his home pleasant while he was about. After a while he used to disappear for weeks, spending the time in low haunts in the city, or none knew where. Last year Mrs. Lane's father died, and she came in under the will for more than a million dollars' worth of property. Then Mr. Lane changed his habits. He became most attentive to his wife. He looked to her wants, and appeared to the world as a model husband. But more was going on than we knew. From the little she told me, from the hints she dropped, she must have looked upon him with dread. She failed rapidly in health, and six months ago she died."

"Murdered?" I asked.

"I believe it with all my soul," said Mrs. Knapp. "But there was no evidence-not a particle. I tried to find it, but it was beyond the power of the doctors to discover."

"And his motive?"

"He thought he was heir to her fortune. When he found that she had left it with Mr. Knapp and me, in trust for the boy, his rage was frightful to see. His servants told me of his dreadful ravings. He dared not say a word to Mr. Knapp, but he came and spoke to me about it. I was afraid for my life that time. He said that the money was his, and he said it with such meaning that I felt assured he would stop at nothing to get it. But when he spoke, I cut him so short that he visited the house but once again. Before he had time to put any of his wicked thoughts into action I took the boy to my home, thinking that there I could keep him in safety. Mr. Knapp pooh-poohed my fears, and when Mr. Lane made a demand for the child was in favor of giving him up. 'The father is the one to care for the boy,' he said, and washed his hands of the whole matter."

"Then Mr. Knapp had nothing to do with the affair, one way or the other?"

"Oh, no-nothing at all. I believe, though, that Henry did use his name with the police, to deter them from interfering with our plans."

I remembered Detective Coogan's words, and knew that she was correct in this supposition.

"Mr. Lane," she continued, "threatened legal proceedings. But, knowing his own past, and knowing that I knew something of it, too, he dared not begin them. Mr. Knapp's feelings in the matter had made me unwilling to keep the boy in my house, but at first I thought it the best way of protecting him, and had him with me. Then one night the house was broken into, and two men were discovered in the room where the boy usually slept. I had taken him to my own bed that night, for he was ailing, and so he escaped. The alarm was raised before they found him, and the men fled. Mr. Knapp was confident that they were ordinary housebreakers, but I knew better. I dared keep the boy there no longer, and called Henry Wilton to assist me in making him safe. He found a suitable house for the boy, and hired men to guard it. But after one experience in which the place was attacked and almost carried by storm, Henry thought it better to hide the boy and watch the enemy. The rest you know."

Heaving a sigh as of relief, she went on:

"Mr. Lane was insane, I am certain. I tried to have Mr. Knapp take steps to lock him up. But Mr. Knapp could not believe that his brother was so wicked as to wish to take the life of his own child, and shut his ears to the talk of his madness. I think he was fearful of a scandal in which the relationship should become known, and the stories of his brother's early days should come to the public. But there was a time, a few weeks ago, when I was near spurring Mr. Knapp to action. It was at the time of his trip to Virginia City. Mr. Lane came to the house while I was away and scared the servants into fits with his threats and curses. Luella had the courage and tact to face him and get him out of the house, and I telegraphed for Mr. Knapp."

"I remember the occasion, though I didn't know what was going on."

"Well, Mr. Knapp was very angry, and had a long talk with Lane. He told me that the creature cried and pleaded for forgiveness, and promised amendment for the future. And Mr. Knapp believed him. Yet that very night you were assailed with Luella in Chinatown."

The truth flashed on me. The groans and cries behind the locked door in Doddridge Knapp's office, the voices which were like to one man pleading and arguing with himself, were all explained.

"I think the assault was something of an accident," she continued; "or, rather, it was more the doing of Terrill than of Lane."

"What was the cause of Terrill's enmity?" I asked. "He seemed to take a hearty personal interest in the case for a hired man."

"For one thing, a family interest. I think he is a son of Lane's early years. For another, he had a violent personal quarrel with Henry over some matter, and you have had the benefit of the enmity. But I don't think you'll hear of him again-or Meeker either. They will be in too much of a hurry to leave the state."

I thought of Terrill lying bruised and sore at Livermore, and felt no fear of him.

"You took great chances in sending me to Livermore," I said. "It might have gone hard with Mr. Knapp's plans if I had not got back."

"I thought of that. But if the boy had been where I supposed all would have been well. I should have telegraphed you before nightfall to return. But in the distraction of my search I did not give up till midnight. I left a telegram at the office to be sent you the first thing in the morning, but by that time you were here. It was a bold escape, and I feel that we owe you much for it."

At her last words we were at the wharf, and landed free from fear.

An hour later I reached my lodgings, sore with fatigue, and half-dead for want of sleep. The excitement that had spurred my strength for the last enterprise no longer supported me. I slept twenty-four hours in peace, and no dream of Doddridge Knapp's brother or of the snake-eyes of Tom Terrill disturbed my repose.

CHAPTER XXXI. THE REWARD

"I've heard about you," said Luella, when on the next evening I made my bow to her. "But I want to hear all about it from yourself. Tell me, please."

"Where shall I begin?" I asked, looking into the most charming of faces, which shone before me.

"How stupid to ask! At the beginning, of course."

"I was born of poor but honest parents"—I began.

Luella interrupted me with a laugh.

"How absurd you are! Anyhow, you can tell me about that later. Just begin with the San Francisco beginning. Tell me why you came and all about it."

"Very good," I said; "though really this part is much longer than the other."

Then I told her the story of my coming, of the murder of Henry Wilton, of the struggles with death and difficulty that had given the spice of variety to my life since I had come across the continent.

It was an inspiration to have such a listener. Under the encouragement of her sympathy I found an unwonted flow of words and ideas. Laughter and tears shone in her eyes as the ludicrous and sorrowful parts of my experience touched her by turns. And at the end I found—I really don't know how it happened—I found that I was clasping her hand and looking up into her eyes in a trance of intoxication from the subtle magnetism of her lovely presence.

For a minute we were silent.

"Oh," she cried softly, withdrawing her hand, and looking dreamily away, "I knew it was right-that it must be right. You have justified my faith, and more!"

"I am repaid for all by those words," I said. I am afraid I stared very hard at her, but it was pleasant, indeed, to look into Luella's eyes without any reservations or conscientious qualms in thinking of my duty to hang her father.

"You deserve a much greater reward than that," said Luella.

"I want a much greater reward than that," said I boldly.

I did not think the courage was in me. But under the magnetic influence of the woman before me I forgot what a poor devil I was. Luella looked at me, and I saw in her eyes that she understood what I would say.

I do not know what I did say. I have no doubt it was very badly put, but she listened seriously. Then she said:

"That's very nice of you to want me, but I am going to marry the president of the Omega Company."

I turned sick with despair at these words so gently said, and a pang of fierce jealousy, tinged with wonder, shot through me. "Surely she can't be in love with that red-faced brute we fought with in the Omega office," I thought. That was impossible. Besides, we had turned him out. Doddridge Knapp would be president as soon as the new board of directors elected its officers. She couldn't, of course, think of marrying her own father. I could not understand what she meant, but I knew I was furiously uncomfortable and wished I was rich enough to buy up the company. Luella saw my distress as I tried to rise and fly from the place.

"Don't go," she said gently. "What are you going to do with your men?"

"The free companions are to be disbanded," I said, recovering myself with a gulp.

"Are any of them killed?" she asked in solicitous tones.

"No. Porter is pretty badly hurt. We got him down from Livermore to-day. He was in the jail there, with Abrams and Brown. We gave bail for them, and all the men are back at the Montgomery Street place. Barkhouse is getting on all right, and there are a few bruises and cuts scattered around in my flock. But they'll all be in trim for another fight in two or three weeks."

"I suppose you'll be sorry to part with them."

"They are a faithful set, but I've had enough excitement for a while."

"And Mrs. Borton?"

"Is to be buried to-morrow."

"And you, Mr. Dudley?"

This question struck me a little blank. I had really not thought of what I was going to do.

"It's another case of an occupation gone," I said rather ruefully. "With the break-up of the plots and the close of the Omega deal, I am at the end of my employments."

With this view of the question before me, I fell into a panic of regrets, and began to blush furiously at my folly in imagining for an instant that Luella could think of me for a husband.

"No," said Luella thoughtfully. "You are just at the beginning."

The tone, even more than the words, braced my nerves, and once more there glowed within me a generous courage of the future.

"You are right. I thank you," I said feelingly. "I have faith in the opportunities."

"And I have faith —" said Luella. Then she stopped.

"In the man, I hope," I ventured.

Luella did not answer, but she gave me a look that meant more than words. I was a trifle bewildered, wondering where I stood in the eyes of this capricious young woman, but my speculations were cut short by the coming of Mrs. Knapp.

There was no reservation in her greeting. Whatever lingering doubts of me her mind had held, they had all melted away in the fire of that last journey that had ended the struggle for the life of the boy. As we talked over the events of the month, I found nothing left of the silent opposition with which she had watched my growing friendship with the daughter of the house. At last she cried:

"Oh, I had almost forgotten. Mr. Knapp wishes to see you in his room before you go."

"I am at his service," I said, and went at once to the den of the Wolf.

"Ah, Wilton, I find you're not Wilton," he growled amiably. The loss of his brother had not affected his spirits.

"Quite true," I said.

"You needn't explain," he said. "The women folks say it's all right, though I don't quite understand it myself."

"I can tell you the story," I said.

"I don't want to hear it," he growled. "I've tried you, and that's enough for me."

I murmured my appreciation and thanks for his good opinion.

The Wolf waved his hand as a disposal of all acknowledgments, and growled again:

"Have you any engagements that would keep you from taking the place of president of the Omega Company?"

I fell back on the chair, speechless.

"There'll be a good salary," he continued. "Well, of course, you needn't be in a hurry to accept. Take a day to think over it if you like." The Wolf actually smiled.

"Oh, I don't need any time," I gasped. "I'll take it now."

"Well, you'll have to wait till the directors meet," he said.

I gave him my hearty thanks for the unlooked-for favor.

"To tell you the truth," he said, "it was the doing of the women folks."

My heart gave a leap at the announcement, for it carried a great deal more with it than Doddridge Knapp knew.

"I am a thousand times obliged to you-and the ladies," I said.

"Well, I wasn't unwilling," he said indulgently. "In fact, I intended to do something handsome for you. But there's one condition I must make."

I looked my inquiry.

"You must not speculate. You haven't got the head for it."

"Thank you," I said. "I'll keep out, except under your orders."

"Right," he said. "You've the best head for carrying out orders I ever found."

The King of the Street waved me good night, and I went back to the parlor.

Luella was sitting where I had left her, and no one else was about. She was looking demurely down and did not glance up till I was beside her.

"I have won a double prize," I said. "I am the president of Omega."

And I stooped and kissed her.

www.ingramcontent.com/pod-product-compliance
Ingram Content Group UK Ltd.
Pitfield, Milton Keynes, MK11 3LW, UK
UKHW021912190726
13853UKWH00002B/637